Dahlias FOR Dominica

Dahlias for Dominica

In Bloom Series Book 2

KASEY KENNEDY

Dahlias for Dominica
In Bloom Series, Book 2

ISBN-13: 978-1-958942-05-5 (paperback)
ISBN-13: 978-1-958942-06-2 (hardcover)
ISBN-13: 978-1-958942-04-8 (e-book)

Cover and interior design by Alt 19 Creative

Author Website:
www.kasey-kennedy.com

Published by:

*For my dad,
thank you for showing me
what a strong, man of faith looks like*

CHAPTER ONE

NICA TOOK A bite of her veggie omelet as she listened to her cousin Izzy prattle on about the upcoming *quinceañera* for Izzy's youngest sister, Evie. The *quinceañera* would celebrate Evie's fifteenth birthday, a coming-of-age celebration that was an important tradition for their Mexican-American family.

The girls sat in a small booth in their favorite diner enjoying the mid-morning breakfast Izzy was treating them to before their afternoon classes. Max's Coffee Shop was between breakfast and lunch rushes so there were only a few other patrons.

"Even though you refused your own *quinceañera*, you have to get behind Evie's," Izzy said, cutting into her stack of butter and syrup-slathered pancakes.

"Why does everyone think I won't?" Nica threw up her hands and the small chunk of egg on her fork went flying. "Oops," she muttered, thankful no one was at the table next to them.

"Because you change the subject every time it comes up." Izzy flicked her hand in a dismissive gesture and the sun streaming in through the window caused her glittery nail polish to sparkle.

"I do?"

"Yes. The moms are worried about you. You don't talk about boyfriends; you don't listen when they try to set you up—"

"So why don't they stop trying?" Nica's voice rose. This argument was getting old. "The moms" were sisters who, after Izzy's dad had been killed in a car accident when Izzy was little, had combined their families into a large house on the North side of Chicago. The move brought three parents, and eleven children, together in one large, caring family in a boisterous home.

"Because they want you to be happy," Izzy replied. "And to them, being happy means being married and having babies."

"But I don't want that. What about "to each his own"? If they wanted me to be happy, maybe they would ask and *listen* to what I want. I would be perfectly happy with a roommate—I know it won't be you forever, because you are on the hunt for a husband—but I'd like a roommate to share the expenses and to keep the loneliness at bay. As much as I love our family, growing up in a house with eleven kids gave me a lifetime's worth of snotty noses, noise, chaos, and cleaning. Ugh. No thanks."

"Well, maybe I will find a husband and we'll have a big house with an apartment over the garage, or, oh! A carriage house!." Izzy clasped her hands together. "Then you can live in your own little apartment on our property and be close by so you never get lonely."

Nica pushed her dark bangs out of her eyes. "And you get a free babysitter. That's your plan, right?"

"No, no, no," Izzy shook her head vehemently. Her ponytail swung back and forth, and her teardrop-shaped leather earrings brushed her shoulders. "That is not my plan. I will have enough kids so that they can babysit each other. Ha, ha!"

"Wow, you are following the family tradition." Nica finished her omelet and took a small bite of her wheat toast. "When is Evie's party again? I don't think I put it on my calendar."

"October twenty-second," Izzy answered. "Don't forget to ask for that weekend off from work. We have to go home Friday to help get everything ready. It's going to be beautiful. And you need to think about a date. If you go to one more family event without one, the moms will lose their minds! I'm hearing little tidbits that they may be trying to stuff the guest list with eligible bachelors for you."

"No! What about you? Why aren't they trying to do the same thing to you?"

"Come on. Don't be silly. I go to every event with a date. They know I'm looking; that makes them happy."

"They wouldn't secretly tell men that they're trying to set me up, would they?"

"Oh, they would. They definitely would. You better come up with a plan, *prima*."

Nica stacked her dishes and looked out the window. If the moms were going to play dirty and start parading men in front of her, she would have to come up with something. She'd start looking around her classes for a potential date. Unfortunately, the men that came into her workplace, the In Bloom Flower Shop, were usually buying flowers for wives or dates. No eligible bachelors came in to flirt with the help. Maybe she needed to get a second job where single men hung out. A bar? A sandwich shop? Foot Locker? She could really use an employee discount for running shoes.

Izzy's voice brought her back to the conversation. "What if I set you up? You'd be surprised how many single men come into work, to buy hair gel, deodorant, cologne, and whatnot."

"Yeah, no, thank you."

"What? You don't want a guy that takes care of his appearance and smells nice?" Izzy teased.

"Well, of course, those are good qualities, but I don't want you scouting out guys for me. Besides, how would that work? They look at beautiful you and then you say you want their number for your cousin? Ha! They would be hoping and praying that you were hitting on them, not trying to set them up. They'd be disappointed to meet me after you."

Nica wasn't envious of her gorgeous, ultra-feminine, cousin, but she wasn't blind to men's reaction to her either. If she ever dated, she would want to be confident in her relationship *before* introducing her boyfriend to Izzy.

Not that she had any intentions of dating right now. She was too busy to add that stress into her life. She was in her senior year of college, worked a great part-time job, and loved to fill her downtime with DIY projects around their apartment that she would video and share on social media. She hoped to increase her skills and build a following.

Izzy cleared her throat. "Was that a pity party? I apologize if I'm not dressed properly for a party."

The waiter came over with a coffee pot and Nica raised her cup while Izzy declined. He put his hand on Nica's shoulder as he poured the coffee and she had to suppress the urge to jerk away. He walked away and she silently recited the Serenity Prayer as she focused on the warm cup between her hands.

She looked at Izzy and sighed. "Not a pity party. I am just so frustrated at the consistent push to date, date, date. What year is it anyway? Last, I checked it was 2022. Not 1950. I don't need a man to take care of me. I am enough. I have a full life. I'm not less than anyone else just because I'm single. If I decide to date, it will be on my terms. Not yours. Not the moms'. Not anyone else's."

"Okay, okay. I'm officially off your back. And I will work on the moms." Izzy reached for her purse and pulled out her wallet. "Are you ready?"

Nica nodded. "Let me finish my coffee and I will be. Thank you for listening and understanding. People are different. You can't assume you know what someone wants just because of their gender or how they look or where they come from. You have to ask. You have to *listen*."

Izzy smiled from ear to ear. "You are going to be an amazing teacher! Your students are going to love you!"

The feeling of peace Nica had felt when Izzy stopped pushing her about a date was replaced by a feeling of disappointment. How many times had she told Izzy that she was just pursuing the education degree to appease her parents? That wasn't her passion, it was her backup plan. Her dream was to flip houses and feature them online.

Frustration bubbled up and she checked her watch. If they got back to their apartment soon, she would have enough time to go for a run before she had to leave for class.

She'd made some progress with Izzy today. But she couldn't expect everything to right itself in one conversation. She would persist.

One of these days, she'd get up the nerve to sit her parents down and tell them that the physical education degree was the backup plan, not her dream.

It would probably be easier to fake date someone to get the family off her back before she tried to get them on the same page as to her future career.

Baby steps.

CHAPTER TWO

GRADY LITWILLER LIFTED a piece of lumber up to his brother's waiting hand. Matt pulled the board up onto the platform in the large oak in his backyard. "At this pace, you'll finish this treehouse by the time your kid starts high school," Grady teased.

"I want it done right, not done fast. Besides, my kid can't even walk yet, so I've got some time," Matt retorted.

"Precisely. Wouldn't it have been better to do this in the spring? Building a treehouse just before winter for a kid who can't walk seems shortsighted." Grady looked towards the back of his brother's house and saw Matt's wife, Julie, standing at the sliding glass door, holding the future tree climber on her hip. His nephew Charlie was only five months old.

"I don't like to have things hanging over me," Matt said. "We decided we wanted a treehouse so I'm building a treehouse."

"You are the epitome of an oldest child."

"Well, if the shoe fits. But you're not that much different than me, Grady. You're a go-getter. Look at all you've accomplished in your life. Bank branch manager. Owner of your own home. Owner of several rental properties. You're killing it. Financially, at least. I think you work too hard, though, and need to live a little. Life is more than just work and accumulating wealth. It's having fun, exploring, and having a family. Do you know what I mean?"

Grady considered the question, but it was an easy answer. Yes. His focus was on the FIRE movement. Financial Independence, Retire Early. He had a plan. He knew the path to get there. Working. Investing. Saving. That was how he'd get to retire early and travel.

"Yes, everything is great," he replied, ignoring Matt's comments about fun and family. "I've got a couple of investors on board, which will allow me to purchase another apartment building in January. It's in a great location, near the Wesleyan College campus. It'll be my largest building, with twenty-four units."

"Wow." Matt paused for several seconds. "Are you sure you're not stretching yourself too thin? Having to take on investors? I didn't think you wanted to go that route. You'll lose some autonomy that way."

"True. But it'll allow me to buy a sweet property without having to wait. I've become cash-strapped this year with the three other rental properties I purchased."

Matt hammered a board in place and stood, stretching his back. "Sounds like you're close to overextending yourself."

"It's a rental property—in a college town. It's a solid investment. You know I'll never take a risky bet again." Grady suppressed a shudder thinking about the "double your money guarantee" investment that a friend talked him into making the first year out of college. Grady had been so determined to accumulate cash quickly and jump into the FIRE movement that he'd ignored his instincts and poured ten thousand dollars into the scheme. Six weeks later, his money and his friend, were gone.

Matt peered over the edge of the platform and raised an eyebrow at Grady. "Be careful, little brother."

"Look who's talking. How much did you spend on the supplies for this Taj Mahal treehouse?" Grady wanted to deflect the attention away from himself. He didn't want to tell Matt just how much debt he'd be taking on with the new apartment building.

Matt climbed down the temporary steps that he'd nailed into the tree. He'd replace them later with a more kid-friendly staircase. "Not to worry. It's in the budget." He changed the subject. "I'm ready for a break. Julie said she'd have lunch ready at noon, and it's ten minutes to according to my watch. Hungry?"

Grady nodded. "I was doing the heavy lifting, so yes," he teased.

Matt grunted. "With your book smarts, you're only good for grunt labor. So yes, you did the heavy lifting. But I used brain power, measuring, calculating, leveling...and I put in some sweat equity, too."

They walked towards the house, exchanging light physical jabs along with their verbal ones. Stepping into the sliding door of the ranch-style house in the Jackson Woods subdivision of Bloomington, Illinois, Grady inhaled the warm, spicy aroma of the chili that Julie was cooking on the stove. His mouth immediately salivated at the smell. He had no intentions of ever marrying, as it would interrupt his financial plan and slow down his pace to hit financial independence, but he had moments when he appreciated the partnership displayed by his brother and sister-in-law. There was no better team under forty that he'd come across.

Grady and Matt were lucky; they had great role models in their parents. Joel and Tara Litwiller were college sweethearts who'd married only a month after graduation. Matt was born one year later, and Tara left her job as an elementary school teacher to be a stay-at-home mom. Grady was born two years after Matt, and then Cooper was born three years later. When all three boys were in school, Tara volunteered at the school, but didn't want to be committed to a job and unavailable if the boys were sick. She saw child-rearing as her number one job, and she gave it her all.

Grady appreciated that she'd been around while they were growing up. Their dad was on a fast track to an executive position at work, which he secured before he was thirty. That meant a lot of late nights and weekends in the office. The one day they could count on Dad being around was Sunday. That was a rule that Tara firmly enforced: they would be together as a family on Sundays.

Grady knew both parents sacrificed for their family. And he often wondered if things would have been better if both parents had worked. Then maybe his dad wouldn't have had to work as much and miss so many of their activities.

Julie handed Charlie over to Grady. "Here, say hello to your nephew."

"Hello, nephew," Grady said, holding the child out at arm's-length.

Julie swatted his arm. "Hold that baby like he means something to you, Grady!"

Grady placed his nephew in the crook of his arm and rested him against his chest. "Is this better?"

"Much," Julie praised.

Matt smiled from the kitchen sink, where he stood washing his hands. "Every time you hold him, it seems like the first time. I think you need to come over more often and practice."

"So you can continue to get good, cheap labor, right?"

"You are cheap." Matt dried his hands on a towel. "I just wish you were good."

Julie buzzed about the kitchen stirring the chili on the stove, and opening the oven door to check on what Grady assumed was garlic bread, based on the smells wafting across the room. "You two are the worst. Grow up already."

"Won't happen. We're brothers." Matt responded.

"Yes, but you're not children, you're men," Julie chided. "Grady, you can put Charlie in his highchair. We'll eat in just a few minutes."

Grady looked at the contraption. "You trust me to do this?"

"You have a college degree, dork," Julie responded. "You can figure it out. And if he gets hurt, your brother will kick your butt."

Matt put the hand towel back on its hook and turned from the sink. "You got that right, sweetie."

Grady leaned over and managed to lower Charlie into the highchair, even though the baby's little legs kept flailing about. He looked up to find Julie watching him.

"Now just click the belt in place and he'll be all set," she said.

The adults sat down with bowls of chili and garlic bread, but Julie focused on giving Charlie a bottle first.

"Grady, Matt says that you're still not dating anyone," Julie said. Grady dreaded this part of the conversation. It came up every time he visited. Why did married people want everyone around them to be married, too? "You know I ask him all the time. There's a new young lady in my bible study group at church. I can feel her out if you're looking for a setup."

"No thanks, Jules. I'm too busy to date."

"I don't believe that for a second. You can't work one hundred and sixty-eight hours a week."

"A hundred sixty-eight?"

"Twenty-four times seven. One hundred sixty-eight." She picked Charlie up and placed him against her shoulder to burp him.

"Thanks for the math lesson. Once I work, eat, sleep, and work out, I have about three hours left over each week. I usually fill those hours with drum practice. So, no time to date." Grady looked to Matt for help. No luck.

"She's never gonna stop, Grady," Matt said, joining the conversation. "Why don't you just let her set you up?" He took a bite of garlic bread, but the action did not hide the grin on his face.

"When I'm ready to be set up, I'll let you know. How's that?" Matt hoped this would get them off his back. There was no way he was dating. But if he gave them a little hope, maybe they'd back off.

CHAPTER THREE

NICA TIGHTENED THE plumber's wrench onto the kitchen sink's p-trap. She gave it a jerk and a wiggle, but it didn't want to loosen.

"Nica, we can call Trevor to do that. He'd be over here in fifteen minutes, and he's a professional, remember?" Paige leaned her hip against the kitchen counter, peering at her roommate under the sink.

"No!" Nica grunted from the confines of the cabinet. "This is an easy job. I can do it. Besides, I need the practice. If I'm ever going to flip houses myself, I have to be able to do these things without paying for professionals."

"OK. Suit yourself. But if you mess it up, he'll tease you to no end."

"Oh, believe me, I know." She grunted again and the nut came loose. "Ah, ha. Got it, you little—" She shimmied the p-trap loose but was startled when a gush of cold, icky water shot out of the pipe and soaked her hair. "Ugh."

"What happened? Are you ok?" Paige asked.

"Yes, can you hand me a towel?"

Paige handed her a dish towel that was on the counter. "Will this work?"

"No, I need a bath towel. My hair is soaked."

As soon as Paige walked out of the room, there was a knock on the door.

"What now?" Nica muttered, holding the insufficient dish towel to her head. She stood and walked the three steps to the door. Water from her shoulder-length hair continued to drip onto her t-shirt and overalls.

She opened the door to see a man, likely in his late twenties, wearing a blue suit, standing on the porch landing. "Can I help you?"

"What the heck are you doing?" he said, his eyes darting from her dripping hair to the plumber's wrench in her hand.

"What the heck does it look like I'm doing? Plumbing!" she retorted.

"Are you a licensed plumber?" he asked.

"No, are you a licensed jerk? Why all the questions? Who are you?" Nica's nerves were shot. Unclogging the kitchen drain was supposed to be a quick job; she had to get ready and leave for an evening class in thirty minutes.

"I'm Grady Litwiller. Your landlord."

"Oh," she replied. *Shoot, we've been here two years. When has the landlord ever stopped by? Just my luck.*

"And you are?" he continued.

"Nica. It's short for Dominica. Dominica Mendoza. How can I help you?"

Paige walked into the kitchen with the bath towel. "Nica, I've got that towel for you."

Nica turned around and placed the dish towel and plumber's wrench on the counter. "Thanks, Paige." She leaned over and wrapped the towel around her head. Rising, she wiped her damp hands on the denim overalls she used when doing repair projects. Turning back to the door, she said to Grady, "I'm sorry, you caught us at a bad time. Now, what can I help you with?"

He ran his hand over his short and impeccable hair. "First,

what are you doing? And if something needed to be repaired, why didn't you call the management company? They would have sent a plumber out right away."

"Where are my manners? Won't you please come in?" She turned from him and waved her arm towards the kitchen. "The kitchen sink was clogged. We tried drain cleaner and sending a snake down it—didn't work. I wanted to take the p-trap off to see if I could clear it that way."

Grady stepped into the kitchen. "I asked before—are you a licensed plumber?"

"No, but I know my way around household repairs. It'll be faster, and cheaper for *you*, to do it myself."

"I don't know about that. If you hurt yourself and sue me, it would be much more expensive."

"I've got it under control," she replied, angry that he assumed she would get hurt. Just like her dad. Assuming that because she was a girl, she couldn't do it.

"So, like Nica said, how can we help you, Mr..." Paige jumped into the conversation.

"Sorry, I'm Grady Litwiller." He stepped forward to shake Paige's hand. "Please just call me Grady. I'm here to let you know that we are going to be replacing the stairs leading to your apartment. They are old and unsafe."

"Wow. That's great," Paige said. "I'll admit they scare me. Any chance the new ones won't be so steep?"

"Yes, they'll be up to code, and we'll build an extra landing halfway up."

Paige asked, "What will we do while the work is being done?"

"You'll have to use the fire escape." Grady gestured to the back of the building. "The crew estimated it will take them three days to complete the work. I told them there will be a bonus if they get it done in two—safely, of course. No cutting corners. I know using the fire escape will not be pleasant. I suggest you try to get groceries, laundry, etcetera, done before the work starts, so you can limit what you're hauling up and down the fire escape. If you are uncomfortable with that arrangement, I'll pay for a hotel room while the work is being done."

"Really?" Nica joined in. "You'd do that?"

"Yes, I know it's an inconvenience. If I could, I would wait until you all moved out and do the work when this apartment was empty, but you recently signed a new lease, so I would rather get it done now before someone gets hurt."

"Are you old enough to be the landlord?" Nica asked.

Grady chuckled. "Are you old enough to be so blunt? Yes, I'm old enough."

"How old exactly?" Nica pushed.

"Nica," Paige scolded softly.

Ignoring Paige, Nica continued, "How old?"

"Twenty-eight."

"You don't look a day over twenty-seven."

"Ha. You're funny."

"Ha. You're—" she wanted to say sexist, but decided it was better to keep that opinion to herself; the guy controlled the rent, after all. "Never mind. Is that all you wanted? Why did you come in person just to tell us about the stairs? You could have sent a letter."

"Yes, that's all that I wanted. I'm also trying to meet all of the renters. I just purchased the building in August, and I like to know my tenants."

My tenants. Nica wanted to roll her eyes. *Who does this guy think he is? I'll show him his tenants.*

"Well, that's all I originally wanted." The corner of his mouth raised in a smirk. "But now that I'm here and see that you are Wonder Woman trying to fix the drain, can we talk about the sink? Can I take a look?"

"In your fancy suit? Do you even know what you're looking

at? I don't think that's a good idea. A bunch of gunk fell out when I took off the pipe. There's a mess under there. I didn't get a chance to clean it up while I was wringing it out of my hair."

"You should have that checked out," he said, nodding at the towel wrapped around her head.

"Ha, ha, ha. You are a funny landlord in a landlord suit."

Paige backed up. "I think you two have things under control here. I'm going to go hang out in my room. Yell if you need anything. You know, towels and stuff."

Nica squinted her eyes at Paige. "It's under control."

Grady walked to the sink and leaned down, peering under the sink. "It's not a landlord suit. I work at a bank and was making a few stops on my way home."

"Oh, you're a banker *and* a landlord. Got it." Nica wondered if it was crazy to dislike someone within five minutes of meeting them. It was a new sensation for her.

"Am I coming off like a pretentious a-hole?" he asked.

"Who says a-hole?"

"Pretentious people."

They laughed at the same time. Nica felt some of her tension ease. "Finally, you got one right."

"Yeah, I deserve that. Well, it looks like you got it under control. How about this? You finish your project, and if you run into any more issues, you call my management team and I promise you they will have a plumber here ASAP. I'll call and give that direction as soon as I leave here."

"Do you have only certain plumbers you work with?" Nica asked.

"We have a list of preferred vendors, yes. But if they're booked, we will reach out to others. Why do you ask?"

"Paige, the one that was just in here, her boyfriend is a plumber. He's great. I wonder if he's on your list."

"What's his name?"

"Trevor Morrison."

"I'll check. Well, I'll get out of your wet hair, Nikki."

"It's Nica."

"Right. Sorry about that. I'll take off. Here's my business card with my number and the management company's number. Call them if you have any further issues."

He smiled and walked out the door. Nica stared at the card in her hand. "Grady Litwiller. Lit-Up Properties, Inc." Her eyes rolled again. *A pretentious frat boy. Great. Great Grady, what a world-class jerk.* How dare he assume she didn't know what she was doing? Wasn't she dressed for plumbing? Didn't she have the tools? Well, the only way to prove that she could handle it was to do the job, do it well, and *not* call the management company for help. Glancing at the clock, she realized she needed to hustle to get to class on time. She'd finish the plumbing as soon as she returned home.

CHAPTER FOUR

GRADY CHUCKLED TO himself as he walked down the steep steps of the apartment building. He was thankful that only the top floor apartment, housing the college-coeds, had been impacted by the stair rebuild. The other four units in this building were accessed by an internal stairwell.

Nica was a spitfire, for sure. The last thing he'd expected to find when he knocked on the door to the apartment was a cute, petite Latina wielding a pipe wrench. Wait until he told his brother Matt about the young woman repairing the sink—in a rental unit, no less. He'd get a laugh out of it, too. Grady expected college girls to be the first ones to call the management company to complain about any little issue.

Climbing into his used Audi, he pulled his cell phone from the pocket of his jacket and called Linda, his "management company".

"Hey, Linda," he said, once she answered. "Can you make a note on the 171 University St. Apartment E address for me? If they call for a plumber in the next couple of days, can you put a rush order on getting someone over there? I want a plumber there in two hours."

"You got it, boss man." Linda was a friend from college who he'd enlisted when he created his new property management company. "Company" was being generous; it was just him and Linda. "Why the rush, though?"

"Got a fixer living there. Says she can do it herself, but if she can't, I want us to take care of it ASAP."

"She?"

"Yes, *she*."

"Alrighty," she paused. "Interesting. Is she pretty?"

Grady rolled his eyes; thankful they were on the phone. "Yes. Your point?"

Linda laughed. "Methinks Grady might like a lady. It's about time. Your dry spell is reaching epic proportions. There's an office pool and everything."

Grady knew Linda was teasing him. His non-existent dating life was a constant mystery to her. "We don't have 'an office'. It's just you and me, Linda Lou."

"Hey, I have two cats. We have a pool. So, anything else for today, Mr. Non-Committal?"

He ignored the jab. "Yes, is Trevor Morrison on our list of preferred plumbing vendors?"

"Let me check. Hold on."

He listened to the tap-tap of her keyboard.

"Yes, he's on here, but down on the list. My understanding is that it had been a two-person company—Mr. Morrison and his son, but the dad passed away a while back. I've called a couple of times, but the son hasn't been able to accommodate us, so I bounced him down."

"Well, bounce him back up, okay? Let's give him another try. Especially if 171 University, Apartment E calls."

"You got it. Any more back bends for 171 University, Apartment E, and its pretty tenant?"

"No, that's it for now. Thanks, Linda."

"You got it, Gravy Grady."

He disconnected and pulled his tablet out from under the pair of drumsticks he kept in the car. Pulling up the file of tenant information, he found Nica's cell phone number and sent a text.

> **GRADY:** This is Grady (landlord). The office knows plumbing is a priority if you need it. Also, Trevor Morrison is on our preferred vendor list.

He started the engine and put the tablet down, not expecting a quick reply. She had her hands full with a kitchen pipe and a wrench! He'd check when he got home after two more stops to check on his newly-acquired units. He may have overextended himself, but two of the properties, including 171 University, were in his desired location, and they didn't become available often.

To achieve his dream of retiring early, he had to be aggressive and take some risks. Smart risks. Calculated risks. Not silly risks. He pored over balance sheets, income statements, occupancy rates, location and demographic reports, and any other piece of information he could get his hands on to analyze and calculate the risks. He needed to make smart money moves, sound business decisions, and avoid risky investments.

If he continued to be smart about his money and investments, he'd be able to retire by the age of forty-five, then he could live his dream and travel the world.

There was no time for relationships, no time for extracurricular activities, no time for spunky brunettes with bright smiles and wrenches. He chuckled again, thinking about Nica's feisty spirit and stubborn attitude. Thank goodness he wasn't in the market for a relationship because someone like Nica could be a disruptor to his life plans.

Not only did she have a very pretty face and engaging smile; he really appreciated her can-do attitude to save some money. If she managed to fix the issue on her own and not call a professional plumber, it was a savings to his bottom line. He'd take it.

If he could keep the rental properties for the long term and invest in new property development, he'd be all right.

He pulled into the next apartment building on his list, 8808 Linden Avenue, a building with twelve units that had seen better days. The landscaping was non-existent and there was peeling paint and drywall damage in the small, outdated lobby. Four of the units were empty and he was having a hard time getting them rented. Non-rented units meant thousands of dollars a month not coming in to pay the bills and invest in more property.

Entering the lobby, he looked again at his surroundings. The nineteen-seventies-decorated lobby was atrocious. The lime-green wallpaper with gold foil accents, orange shag carpet in the sitting area, and purple-speckled linoleum flooring leading to the stairway, were a confusing and overwhelming mix of colors. He sighed as he surveyed the pitiful room. He needed to hire a contractor to come in and give him estimates to replace all of it, but with what? How could he remodel on the cheap and have it still look good for years to come? He would not be able to remodel every couple of years to stay trendy, even if that's what college kids wanted. He needed to be smart about this. Needed to use products that were sturdy, reliable, and good-looking.

He checked the ancient "suggestion box" in the lobby and made a mental note to ask Linda to investigate an online ticketing system where tenants could submit ideas and complaints. Then they could use analysis to evaluate requests based on data—what was the cost-benefit of the request, how many people reported it, what was the risk assessment score, and other such factors. No more responding to requests because the requester screamed the loudest—or was the prettiest petite brunette with a wrench.

He shook his head. It was going to be a while before he got Nica off his mind.

CHAPTER FIVE

NICA STOOD IN the kitchen with a cup of coffee in hand, admiring the ease with which the water drained from the sink. She leaned over and turned the water off, pleased with her accomplishment.

She picked up her phone and looked at the text message from the annoying landlord. She smiled to see that Paige's boyfriend, Trevor, was on the preferred plumber list. She would let him know the next time she saw him.

She chewed on her lower lip, debating whether to text Grady back or not. He was probably too busy, too important, and too pretentious to give a text from her more than passing notice. But she wanted to tell him that she'd fixed it on her own. No help needed, thank you very much.

NICA: I fixed the drainage issue in our sink. No need to call a plumber. Thought you might like to know.

No, that sounded weak. Too weak. She deleted it and tried again.

NICA: Fixed the sink. On my own.

She hit send and smiled. She'd love to see his face when he read it. She imagined his surprised look, his disbelief.

She put her phone and coffee mug on the counter. Lifting her right foot, she placed it on the counter and leaned over to stretch her hamstring. She held the stretch for several seconds, then repeated it on the other leg. As she continued stretching, her phone beeped.

> **GRADY:** Wow, look at you. Smarty pants with the wrench. So, are you sending me an invoice?

Wow. He actually asked for a bill? Just because she was a woman, he probably expected to get a bargain. Well, no way, José. And she wasn't referring to her cousin José. She was going to send a bill. She'd confer with Trevor first. What would he have charged for the job? She would bill Grady for the same amount that Trevor would have. That was only fair.

Izzy walked into the kitchen, wrapped in her long pink bathrobe. "Would you get your foot off the counter? That's disgusting."

"My feet are clean, I just showered!" Nica protested. She hadn't realized she had put her foot back up, but she took it down.

"Who's texting you this early? Is everything *bueno*?"

"How did you know...?"

"I heard la beep, beep." Izzy poured herself a half cup of coffee and filled the mug with cream. Nica winced to see the amount of dairy in the mug.

"Yes, everything's fine. It was the landlord. I let him know I fixed the sink and he asked if I was going to send him a bill." Nica smirked.

"And he said what exactly?"

"He called me a smarty pants with a wrench and asked about an invoice."

"Are you really going to send the landlord a bill for something you didn't ask permission to do?" Izzy gulped (gulped!) her coffee. Easy to do when it was lukewarm at best with all that cream.

"Since he was a beast about the whole thing, I think I will. I'll check with Trevor to see what he would charge."

"Double it."

"Ha. Great idea! But, no, that wouldn't work. That would look childish. I want to show him that a woman should get equal pay for the same job."

"Way to stick it to the man. Tell me more about the landlord," Izzy continued. "Was he old and fat? Bald?"

Nica thought about the annoying man that came to their apartment. Not old. Not fat. Not bald. "The complete opposite of all those things."

"Oh, yeah? Maybe I should be home the next time he comes."

"I don't think he's going to make a habit of stopping by to tell us when work is going to be done on the building, Iz. He's a businessman. Doing business things. Being busy and important." Nica held onto the counter and started calf raises.

"Are you running this morning? What's with all the stretches?"

"No. I feel tight."

"OK. Back to the landlord. He sounds like a dull, boring human. I hope I'm not home if he ever stops by."

For some reason, that pleased Nica. She usually wasn't jealous of Izzy. But Izzy was a knockout and attracted men like sugar water attracts hummingbirds.

"What are your plans for today?" Nica asked.

"I work from noon to four, then I have a date with Evan."

"Evan? Have I even heard of Evan?"

"Um, no. I met him last night at the gas station."

"Is dating him so soon a good idea?"

"Strike while the iron is hot. And this guy is hot, hot, hot." Izzy did a little shimmy as she described Evan.

"Your number one quality in a man. Just be careful."

"I'm good. Bought a mini-can of pepper spray for my keychain. What are you doing on this glorious Saturday?"

Nica glanced out the window in the exterior door. It was a beautiful early fall day in central Illinois. "Now that you mention it, I am going for a run. After that, I will catch up on homework."

"You're not working today?"

"No, a rare Saturday off. I'm going to take advantage of it."

Izzy poured herself another coffee and cream combo and went back to her room. Nica rinsed out her cup and put it in the sink. She picked up her phone and looked at Grady's text again. She was going to send him a bill, it was a matter of principle now.

NICA: Send the invoice to your mgmt co?

GRADY: No. Email me. Litup1994@litup.com

Nica frowned. That probably meant he wasn't taking her seriously. Why wouldn't he want it to go to the management company? She decided this was a good problem to mull over while she ran, so she put on her shoes and left.

AFTER HER FOUR-MILE run, Nica showered and called Trevor to confer on an appropriate charge for the clogged pipe repair. Then she plopped on the couch with her laptop and sports psychology textbook. Before she settled into reading and studying for her exam on Tuesday, she crafted her invoice for Grady and hastily created a company name for herself.

To: Grady Litwiller
Lit-Up Properties

From: Dominica Mendoza
Dom's Domestic Industries

Re: Invoice 101

Dear Sir,

This invoice is for services provided on October 3, repair of clogged kitchen sink at 171 University, Apt E.

Amount Due: $125
Due upon receipt.

Sincerely,
Dominica Mendoza, President

She reread the email and smiled. Perfect. She thought about putting "non-negotiable" in the invoice but decided against it. She would see how he responded first.

CHAPTER SIX

OME FROM THE gym, Grady booted up his laptop in his office. It was the smallest bedroom of his two-bedroom, one-bath mid-century modern duplex. He lived in one unit and rented the other to a fellow bachelor, Lionel. It was the first property he'd bought, three months after college graduation. All through college, he'd saved at least fifty dollars a week in a non-touchable account called 'House Fund'. Any extra money after paying for school and living expenses had gone into the account. He wasn't just frugal in college, he was FRUGAL. Girlfriends didn't stick around long after they realized he wasn't going to shower them with gifts and fancy dinners. That was fine with him; marriage and family were not part of his near-term goals.

Waiting for the laptop to boot up, he went into his kitchen to get a Coke out of the fridge. He loved the burst of flavor and sugar after a workout. He drank plenty of water before and during his workout for proper hydration; the Coke was a treat.

In the office, he nudged his solid gray cat, Chad, named after his favorite drummer, Chad Smith of the Red Hot Chili Peppers, off the office chair. "Sorry, buddy, I have to get on the computer. You can have the chair back when I'm done."

Opening his email application, he thought about the note he

needed to send Linda with a list of items for her to follow up on. There were several open apartments that he hoped could be leased soon. It would be a challenge now that the school year was underway. Not a lot of college students had the time or desire to move-in during the months of October, November, or December. Maybe they could advertise holiday move-in specials and interest students wanting out of bad roommate situations for the spring semester.

Once the email application opened, he saw an email from Dominica at the top. He smiled as he read it. He paused looking at her "company name". It sounded like something she probably didn't intend. He quickly sent a short response.

> Re: Re: Invoice 101
> To: Dom's Domestic Industries
>
> Dear Ms. Mendoza,
>
> We will process the payment soon.
>
> I would also like to suggest that you consider changing your company name. "Dom" probably isn't the best abbreviation if you think about it. And, "domestic" could refer to cleaning houses vs. repairing them.
>
> Sincerely,
> Grady Litwiller–President, Lit-Up Properties

Skimming the rest of his emails, he saw one from his Grandpa Fred. He read the note and pulled a drumstick out of his pencil cup. He started tapping on the desktop in frustration. His grandfather had received an offer for his farmland—an offer that might be too good to pass up.

Grady cursed the timing. If only his grandfather had mentioned the possibility of selling the land six months earlier, Grady could have considered buying and preserving it. He'd hoped for a long time that when his grandfather finally decided to retire, he'd be able to afford to buy the family farm and ensure it wasn't busted up or sold to a corporation that cared only about profit and not about legacy and the environment. If he bought the farm, he'd look for someone to lease the land for farming.

As it was, Grady had bought three apartment buildings recently, and now all of his cash was tied up, and his debt was over seven digits. There was no way his bank, or any bank, would take that kind of risk on an unproven businessman. If his grandfather seriously considering selling it soon, Grady would be unable to save the family farm.

A quick look at the clock told him it was only 2:00 p.m. He would send his email to Linda, shower, and take a drive to Armington to see his grandpa and talk about the options. More than anything, Grady wanted to tell his grandpa that he would like to buy the farm. At least, he hoped to be able to convince Grandpa Fred to wait to sell and give Grady time to get a plan together. Maybe he could ask his brothers if they would be interested in going in with him to buy their grandpa's property.

Matt would have to consult with Julie. Cooper was only twenty-five and still finding himself. Meaning, he had dropped out of college and was a server at one of the steakhouses in town. He might not be in the best position to invest now, but maybe this opportunity would spur Cooper to get his financial act together. Grady could only hope.

SITTING ON ONE of the many rocking chairs on the porch of his grandpa's farm, drinking his second Coke of the day, Grady surveyed the autumn landscape. The leaves on the trees were turning and beginning to fall. The large yard was littered with their orange, yellow, and gold discards. The trees would be bare in a few more weeks and the fields would be harvested soon.

Grandpa Fred said he thought he'd have his completed by early November if the weather remained dry.

"Do you need to hire extra help to harvest this year, Grandpa?" Grady asked, setting his empty soda can on the floor of the porch, next to his chair.

Grandpa Fred rocked slowly, like he didn't have a care in the world. "Naw, Bob and I will manage just fine. Not planting the forty acres behind Miller's Creek this season kept the workload doable. Don't you worry about the harvest, Grady. We got it under control."

"What about this offer you received, are you seriously considering it?" Grady thought about Cooper's dream as a child to take over the farm. As he got older and began helping his grandpa out, he'd realized the work was hard and dirty, and he'd decided he didn't like getting dirty.

"Honestly, not sure. It's a good offer, and it's from someone who says he wants to farm it, not break it up, develop houses on it, or create commercial sites. So that's appealing. Sure wish one of you boys would have gotten the farming bug. Would have liked to see it stay in the family."

"I know. I do, too."

"Don't get me wrong. I'm proud of all of you. You're smart and hard-working. Would have been nice if your grandma and I had been able to have more kids; maybe the farming gene would have passed on. But your mama did us proud. Married a good man and raised three amazing sons. We did something right."

Grady smiled, thinking about Grandma Miriam. She'd been a tough lady that would chew you out if you were doing wrong, kiss your boo-boos, and make a perfect batch of peanut butter cookies, Grady's favorite. He secretly thought he was her favorite grandson because she'd always made peanut butter cookies even though Matt and Cooper preferred chocolate chip.

"Yes, you did." Grady watched a hawk swoop down into the field. "Back to that offer. If there was a way I, or more likely, my brothers and I, could buy the property, do you think we could lease the land for someone else to farm? Are there any farmers nearby looking for additional land who might go into a lease agreement?" Grady leaned forward and stopped rocking, closely watching his grandpa.

"Huh," Grandpa Fred looked off into the distance. "Someone to lease. Interesting. And you would consider buying the property?"

"Yes, I would. I would like the property to stay in the family. Who knows, maybe someday Matt or Cooper will have a kid that wants to farm it. Maybe the gene just jumped two generations." He smiled at his grandpa.

"What about you?" Fred asked. "Couldn't you have a kid that wanted to farm?"

"I'm too much of a loner to consider myself marriage material, much less father material. I work sixty to seventy hours a week now. And I love it. I can't imagine cutting back on the work, and that wouldn't be fair to a woman. Or a family."

As he answered, an image of Nica and her pipe wrench appeared in his mind. He grinned, and hoped his grandfather wouldn't question the look.

"You're a workaholic. That's not good. You'll likely die of a heart attack before fifty. And they say farming's hard."

"It is hard, Grandpa! You're the hardest worker I know. Besides, I take care of myself. I went to the gym today, and I usually go a few times a week."

"Yeah, those sodies will kill ya though."

Grady laughed. His consumption of soda had always been a worry of his grandparents'. "Maybe so, old man. Maybe so. But do you think getting someone to lease is a possibility?" Grady still didn't know how he (or they) would secure the loan.

"I got a couple of folks in mind. I'll feel them out. Would love to see it stay in the family." He sighed and looked at Grady. "Wish I could just turn it over to you, but I had to take a loan out on the property a few years ago, shortly after your grandma died. I just couldn't keep up; I was grieving for her, for what I lost. My mind was so consumed, I made a few mistakes, and lost most of the crop yield that year. And I won't turn any debt over to my kin."

Grady thought of his own debt. Good thing he didn't have a wife or kids to be saddled with debt along with him. He was comfortable managing it on his own but wouldn't want his spouse to bear the burden. "I understand that. Well, let me know what you find out. I'll talk to Matt and Cooper. Maybe Dad would be interested in going in on it, too."

He pushed back to start rocking again. He soon matched his grandpa's pace, and they rocked quietly, enjoying the peaceful country view and the beloved companionship.

CHAPTER SEVEN

THE FOLLOWING WEDNESDAY, Nica was at In Bloom, the flower shop where she worked. It was a busy day, and most of the employees were there, along with Anna Lee, the owner. The only one missing was Tilly.

This weekend was the annual Pumpkin Festival in Morton, and Anna Lee was leading the team in making the final flower arrangements and crafts that she would be selling in her booth there. They were making both live and dried floral arrangements featuring fall colors of yellow, orange, tan, and deep crimson. Morton was proclaimed the "Pumpkin Capital of the World" by the Illinois governor back in 1978, as eighty-five percent of the world's canned pumpkin was processed there.

Anna Lee brought a large bucket of dahlias to the worktable. Most of the flowers' largest petals were raspberry-colored, with smaller coral-colored petals, and centers a shade of sweet peach. Orange blooms with pink and gold highlights added extra fall color.

"Where do these flowers come from?" Nica asked.

"I grew all of these in my own garden. The coral and raspberry ones are called Belle of Barmera, and the orange ones are called Mango Madness. Aren't they beautiful?" she asked, pushing her long, silver bangs back behind one ear.

"They're gorgeous. I'm surprised they grow so well here. Did you know that the dahlia flower is the national flower of Mexico?" Nica pulled a stem from the bucket and snipped off the leaves. She put three stems into a tall white glass vase. One vase down, nineteen to go.

"I did know that, Cricket," Anna Lee said. Nica wondered if she was the only worker at In Bloom with the nickname "Cricket". She'd have to ask the others. "They can't survive the harsh Illinois winter though." Anna Lee swept a few leaves off the table, into her hand. "I have to dig up the roots after the first frost. I usually ask for helpers for fall yard cleanup. I can do the ongoing maintenance myself, but the fall cleanup is intense and my ol' bones can only take so much."

"Sounds interesting. I'd love to help." Nica thought about the physical benefits of gardening. While helping Anna Lee, she could document which muscles were being worked. It would be research for an upcoming paper she needed to write on occupational fitness.

Paige placed a box of additional vases on the worktable. "You're in the best shape to help, Nica. I helped last year, and I was sore for a week afterward. I think Lauren took an hour-long break after breaking a fingernail," she joked.

Nica was still getting to know Lauren. Though Nica had started working at In Bloom back in May, Lauren had left in mid-May to go on a backpacking trip across Europe. She had returned in August, but since they were back in class, Nica and Lauren had not worked together very often.

"No. That's an exaggeration, Paige." Lauren declared. "I took a quick break to get a bandage on my finger. Anna Lee can attest."

"What? I don't recall. I think I heard the doorbell jingle," Anna Lee said, exiting the room.

The girls fell back into their easy rhythm filling the vases and talking about fall semester classes and activities. After all the dahlias had been arranged and the vases set on shelves against the wall, they began setting up to arrange artificial flowers in craft pumpkins. Lauren cut the tops off the artificial pumpkins, Paige stuffed the pumpkins with biodegradable floral foam and Nica trimmed the piles of artificial flowers with wire cutters. Then, she cut and sorted the flowers into color groups.

Lauren cut the last pumpkin open and put it on the table. She picked up one of the pumpkins that Paige had stuffed and began arranging floral picks in it according to the sample that Anna Lee had made. "Paige, how's Trevor? I haven't heard you mention him for a week."

"Oh, he's great," she smiled. "Things are going well. I've just been so focused on classes and work, trying to get the right study schedule in place. I have a heavy class load this fall so I can graduate in the spring even with attending the internship, so I haven't been able to see Trevor as much as I'd like."

"I can vouch for that," Nica added. "Haven't seen Trevor at the apartment in a while."

"I told him I have to focus on schoolwork. He's very understanding. Since I'm not working on Saturday, we're going to the Pumpkin Festival."

"Yes, please stop by and say hello," Nica said. "I want you to see the booth that I designed. I think Trevor will be impressed with my handiwork."

"And, Lauren," Paige said, turning to the pretty blond, "I'm hoping Trevor's friend, Hawk, will be with us. I want to introduce the two of you. I think you'll like him."

"Oh, yeah? You've talked about him enough; I would like to finally meet him. Let's see if there's any attraction on the part of either party." Lauren said, sounding like a lawyer. She finished her first pumpkin arrangement and spun it around so the others could see it. They nodded in appreciation. "Does Trevor have a friend for Nica too?"

"Doesn't matter," Nica quickly responded. "I'm not interested in being set up. No, thank you!"

"Come on, Nica," Paige jumped in. "You haven't dated a single person since I met you. It's not healthy."

"Not interested."

"Wait!" Paige held up a hand and shot a cunning smile at Lauren. "What about our landlord? He was very handsome, and I swear there were some sparks flying."

"There was something flying all right. His ego and the ridiculousness he was spewing."

Paige laughed. "No, that's not what I saw."

Nica's heart raced. She was still trying to figure out what she thought about Grady and she wasn't ready to discuss him with her friends.

Her stomach knotted. She felt it every time she wasn't heard. It felt like a barbed wire fence was separating her from whoever wasn't listening to her. It was usually a feeling she got when talking with her parents.

"He called me Nikki, for goodness sake," she exclaimed. "He's a world-class menace. And I'm sure he has a perfect girlfriend. Perfect life. But I don't care. Not interested."

"Nica! That's not nice. And not like you. I've never heard you talk about someone in such a negative way. Are you okay?" Paige leaned over and wrapped an arm around Nica's shoulders.

Nica slumped. This *wasn't* like her. She normally saw the positive in everything and everyone. Maybe the stress of school and pursuing a degree she didn't want wholeheartedly, was weighing her down.

Besides, she was still embarrassed about the email exchange with Grady. She had been pleased with the company name she'd come up with when she invoiced Grady for the sink repair. But then he had to go and point out that there was a potential double entendre in "Dom's Domestic Industries". And he said it so coldly, so matter of fact. She acknowledged that it was in an email, and they tended to be cold, and it could be hard to interpret someone's meaning. But still, he could have been nicer about it.

She needed to buck up. She was sloppy with her on-the-fly company name, and he just pointed it out. He was probably trying to help. She should talk to Lauren about a company name, she would have good advice.

Lauren came around the table as well and patted Nica's arm. "Hey, now. Just forget all about him. And you say the word and we will be on the hunt for a suitable match for you. You just tell us what you're looking for and, when you're ready, we're here to help. And if you are happy being single, then more power to you."

Anna Lee returned to the workroom. "What's going on, ladies?" Her brow furrowed as she hurried over to where Paige and Lauren were clustered around Nica in a protective way.

"Nothing. I'm fine. I'm fine." Nica sat up straighter and smiled at the others.

"That face doesn't look fine. Spill." Anna Lee put her hands on her hips and stared Nica down.

"I was just feeling frustrated with our landlord. He sort of put me down for working on our sink when he stopped by. He acted like, of course, I couldn't do it because I'm a girl. I hate that." That wasn't hard to admit, Paige was already aware of that issue. She wasn't going to embarrass herself again and tell these women about her misguided "company name".

Maybe she was a little jealous of Grady. He seemed to be on top of his business game while she was still working hard to make it through college before she would start to pursue her passion. He had the investment and business experience that she would need to flip houses.

Not that there was a reason to continue to talk to him or see him, but she could probably learn something from him. And he was very easy on the eyes. She'd never admit it to Paige, but he made her think about dating again.

Anna Lee nodded. "Well, his opinion don't amount to a hill of beans. Forget it. You are an amazing, talented, fierce woman. Don't let no man's opinion, comment, or expression derail you."

"What about parents' opinions?" Nica was sure Anna Lee would say to listen to her parents.

"Nica. You're an adult. Adults make mistakes. Adults do things their parents don't agree with. Believe me. I know."

Nica noticed that Lauren and Paige exchanged a look. They had told Nica that they were curious about Anna Lee's past. She didn't share much with them.

"But," Anna Lee continued, "You have to decide what's best for you. What's right for *you*. And yes, I'm supposed to say listen to your parents, but shoot, when do I say what I'm supposed to?" She laughed and looked around. "Well, are we gonna finish up today, ladies?"

Lauren took charge. "Yes, we are!"

They all turned back to the worktable and restarted. That was just what Nica needed.

CHAPTER EIGHT

FTER A LONG Thursday filled with meetings with the loan officers in his branch, Grady was ready to head to the gym to work out and release the tension pulling on his shoulder blades. Thursdays were tough due to the number of house closings on Fridays. There were always last-minute issues with paperwork and decisions that needed to be made.

He admired the team that was in place at his bank—especially because he'd been able to hire both loan officers himself. To have a great team is to make a great team. And accountability for this branch's success rested firmly on Grady's tired shoulders.

Settled into his car for the commute to the gym, Grady pulled the business card from the interior pocket of his suit jacket. He propped the card up behind the gear stick. On the back of the card was the bulleted list of items he wanted to go over with Linda during the drive. They often exchanged emails throughout the day, but he limited the time he focused on the property management business while working at the bank.

Grady was thankful that Linda was a good sport about the crazy hours. They started each workday with a 7 a.m. call and ended it with a 5:30 p.m.-ish call. Long hours, but Grady knew Linda took an extra-long lunch to compensate.

He started the car and resisted the urge to pick up his drumsticks. He needed to concentrate on navigating his way out of the parking lot and onto a busy Veterans Parkway.

Linda answered on the second ring. "Hey, Grady. How was your Thursday? As busy as you expected?"

"Busier. I thought home closings would have slowed down now that we're in late September, with kids back in school and all. But, we have eight closings tomorrow. How was *your* day? Were you able to schedule those showings that we talked about this morning?"

"Yes, they are all scheduled for tomorrow or Saturday. So, hopefully, we'll get a few takers for the empty units on Linden."

"From your mouth to God's ears." Grady chuckled at his use of one of his grandmother's favorite sayings. "Keep me posted on those."

"Of course. Next up, I got the check ready to go for Ms. Mendoza. I assumed you wanted me to mail it, so I dropped it in the mail today."

Grady winced. He had wanted to drop off the check at Nica's apartment personally and compliment her on the fix. And it would've been nice to see her again. Maybe seeing her would help get her off his mind. He didn't have time for the distraction. "That's fine."

"Good. You seemed interested in her before, so after I mailed it I had a brief pause, thought maybe you'd want to do something else." There was a teasing tone to her voice.

He needed to change the subject pronto. "No, you did right. Now, about those suggestion box tickets that I dropped off to you the other day. Anything urgent?"

"No." He could hear Linda typing, diligently checking her notes. He appreciated her thoroughness. "They were mostly complaints about the lighting in the parking lot. I called three electricians for quotes to get it fixed. I'm waiting on the last estimate. Hopefully, I'll get that tomorrow and be able to assign the work."

Grady glanced down at his card, as he turned onto Empire St. He had to make a stop at the post office before the gym. "Thanks for following up on the electrical work. Make sure you consider timeliness to commit to the repair, not just the cost, in the decision."

"Do you want to see the specifics before I make a decision?"

"No, I trust you. Let's just get it done quickly. If potential renters drive by at night, the poor lighting may turn them away."

"Got it," Linda replied.

"How are things coming on the contractor to replace the stairs at 171 University?"

"Scheduled to start on October third."

"Good. Will you remind them of the bonus for getting the work done in two days, please?"

"You bet," Linda answered. "I have a call scheduled with Mr. Peña on Thursday to confirm everything. I also have a letter to send to the tenants on Tuesday to remind them."

"Can I take a look at that letter before you send it?"

"Sure. Hmm."

"What?"

"You sure are interested in that property. I'm not sure if it's the property or the tenants. Or one certain tenant. She must be special."

"Yes, she is." Grady smiled. Nica was special. Beautiful. Energetic. Feisty. With a wrench in her hand. A surprising combination.

"Interesting. Isn't there a rule in your rule book about dating tenants?"

Grady thought about the Method of Procedure document that he and Linda had written up as he began his property business and added Linda as his first, and only, full-time employee. "Ha, ha. Nice try. Of course I'm not going to date a tenant. She's a fiery Latina and a hot mess." He thought of her dripping hair. "She's probably just in college to find a husband. You know they all want a dozen kids and to stay at home while the husband pays the bills and takes care of them. No, thank you."

"Oh, my word. You could not sound more sexist if you tried, Grady Litwiller. Rethink your life choices and call me back when you've got more sense." She hung up on him.

"Ah, for the love of Slovak," Grady swore, invoking the memory of the Red Hot Chili Pepper's original guitarist. He pulled into an empty parking space at the post office. Turning off the car, he grabbed the drumsticks and began tapping out a favorite drum fill pattern. The regular rhythm began to ease his spiked blood pressure after a few minutes. It was great that Linda was a close friend, but there were times, like now, that tensions arose despite, or because of, their ease with one another.

After five minutes of banging out his frustrations on the steering wheel, Grady leaned back and let out a heavy sigh. "She's right. I hate it when she's right."

He redialed Linda's number and waited. She let it ring four times before answering, and when she did answer, she didn't say anything. She sat in silence.

Grady waited a few seconds to see if she would greet him. When she didn't, he sighed again and began apologizing. "Linda, you are absolutely right. I apologize. That was a terrible assumption and statement that I made. I'm sorry and I appreciate that you hold me accountable." He waited.

After another pregnant pause, she spoke. "That's better, Grady. You know I care for you, and I will call out your misogynistic b.s. every time. You know better. You need to do better."

"You're right. Thank you. Now, can we continue?"

Grady could hear the smile in her voice when she spoke next. "Can you first define your amends?" This was a running practice between them. When one called out the other one for a faux pas, they had to make "amends".

"Hmm," he stalled, thinking. "I will make a hundred-dollar donation to the Red Cross."

"Close, but I think something Hispanic would be appropriate in this case."

He grunted, then asked, "Do you have something in mind? I'm afraid I'm at a loss here."

"That's part of the problem, Grady. I have an idea. Have you heard of The Immigration Resource Center?"

"No, what's that?"

"It's a non-profit organization providing legal assistance to immigrants. My roommate's boyfriend volunteers there."

"Great. I'll donate to them. Now, can we continue our regular meeting?"

"Well, it's a step in the right direction," Linda conceded.

"Good. Can you make a check out to them?"

"No, no, no. This isn't coming out of the business account, Grady. This needs to come out of your personal finances."

"Fine. I'll send a check this weekend. Will you send me an email to remind me?" Grady exited the car and walked towards the post office.

"Of course, boss. Now, I have to bring something to your attention. And I hate doing this. It's not good."

Grady reached out for the door handle and paused. First, he'd been reprimanded by Linda, then hung up on, and NOW she had bad news?

"Yes?" He got out of the car and walked into the post office, hoping the movement would ease his stress.

"Tom and Marty called today." She paused.

Tom and Marty were the investors that Grady had courted to invest in the apartment building on East Chestnut, just two blocks from the Illinois Wesleyan campus. "And?" Grady prompted.

"They've been reviewing the financial statements that I sent over. They are not pleased with the vacancy rate in Linden. They're worried about your cash flow."

Another reason Grady appreciated Linda's friendship was that she knew every detail of his professional finances. She kept her eye on the flow of every receivable and expense.

"There's nothing to worry about!" Grady shouted, his words vibrating off the walls in the (thankfully) empty lobby. Lowering his voice, he continued. "Are you kidding me? There are only four empty units."

"Out of twelve, that's thirty-three percent."

Gah. Grady knew that. He didn't like hearing Linda spell it out. "I know. What did they say? Are they having second thoughts?"

"Yes, you could say that. They said if you don't get at least three of those units leased by December first, they will not go through with the backing for Chestnut. Sorry, Grady."

Grady pulled the phone away from his ear and faked a punch to the brick wall. He tapped a fist against it while thinking. There was no easy answer. Putting the phone back to his ear, he heard Linda typing. "Back to the electrician. All emphasis on speed, okay?"

"Yes. Got it. Potential bonus?"

"Sure." Ugh, these bonuses weren't great for the bottom line. "I need to come up with a solution to get renters in there. First month free?"

"Grady, you've seen that lobby, right? You might have to give several months free to get people in there. It's hideous."

Ouch. She was right. What was cheaper, remodeling or free rent? Free rent might just be a short-term fix. Long term, it needed to be remodeled. If only he could do it on a budget.

"Thanks for the news flash."

"Hey, just trying to keep it real, boss. Anything else on your list?"

Grady got the stamps he needed out of the vending machine and exited. His mind was swimming, and he couldn't remember what else was on his list. "Whatever it is, it can wait until the morning. Have a good evening, Linda."

"Later, Gravy Grady."

CHAPTER NINE

THERE WAS NO escaping the smell of fall in the air. And by fall, Nica meant pumpkins and spice. Lauren brought each of them an extra-large pumpkin spice latte and Nica took a moment to inhale the aroma and take two large gulps of the creamy, sweet goodness. Normally, she wasn't a sweets person, but working Anna Lee's booth at the Morton Pumpkin Festival was going to require a caffeine boost.

Anna Lee's natural energy was bubbling over. She loved nothing more than to meet people, and with thousands of festival attendees, she would be in her element today. She finished setting out the last batch of pumpkin princess wands—twelve-inch wands with a small pumpkin glued to the top and ribbons, flowers, and orange sparkles aplenty.

"Anything else to set out, Anna Lee?" Lauren asked, putting her latte on the card table that sat in the middle of their booth space. The outside of the booth was rimmed with eight foot long, two-foot-wide folding tables lined with items for sale. There were boxes and boxes of additional products to sell under all the tables, hidden by tablecloths.

"No, we're good for now. Just remember, when you start to see stock dwindle, add more," Anna Lee directed, finally standing still for a moment, and shrugging her shoulders to loosen the apparent stiffness in them.

Nica tightened the In Bloom apron around her neck. The large pocket on the front held money for change, a small sales pad to record sales and provide receipts to shoppers, and a stash of M&Ms, her go-to junk food—it was easy to only eat a few at a time to get the small sugar rush but not go overboard. Though she suspected that today she'd eat the full, king-size bag and regret it later.

Lauren looked at her watch. "It's seven forty-five. Shoppers should start coming by soon, right?"

Anna Lee nodded. "I'm surprised they haven't started already. Like a garage sale, the early bird gets the worm. Or the pumpkin arrangement, in our case." She laughed as she put on her own apron. "Nica, I have to tell you again that the facade you designed is amazing. We are going to get so many compliments on it today. No other booth looks as good as ours!"

Nica smiled at Anna Lee's enthusiasm. She hoped she would get to the point where she could say whatever she wanted without feeling like she had to tamp down her passion or hold her tongue when she disagreed with whatever was being said to her. She agreed with Anna Lee, the fake flower shop building was special, and Nica was excited to see the booth facade set up and in use for the first time. She had worked on it all summer long. When she first met Anna Lee back in the spring, Anna Lee had been preparing for a steampunk festival and said she wished she had a more striking setup for her flower booth for street fairs and festivals.

Nica had never heard of steampunk before coming to college. She discovered that it was a subgenre of science fiction that celebrated a retro-futuristic fantasy world where steam power reigned supreme. She loved attending her first "Cogs & Corsets" festival in Bloomington to see the fanciful costumes that mixed looks from the Victorian Era, technology, and the American Wild West.

Anna Lee and Nica had brainstormed ideas and Nica created an easily assembled pop-up booth surround that looked like a Paris flower market. The "building" was a deep green with "In Bloom Flower Shop" hand-lettered on the "door" in a fancy script. Nica cut out squares of the plywood and filled them with sheets of plastic to resemble windows, and Anna Lee painted rows of flowers in buckets on the plastic. The colors popped and made a striking display. The plastic windows helped keep the setup lightweight and easy to assemble. Some of the windows were easy to replace, according to the season or particular festival. For the steampunk festival, Anna Lee designed windows with cogs, clocks, wheels, and bolts in keeping with the steampunk aesthetic. For today's event, Anna Lee had painted the windows with fall leaves, pumpkins, and dahlia flowers. The colors were incredible—vibrant and fun, and the drawings themselves were realistic.

"And the windows you painted are the icing on the fancy cake!" Nica said, putting an arm around Anna Lee. Her petite stature put her shoulder to shoulder with the older woman.

"Speaking of cake, who's running after pumpkin donuts? I'm famished!" Anna Lee pulled a twenty out of her apron pocket and held it out.

"I'll go," Nica responded. She knew that once the festival got going, they would be busy and she might not get another chance to look around. "I saw a donut booth at the end of the first aisle. I'll be right back."

She walked along and looked at each booth—she was constantly looking for new ideas for her own crafts, and this fair did not disappoint. She saw decorative porch signs done up in fall colors, with heavy pumpkin accents, of course. She stopped briefly in front of a booth selling picture frames that had window screens stapled inside of them for hanging earrings and other jewelry. She made a mental note to craft something similar for her cousin Izzy, who was a jewelry hoarder, and her sister Lucia. Maybe even one for Evie—it would make a cute *quinceañera* gift.

When she finally made her way to the pumpkin donut stand, she groaned. There were at least thirty people standing in line in front of her. She pulled her cell phone out of her back pocket, snapped a picture, and sent it to Lauren, asking her to tell Anna Lee that she'd be back as soon as she could. Anna Lee still carried a flip phone and claimed it couldn't receive pictures. The girls in the shop weren't so sure about that. They speculated that Anna Lee just didn't want to learn how to send and receive pictures.

Twenty minutes later, she left the donut stand with a pack of six donuts. She was almost positive that she wouldn't eat any—all that sugar—but they smelled like warmth and pumpkin and heaven and cinnamon all rolled into delicious dough. The Pumpkin Festival only happened once a year, and where else would she get hot, fresh pumpkin donuts?

Back at Anna Lee's booth, Nica wasn't surprised to see it surrounded. She heard the oohs and aahs even before she approached. She walked behind the booth and entered, putting the warm donuts on the table in the middle. Walking to the side that was not manned by either Anna Lee or Lauren, Nica asked a customer if she needed any assistance.

The next three hours flew by. They helped customers, restocked tables, and chatted with passersby. Lauren even had to make a run to the van to get more boxes of floral crowns.

The flow of customers began to slow so Nica grabbed a second donut. She thought about giving away the pack of M&Ms in her pocket—if she ate them after the two delicious baked items, she would come down hard from a sugar high later in the afternoon, probably when they were at their busiest. She didn't want to be a grumpy grouch in front of Anna Lee.

Anna Lee looked at her watch, a skinny Timex face on a brown band. "Well, ladies, we may see a slow-down now that people will start thinking about lunch. We should think about lunch ourselves," she said, taking the last bite of her donut.

Lauren sighed, taking another bite of hers. "Can't we just get more donuts for lunch?"

"No way!" Nica exclaimed. "I cannot eat any more sweets today. And I recommend you don't, either. I brought an extra-large salad filled with veggies and chicken. I'd be happy to share."

"Oh, Nica," Lauren said. "You sure know how to burst someone's bubble." She smiled fondly and her blue eyes sparkled. "You're certainly right, though. I would regret more donuts. I brought a peanut butter and banana sandwich, so I'm good. What about you, Anna Lee, do you need lunch?"

"Nope. I brought—"

"Hello!" a woman called. They all turned towards the front of the booth and saw a local cameraman and newscaster standing there. The woman continued, "Wow. This booth is absolutely gorgeous. The exterior is amazing. Can we talk to you about it and film it for the local news station?"

Anna Lee beamed. "Why, yes, that would be terrific. And you're in luck because the person who designed and built the exterior is here with me today. Let me introduce you to my team. This is Lauren." Lauren stepped forward and shook the woman's hand. Anna Lee continued, "And this is Dominica. Nica. Nica designed and built the exterior. I'm Anna Lee Foster. I own In Bloom."

"You don't say. I'm impressed." The woman's eyes dropped down to Nica's tennis shoes and back up again. Nica tried not to stiffen. "Was it built specifically for this festival?"

Anna Lee answered, "Not specifically. I'll use it for all festivals going forward. When I first met Nica, I was preparing for the steampunk festival in Bloomington. I thought about how elaborate and unique that festival was, and I talked to Nica about wanting to have something that stood out. She listened to my ideas and then ran with them. She came up with some design options, we discussed them, and finally decided on the Parisian floral shop."

"Fantastic. Was it built in time for the steampunk fest?"

"No, I didn't give God enough time to build something for that fest." Anna Lee laughed. "This festival is the debut."

"Fantastic." The woman nodded to the cameraman. "Can you get some shots of the booth? I'll stand back. Ladies, smile and chat amongst yourself for a few moments. After he gets those shots, I'll ask Anna Lee and Nica to come around to the front for a short interview. Sound good?"

They did as requested, and Nica felt a shiver of anticipation. A feature of her work on TV would be fabulous. What a way to get her work out there! It would be extra-fabulous if her parents could see the feature. Hopefully, she could find it online and send it to them. Maybe then they would take her designing seriously. One could dream.

After the interview, Lauren gave each of them hugs. "You guys were marvelous! Anna Lee, great visibility for the shop, and Nica! Good exposure for your work, too! You have to find a way to take advantage of this. Do you have a website yet?"

Though her parents had encouraged her to become a lawyer, Lauren stood up to them and was pursuing a business degree. She was always thinking of marketing and the bottom line. She had made several suggestions to Anna Lee on cutting costs and reusing work assets to expand her business.

"No, I don't," Nica replied. "I didn't think I needed one yet. I can't focus on the design effort until I get my degree and start teaching. Then I can get my parents off my case and have more control over what I do."

"Hmm," Lauren murmured. "I can help you set up a website. It would just take us a couple of hours. Then you could start highlighting your work, and you could even set up a way to take on clients. At the very least, you could add your services and contact information. I wouldn't recommend putting any sort of pricing on your site; you'll need to estimate each job and write contracts to protect yourself."

Nica wondered if Lauren was getting ahead of herself. Contracts? That sounded complicated. How would she balance jobs that required contracts, schoolwork, and working at In Bloom? It could be too much.

Maybe they were being overly optimistic, but Nica was willing to take that leap of faith. They made plans to get together on Sunday afternoon to plan a website and to talk about Lauren's business major. Nica wanted to get an idea of what it would take to get a business minor along with her physical education degree. Maybe she wouldn't even need to tell her parents about the minor degree.

Several customers strolled up, and the booth got busy again. Twenty minutes later, they took turns eating lunch, taking bathroom breaks, and stepping away from the booth for a few minutes to recharge.

After 1 p.m., just when Nica was beginning to feel the sugar crash, Paige and Trevor approached the booth.

Lauren squealed when she saw them. Anna Lee smiled and sat down in a folding chair.

"You guys!" Paige exclaimed. "There is a murmur throughout the festival about the incredible flower booth! I've heard several people discussing it. Even without seeing it, I knew they were talking about this booth. Nica, even though I saw you building the pieces of this in your room, this just goes beyond my wildest imagination. It truly is amazingly amazing!"

Nica smiled at her roommate's praise. She finally knew that 'amazingly amazing' was a nod to Paige's favorite book, *The Hitchhikers Guide to the Galaxy*. "Thank you, Paige. I appreciate your kind words. What do you think, Trevor?"

Having worked with Trevor on the restoration of his house, she was especially curious to see what he would say of her handiwork.

"It's incredible!" He gently shook one of the panels. "Sturdy. It's not going anywhere."

"Had to make sure they didn't fall over—either inward or outward." Nica explained. "They're laced together with heavy-duty ratchet straps and anchored in the back with concrete blocks. They're a bear to haul, but not so bad with an industrial dolly."

Lauren jumped in. "Anna Lee and Nica were interviewed for the news. We all need to be watching. Hopefully, they'll feature it online, too."

"All right! You're stars!" Paige high-fived everyone, including Trevor. Afterwards, he pulled her close to his side. Nica was happy to see her friends so in love.

"Well," she asked them, "tell us about the rest of the festival. What have you seen?"

Paige filled them in on the activities happening throughout the festival. There was a Big Wheel Race, a pumpkin decorating contest and later in the evening there would be a lip sync contest.

This year's festival theme was the eighties, and Paige and Trevor told them about the eighties-themed pumpkins. Their favorites were a pumpkin decorated as Garfield the cat and another display with characters from the *Ghostbusters* movie, including a Stay-Puft Marshmallow Man—his arms and legs were made of very small pumpkins, and his body and head were larger pumpkins—all painted white.

"I called Tilly," Paige said. Tilly was the other In Bloom employee who was handling the store on her own. "I told her she has to come here when she closes up In Bloom. Maybe she'll stop by and see you. If she gets here in time, we're going to watch the lip sync contest together. Trevor and I will stop and help you tear down and pack up when the craft fair closes, too."

CHAPTER TEN

GRADY WATCHED THE sky lighten Sunday morning, but due to clouds and rain, he couldn't say he watched the sun rise. Trying to come up with a quick, cheap, and effective solution to rent out the Linden apartments was still needling him. He had put in a day in the bank office on Saturday, using the resources available to him there—mainly an eight-foot long white board and a plethora of colored dry-erase markers to drum up ideas.

As energizing and creative as the brainstorming process had been, it had only generated a list of ideas on paper. A few of them were actionable, but most of them would take too much money or too much time to give him the results he needed.

He was frustrated at his lack of progress, so he woke early. All right, sleep was eluding him, to be honest. He awoke before daybreak and found his cat Chad sleeping on his pillow, just above his head, likely looking for body heat. Grady went to bed with the window open, even though the overnight low was predicted to be upper-forties at best.

He rolled out of bed without disturbing Chad and hit the shower. He'd go to the gym later and work out, which would require another shower, but for now, he thought the water would help clear his head and get the creative juices flowing.

Thirty minutes later, he was at the kitchen table, cup of coffee in hand and pages of notes spread out before him. He reviewed all the notes from Saturday's brainstorming session and reminded himself that he was full of ideas, just no great ones.

Grady ran his hand through his medium-brown hair, still damp from the shower, scraping down the close cut in the back. He opened his laptop to search for The Immigration Resource Center. He trusted Linda, and if she suggested the charity, he was sure it was legit, but he wanted to better understand what they did before he sent a donation. He spent several minutes perusing their website, noting their services and volunteer activities. He wasn't bilingual, so he didn't think he had a lot to offer. Well, he'd promised Linda he'd make a donation, so he clicked the donate button, sent an online payment, and signed off.

He hoped his donation would make a difference in someone's life and he said a prayer, asking forgiveness for the stupid comment he made about Dominica the other day. "Know better, do better," he told himself.

He turned on the TV to provide some background noise while he continued his efforts and grabbed a bottle of orange juice out of the fridge. He sat back down to work as a perky reporter began singing the praises of a festival. It was way too early for that kind of perkiness. He reached for the remote to turn the TV off, but when he glanced at the screen, he saw a familiar feisty Latina. Dominica. She was on TV. Instead of turning it off, he turned the volume up.

The reporter continued, "I was blown away when I saw this incredible booth at the Art and Craft Fair this morning, and the festival-goers we've talked to have said the same thing. Just look at the features of this beautiful flower booth. This was the brainchild of Anna Lee Foster, who owns the In Bloom Flower Shop in Bloomington, and her employee, Dominica Mendoza.

Both of these ladies are here today. Anna Lee, tell us again where the idea came from."

An older woman, late sixties if Grady had to guess, spoke next. "Back in the spring, I was preparing for the Cogs and Corsets Steampunk Festival in Bloomington. I was excited to be attending that festival again. I created some unique floral arrangements for it. And I love the atmosphere. I dress up. I love seeing the attendees dress up. It's just so unique! Well, I had just met Nica, and I lamented at how boring and plain my typical booth set up was. White tables, white tablecloths. Downright boring! She told me she was interested in designing solutions for homes and she said the booth would be a fun challenge. She took some time to think about ways to dress it up and brought me several designs. We quickly settled on the Parisian flower shop with these fantastic faux windows which I can change out, based on the event."

The reporter leveled a question to Nica. "Dominica. So, you're a designer. That's fantastic. Tell me more about what you did here."

Nica smiled, and Grady was surprised to feel himself smile along with her. His worries about the empty rental units faded, and the angst of what to do about the investors vanished as he listened to her speak.

"Well, I would compare the concept to making gingerbread houses. I took pieces of a sturdy but thin plywood, cut them to the right size, and cut out holes for the windows. After that, I painted them, added accents like the door handles and the trim pieces to give it a three-dimensional effect. I devised a connection system that would offer stability and portability. But all in all, I'm just happy that Anna Lee is happy." She stopped speaking and looked at the older woman with caring and appreciation.

"Well, kudos, young lady. How can our viewers find you? Assuming you're available for other special projects?" The reporter prompted.

"For now, the easiest way to find me is on Instagram. My handle is NiftyNica01."

The reporter turned towards the camera and Anna Lee put her arm around Nica. Everyone smiled at the camera. "There's so much to see here at the Morton Pumpkin Festival, and the weather is perfect—if you have a light jacket. Come on out and enjoy the day!"

The news shifted back to the anchors in the studio and Grady was not in the mood for their banter. He shut the TV off and leaned against the counter. Nica had design experience. She seemed to balance aesthetics and functionality well with the booth design. Maybe she could help with the Linden lobby situation. Hmm. With all the stress he had going on now, did he have the energy to put up with her sassy attitude? Well, he could put Linda in charge. Then he wouldn't have to get involved. Being involved could be fun. Or it could be infuriating. But it could be fun.

"WHAT'S UP, GROOVY Grady?" Linda asked, answering her phone Monday morning.

Sunday was the one day of the week Grady tried not to talk to Linda. If there was an emergency, she would reach out to him. Even though Grady was itching to get something started on Sunday, he waited until their normal morning call on Monday before involving her.

"Morning, Linda," he answered. "I did some brainstorming this weekend on what to do about the Linden lobby to get the apartments rented out. I think I might have something."

"Oh? Great. Lay it on me."

"I'd like to reach out to Dominica Mendoza to see if she can come up with a creative and cheap solution to make over the lobby." Grady braced for a snarky remark.

"Dominica?" The doubt in Linda's voice was clear. "The tenant that fixed her sink? Are you sure she's qualified?"

"Hear me out. She was on the news yesterday morning. She was interviewed by a reporter covering the Pumpkin Fest—the one in Morton. She had designed and built a clever facade for a craft booth. She works at the In Bloom flower shop here in Bloomington and she made it for the owner."

"Oh, I know that florist. They do great work. But that's flowers."

"Right. Look. She didn't make an arrangement. She took plywood panels and made it appear as though a building was standing around the booth. It was eye-catching, unique." *Just like the girl herself,* he thought to himself.

"Interesting. I'll see if I can find the news story online." Grady could hear her scratch a note on paper. "So, what's the next step? How can I help?"

"Could you draft a contract with just the basic language? I'll swing by her apartment this evening and talk to her. See if we can brainstorm and come up with some ideas."

"And..." Linda prompted.

"And?" Grady wondered what she was getting at.

"See if she's even interested. See if she has time. You can't just assume she's ready to jump in and do your bidding. You're persuasive, Grady. I'll give you that. But from what you told me about your initial run-in with her, I wouldn't assume she'll be gung-ho about working with you."

Dang. She was right. There had been a heated moment in their exchange. He knew she had been frustrated with him. But he'd shown up, he paid her for the work. Surely, that would count for something.

"Well, I won't know until I ask. Get the basic contract ready. Now, let's touch base on a few other things."

Grady needed to get his mind off Nica. Linda was right. There was a chance that Nica wouldn't agree. He wouldn't let his brain play out that scenario right now.

He was going to keep a positive attitude and use all of the charm he possessed to try to get Nica to see the benefits of this plan. Money for her, a really good project for her portfolio and the chance to work together. He didn't typically roll up his sleeves and do the manual work, but if it gave him a chance to work alongside Nica and get to know her better, he could see himself enjoying it. The work of course.

THE BANK WAS hopping all day Monday. He held his normal Monday planning meeting with his staff. They celebrated last week's wins and planned for an even better week ahead. One of the things Grady liked most about his role as branch manager was helping his team succeed in their goals. Of course, helping them achieve their goals helped him achieve his own. A real win-win.

He tossed his computer bag in the trunk, alongside his duffel bag, which was filled with workout clothes and running shoes. After he stopped at Nica's to talk to her about the Linden lobby, he would go to the gym and get a workout in before going home. He had a treadmill and a set of weights for at home workouts, but he met a couple of friends at the gym three days a week. He'd met his friends, Lucas and Truman, in college. They all attended Eastern Illinois University together. Just like with his brothers, Grady was the "middle child" with his friends. Truman was two years older, and Lucas was one year younger. They belonged to the same fraternity and bonded over beers, finance degrees and MBAs.

His call with Linda was quick. She had a draft of a renovation contract drawn up; she just needed some details from Grady. Everything else on the business front was quiet; thankfully, there were no more calls from Tom and Marty.

Pulling up to the curb in front of Nica's building, Grady considered whether he needed to take anything with him. Deciding not to, he jumped out of the car, checked that his cell phone was in his suit jacket, and jogged up the rickety old stairwell. He'd be glad when it was replaced, and he didn't even live here.

He knocked sharply on the door and waited. Moments later, the door opened and a beautiful young woman that he hadn't met stood in front of him with an egg turner in her hand. She was tall and dressed in pink from head to fuzzy socks.

"Hello. I'm Grady Litwiller, the landlord. Is Nica in?"

"Oh no. What did *mi prima* do now?"

"I'm sorry. Your what?"

"*Prima*. Cousin. I'm Isabel but everyone calls me Izzy." The beauty shifted the spatula into her left hand before reaching out to shake his hand.

"Nice to meet you. I was looking for Nica," he reminded her.

Izzy's eyebrows pinched together, and one side of her mouth scrunched. "She fixed the sink. It's not getting backed up anymore."

"Great. But that's not why I'm here. I wanted to talk to her about taking on a new project for me."

"Ay! Okay. Good. She's at work, won't be home until seven."

"At the flower shop?"

"Yes. They had some extra work because of the festival over the weekend."

Grady looked at his watch. He had thirty minutes before he was expected at the gym. He could stop by In Bloom to chat quickly with Nica. He had looked up the address and it was on the way to the gym. "Thanks. I'll try stopping by there to see her. Thanks, Izzy!"

Ten minutes later, he walked into In Bloom and was greeted by the owner, Anna Lee Foster, herself. He recognized her from the TV interview. "Hello," she called.

"Hello. I saw you on the news yesterday. Congratulations on the feature. I hope it brings you continued business."

"Thank you. How can I help you?"

"I'm looking for Nica. I stopped by her apartment and her cousin said she was still working."

"You a suitor?"

Grady grinned. "No, ma'am. I'm looking to hire her for a renovation project. I was impressed with what she did for your flower booth."

Anna Lee's expression was similar to Izzy's. Scrunching up her face, she asked, "How'd you find out where she lived?"

"Oh." The lightbulb went on for Grady; she was creeped out. "I'm her landlord. I met her a couple weeks ago at their apartment."

He wondered if this was moving him out of the creep factor.

Anna Lee nodded twice, sizing him up and down. "I'll be back," she said.

Grady looked around the showroom. There were premade flower arrangements, gift items, and an orange tabby cat circling his legs. He reached down to scratch the cat behind the ear. "Are you the watchdog? Do you keep the mice and bad characters away?"

"He's a watch cat, not a dog. Obviously," Nica said, entering the room.

Grady gave the cat a final soft pat on the head before standing up. "Obviously," he parroted.

"How did you know where I was?" she asked, leaning a hip against the counter. Grady took a mental snapshot of her instantly. She was wearing sneakers and black running tights that hugged every curve of her shapely, though short, legs. She had on a plain, turquoise-blue sweatshirt that skimmed the top of her hips, with the sleeves pushed up. Her short hair was pulled up into a clip on top of her head. The back of it swung loose, brushing the collar of her sweatshirt. She wore no jewelry that he could see and either no makeup or natural-looking makeup.

"I stopped by your apartment. Your cousin told me you were working. I saw that TV interview yesterday, so I knew where you worked." He thought she would be pleased that the TV spot had prompted his stopping by, but she still looked reserved and cautious.

He plowed forward. "Anyway, I have a rental property that needs a face-lift." He saw her begin to shake her head. "Not the whole place, just the lobby." Her head stopped moving and it tilted. "The building is old and was last updated in the sixties or seventies. So, whatever you may be thinking, it's worse. Shag carpet. Foil wallpaper. Dingy light fixtures. It's awful. I'm having a hard time getting it to full occupancy. The lobby is a big turnoff, and I was hoping, after seeing that TV segment, that maybe you could work some of your magic on it."

"Why me?" She asked, still cautious.

"You're talented. I saw what you did for the flower booth. It rocked. It was creative. Well designed. Functional. A perfect package." He smiled and hoped she saw this as genuine praise, not patronizing.

"I don't know," she said. "I don't have a lot of time between school, work, and staying healthy. I don't know that I have more to give."

"Well, you haven't even seen the place, so I wouldn't expect an answer today. Let me at least show you the building, talk about what needs to be done, and brainstorm some ideas."

"So, what I'm hearing is, you want to get my ideas before you go and hire some dude bros."

Grady clenched a fist and released it. He needed that workout tonight. He'd be on the punching bag for sure. "I did not say that at all. I want to hire *you*."

"Why?"

She stumped him. Why was he fixated on hiring her? Because she was talented and would probably be creative—and hopefully within budget. Besides, she was adorable, feisty, and interesting.

"I think you're just what I need." He paused and thought about what he said. He meant it in a purely professional way. But didn't feel he needed to stress that; it was obvious, right? "Think it over. Let me know if you might be interested. I'll leave you my card." He stepped toward her, and she stood up straight, taking a small step backwards.

"I have your number, remember?" she snipped.

"Right. Wasn't sure if you'd deleted it." He put the business card back in his pocket.

She sighed. "Sorry, I'm being peevish. Not one of my better qualities. Let me think it over. I'll reach out."

"If I don't hear from you…"

"If you don't hear from me by Friday, call me. I have a busy schedule this week."

"Sounds like a plan." He said, turning towards the door. "Tell your boss I apologize for pulling you away from work. Take care, Nica."

CHAPTER ELEVEN

NICA STOOD STARING after Grady for several moments. She was oddly thrilled that he stopped by to see her. Surprised, for sure. Surprised by the fact that he came and that seeing him again gave her a mix of joy and trepidation.

Hmm, he'd met Izzy. Most guys became infatuated with her as soon as they met her. Nica didn't see any signs that Grady felt that way. He didn't act flustered or appear smitten when he mentioned her cousin. Could it mean he was immune to Izzy's looks and charms? If so, he might be the first one.

Nica thought about his request. Seriously? Remodel a building lobby? She was interested in rehabbing houses, not commercial buildings. There were probably standards for commercial that she hadn't even heard of. How would she pull that off?

The exposure could be good though. Her Instagram followers had doubled in twenty-four hours just based on the TV spot—and that was a local program.

But she needed to keep her house flipping ambitions under the radar. Her parents might threaten to pull their financial help if they thought she wasn't serious about college. They weren't well-off and weren't covering everything—she still had to take out student loans—but they did help with a monthly stipend for room and board. And her mother, Juanita, clipped coupons to buy staples, pantry items, and health and beauty items cheaply. Every time Nica or Izzy went home for a visit, they were sent back with bags of household cleaners, shampoos, lotions, and makeup. Juanita seemed to forget that Izzy worked in a beauty supply store and got an employee discount.

Anna Lee entered the retail space and walked to the door flipping the *Open* sign to *Closed* and locking the front door.

"Nice young man," she said, turning back to Nica.

"I guess," Nica responded.

"What'd he want? He said something about renovation. Is he raisin' your rent? They all seem to be doing that these days." Anna Lee moved around Nica and approached the register. She pulled a zippered cash bag from the pocket of her apron and began taking the cash out of the drawer.

"No, thank goodness. He asked for help on a renovation project for one of his apartment buildings. Not the one we live in."

"Ah. He'll be raising their rent then," Anna Lee chuckled.

"Maybe. I don't know if it's a good idea to help him, though. Bankers and property owners are always putting up barriers for us."

"Us?" Anna Lee asked.

"Well, immigrants. Students. People of color. You know."

"I know, Cricket. Men in power, they like staying in power. And money provides power. Money is power. I've been bucking that system for fifty years. It's not easy, but it's gotta be done. And you girls have to help carry the torch." Anna Lee closed the cash drawer and pulled the receipts out of the small coffee tin next to the register.

Nica thought about those words. How could she buck the system if she helped Grady? If she helped Grady, would he raise the rent on unsuspecting college students? Could she live with herself if she contributed to that? Definitely not.

But maybe she was judging him too harshly. She didn't know a lot about him. She just knew that he was attractive and infuriating.

She didn't mind the attractive part, but she wouldn't be able to tolerate the "I'm the boss" vibe. He didn't seem like the type to like to get dirty, so maybe he wouldn't be around, and she could work in peace. She'd have to sleep on it and see how she felt in the morning.

Paige came out of the back room. "Everything is put away in the back, Anna Lee. What else needs to be done up here?"

"If you two would put out the package of greeting cards and the leftover pumpkin arrangements up here," Anna Lee said, "we'll be all set. I'm going to the office to do today's bookkeeping. I'm sure you'll be done before me, so go on home when you finish."

TACO TUESDAY MEANT Nica, Izzy and Paige were at La Casa de Suerte having tacos and margaritas. Paige was abstaining because she had an 8 a.m. British Literature exam. Izzy refused to take a class before noon, so she was ordering the extra-large margarita. Nica was comfortable sipping her small strawberry margarita.

"So, tell us again, what does the landlord want?" Paige asked as she took a bite of her cheese enchilada.

"He said he needs a lobby makeover..."

"I'd make over his lobbyyyyy," Izzy purred, somehow trilling a y sound. The margarita was working on her.

"Slow down, Iz," Nica scolded. "You're gonna pass out before we finish dinner." Turning to Paige, she continued. "He has an apartment building that needs a reno—he's having a hard time renting out the apartments. I'm just worried that he's going to turn around and raise the rent on all the tenants as soon as I'm done. And I don't want to contribute to padding his bottom line at the expense of college students or even families. Everyone is getting squeezed when it comes to housing. Corporations are buying up houses and making it harder for working families to afford them. It's a crisis!" Her hands never stopped moving as she talked.

"That definitely sounds like a conundrum," Paige responded. "On one hand it would be great experience for you. You could showcase the before and after. And I'm sure with your creativity, you'd kill the assignment. On the other hand, I get your point. It would be hard on any of us if our rent was raised suddenly. At least, I know it would be for me."

"Would be for us, too," Izzy answered, sobering at the conversation. "You can't do it, Nica. No matter how *caliente* our landlord is."

"His looks have NOTHING to do with this decision!" Nica exclaimed. She sighed when the heads of the couple at the table across from them swiveled in their direction. "But it would be good experience. I think. I haven't even seen the place yet."

"And good money, I imagine," Izzy said. "And with Evie's *quinceañera* coming up, the extra cash would be helpful. *Mamá* is freaking out at how much the party is going to cost. She's asked all of us to chip in and I'm not sure where I'm going to get extra chips."

The waitress passed by. "Extra chips? Right away."

The girls laughed.

Nica grumbled inside. She didn't know that her aunt, Tía Maria, had asked her cousins for financial help. She assumed her siblings hadn't been asked, since she hadn't been asked. If she took the job, hopefully she would get paid before Evie's party. The party was just over three weeks away. Maybe she could get paid weekly.

Izzy took a bite of a chip and continued. "Speaking of Evie's *quince*, do you have a date yet?"

Nica glared at her cousin. "No, I told you I'm not taking a date, especially if money is tight."

"That is not going to pass as an excuse, you know. Not with the moms, not with your dad or the other family members. If you don't commit to taking a date, they will find one for you. Pick your poison." Izzy took a big sip of her margarita and turned to Paige to ask about her work schedule.

Nica took advantage of their preoccupation and pulled her phone out of the tiny backpack that served as her purse. She scrolled through her text messages until she found the text exchange with Grady.

NICA: I'd like to see the lobby. BUT! No decision yet.

She put the phone on the seat next to her leg and reached for her drink. She listened to Paige talk about her plans. Nica was helping Trevor sand and refinish hardwood floors in his old farmhouse. They would be done Sunday, and he hadn't said there was another project to start. So maybe she could work Grady's project into her schedule after all.

A few minutes later, she felt the phone buzz by her leg.

GRADY: Would Thursday evening work for you?

NICA: After 5, yes.

GRADY: Great. Let's meet at 6. 8808 Linden Ave

NICA: I'll be there.

GRADY: (Thumbs up emoji)

Nica groaned. She disliked that emoji.

CHAPTER TWELVE

NICA PARKED IN the small parking lot behind 8808 Linden in a designated 'visitor' spot. She got out and grabbed the mini backpack and her sketchbook. She walked slowly around to the front of the building.

She snapped a picture of the front door, to remind herself later of the peeling paint, the faded and outdated door sign, and the busted decorative seagull hanging above the door.

This is problematic on so many levels, she thought as she entered the building. Inside, she moved to the center of the lobby and slowly turned, taking pictures of the four walls. Just as she turned towards the front wall and the entry-way door, Grady walked in. She smiled to herself as she realized she'd gotten a great picture of him with a broad smile. She would be studying that picture later.

"Hey, lady!" Grady called to her, and she was certain there was a teasing tone in his voice. He strolled across the lobby, stopped, and shook her hand.

She wanted to scoff at being called a lady. She was here in her running tights, tank top, a light sweatshirt, and running shoes. Her shoulder-length hair was pulled back in a messy bun. She planned to go to the campus track and run after this appointment. But Anna Lee had taught her to accept, not fight, compliments. She was still working on the skill.

"Mr. Litwiller," she said, shaking his hand. She hoped he didn't sense the electricity that seemed to flood her body as his hand touched hers.

"Please call me Grady," he said, smiling and the small lines around his green eyes told her that he smiled a lot. "Have you been here long?"

"No. Five minutes. Just taking a few pictures. Tell me again what you're hoping to accomplish." She pressed her palm against her thigh, and it felt as though the electricity passed from her hand to her leg.

"Well, I'm open to all suggestions. This lobby is the pits, as you can see. It needs a refresh. More modern. Clean lines. Trendy, but classy, colors."

"Trendy but classy. I think that's an oxymoron." Nica smiled. "It's a bit of an investment. Why are you doing it?" She wanted him to confess that he planned to raise rents; then she could pick a real battle.

"I care about the tenants. I want them in a clean, cool place. Hopefully, they are happy and they stay longer."

"And you can bump up their rents. Line your pockets with more profit, right?" Nica challenged.

"Ouch. That's a little harsh. No, that's not my plan. I need tenants and if I jack up the rent, I can't keep them. To be honest with you…" he trailed off and broke eye contact. Turning back to her, he gestured to the chairs in the corner. "Can we sit for a moment?"

He wanted her to sit down? This wasn't going to be good. They settled into two uncomfortable wooden chairs. She waited for him to continue.

He rolled his shoulders and went on. "There are only twelve units in this building and four are currently empty. We get people to look, but they won't sign leases. Mostly because of the lobby. Financially, it's not a great time for a big renovation, but I'm not under water. I wasn't stressed about it…"

"Until?" she prompted.

Grady looked at his hands briefly before meeting her gaze again. "I'm working with a couple of investors to buy another building. Expand my holdings."

Nica heard "empire" when he said "holdings".

Grady continued. "The investors have gone over the financial numbers, and they don't like the occupancy rate of this building. If I don't get these units rented by December, they're going to pull the investment dollars that I'm counting on to buy that other apartment building." He ran his fingers through his hair and Nica noted how full and soft it appeared.

"And with this reno you can raise rent on existing tenants. That would help your financial numbers, right?" Nica felt tension building in her shoulders, she needed to stretch out.

He looked puzzled. "You're worried I'll raise rents?"

"Yes, isn't everyone these days?" she asked. "Do you even watch the news?"

"Every morning. Look, Nica. I'm not trying to run off the tenants I have by raising their rent. I need to keep them here. It's a delicate balance. I have to ensure tenants have a place they can afford; I have to cover the bills, and I have to bring home some profit. But I'm not doing this reno specifically to raise rent."

"Oh." She fell quiet. She wanted to trust him, but there was something that held her back. Maybe if she knew him better or knew his people, where he came from, it would help. Her dad always told her you didn't know the nature of a person until you knew how they were nurtured.

Grady leaned back in his chair and studied her. She felt uncomfortable but she wasn't going to back down or break eye contact.

"So," he said slowly. "What if we work into the agreement that I won't raise rent on existing tenants for at least two years. Would you be comfortable with that?"

She nodded slowly, keeping eye contact. "That would be a great idea. Let's talk over all you want done, then I can put some ideas together. I can't do all the work myself, though, Grady. I don't have the proper licenses. Like electric. Or plumbing…" her eyes moved around the lobby. "If that's even needed."

"I have a network of contractors that we can utilize. I knew that coming in. How long do you think it will take to come up with your ideas?"

She stood and glanced around the lobby. "A few days."

Grady stood as well. She could sense his tall body just behind her. "Do you think you could have something by Saturday?"

"Saturday afternoon, yes. I'll probably do most of my work Saturday morning."

"All right. Reach out when you're done and maybe we can meet up, go over your ideas."

They walked around the lobby and talked about what needed to be done. Nica asked questions, took pictures and measurements, and jotted notes in her sketchbook.

"Okay, I think I have what I need. If I want to run back over and look around, will that be a problem?"

"Not a problem."

"Well, I should go. I'm going to the campus track to run and I'm losing daylight."

Grady glanced towards the door. "I think you've lost daylight. I'm heading to BB's Best Fitness for my workout. I have a guest pass if you'd like to join me."

"You do? Sure! I've wanted to check that place out. I can't afford it on my student budget but would love to see it. You sure you don't mind me tagging along?"

"Not at all." He smiled and Nica wondered how it was possible that this man could make her feel so irritated one minute and warm and giddy the next. It was confusing.

GRADY PULLED INTO the gym parking lot and watched Nica drive her small pickup truck into the spot next to his. He wasn't sure what his friends were going to say when he walked in with a female in tow.

He grabbed his duffel bag out of the trunk and turned to Nica, noticing that she was just carrying her tiny backpack. "Let me know if you need anything. Water. Towel."

"Deodorant?"

Grady startled. "You want to borrow my deodorant?"

"No," she laughed. "Just seeing what you'd say."

"You're nuts." He grinned as he turned towards the building. "Ready?"

"You bet."

Entering the building, they walked to the counter so Grady could sign Nica in as a guest. Grady stiffened when he saw the attendant, Javier, a charismatic flirt who was rumored to have broken more than a few hearts in the gym.

"Hello, Grady and *hola, bonita*," Javier said, greeting them. Grady's bicep flexed involuntarily.

"Hey, Javi," Grady replied, squelching the urge to push Nica behind him and out of Javier's eyesight.

Nica beamed at Javier. "*¡Hola!*" She then rattled off some Spanish, and Grady felt left out.

Javier answered her and they laughed. Nica turned to Grady. "Sorry. That's rude. I apologize."

"Can we get her a guest pass, please?" Grady wanted to finish up with Javier and get into the gym.

"Of course. *Un momento.*" Javier winked at Nica.

Pass in hand, they entered the gym. Grady located Truman and Lucas at the free weights and led Nica to them.

"Gentlemen," Grady began, "I want to introduce you to Nica Mendoza. She's helping me out on a building project, and I invited her to see the gym." Turning to Nica, he said, "This big, burly dude is Lucas, and the lightweight is Truman."

Nica smiled at both and stepped forward, shaking their hands. "Pleasure to meet you both. I'm going straight to the treadmill to get my run in. I was going to the track to run, but Grady pointed out that it was dark, and he invited me here. I've always been curious about this place. Anyway, I'll leave you boys to do your thing."

She left all three of them staring after her. At the treadmill, she reached into her bag for headphones and a water bottle. Grady noticed that they were wired headphones. Ancient technology, he thought.

Lucas broke the silence. "So, not a date?"

"No," Grady answered. "Not a date, just an acquaintance. She's actually a tenant and a talented designer. I'm going to the locker room to change. Back in a few."

In the locker room, Grady changed quickly and put his things in a locker. He thought back to the exchange between Nica and Javier. He was going to warn Nica to be careful.

Back in the gym, Grady glanced at Nica, running on the treadmill. He joined Lucas and Truman at the free weights.

Truman finished his reps with the barbells and put the bar on the rack. "I'll spot you next, Grady."

"Fine. But I need to add another forty pounds to the bar," Grady chuckled.

"Whatever, strong guy. So, if she's not a date, can I ask her out?"

Grady paused and looked his friend in the eye. "No."

"Why not?" Truman challenged. "Are you interested?"

Before Grady could answer, Lucas asked, "Can I?"

Grady focused on the task of adding weight. "No. Look, guys, I'm going to have to work with her. I don't want her dating one of you and making things weird. Lay off, all right?"

"Hmm," Lucas said, in a knowing tone. "Okay. She's a hottie. I predict you ask her out within a week."

Grady had thought earlier about asking Nica to dinner Saturday night. Assuming she was ready to share plans Saturday afternoon, why not meet over dinner to review them? They each had to eat, and he could write off the expense. That wouldn't count as a date.

"No way. A) I don't mix business and pleasure and B) I told ya before, women get in the way of building wealth. They expect gifts, they distract you, they want to get married and bog you down with two point five kids. No, thank you."

"Grady, come on," Truman chimed in, putting his hands on his waist. "That line made sense when we were twenty-two, but we're getting older, and it's time to think about settling down. Making bank is not the purpose of life. It's nice but it's not going to fulfill you like a relationship will."

"Man," Lucas jumped in. "When did you get soft? I'm with Grady. Date the ladies, don't wed the ladies."

"You're both still boy-men," Truman replied. "You'll come around."

Grady lay back on the bench and grabbed the weight bar in his hands. "Fat chance, Tru." He had no intention of dating anyone seriously. Someone always got hurt. Better not to let things get that far.

CHAPTER THIRTEEN

GRADY WAS SURPRISED to see Nica run for thirty minutes on the treadmill. She had stamina. He found it difficult to keep his eyes off her and focus on his own workout. When she finally slowed her pace and walked for a few minutes, he began to finish his routine as well.

Nica finished on the treadmill, drank the last of the water in her bottle, pulled on her sweatshirt, and put her things in her bag. She approached Grady and his friends.

"I'm done. I'm going to go. I'll turn my badge in with Javier." She glanced towards the front of the building.

"Wait, I'll walk you out." Grady said, picking up a towel and wiping his face.

"I'm fine. I don't need a sitter," she replied.

"I'm not watching out for you." Well, when it came to Javier, he was. "I want to touch on a couple more things as we walk."

"Fine. It was nice meeting you both," she said in Lucas and Truman's direction.

Grady ignored the smirks on his friends' faces as he followed Nica. At the front desk, she dropped her badge in the designated bin and said a good night to Javier.

"Hope to see you again, *Chica*," Javier replied.

Grady put his hand on her back and guided her out the door. Outside, he dropped his hand but it felt oddly alone after letting her go.

"Okay. Spill it." She said. "What's going on?"

Grady chuckled softly, "Is it that obvious?"

"Yes. You are giving off a weird vibe."

Grady wasn't used to someone talking about vibes, weird or otherwise. They reached the cars and she turned to him, waiting.

"I want you to be careful of Javier. He's got a reputation as a ladies' man. He's dated so many women at the gym that it's easier to assume he's dated someone than not."

"Oh," she said, looking down, seeming to be thinking through his words. "Drats."

"I guess he's good-looking. For a guy. And Hispanic—that's got to appeal to you too."

Nica's eyes flashed up at him. "You think I should only date my kind, don't you?"

"Hey, I didn't say that! I just said—oh, never mind. If you want to date him, fine. I don't care. But, later, I will say I warned you."

"Grady, I'm not some peach that bruises easily. I can handle myself. I don't date a lot. I have too much going on. I need to finish college, then start teaching and building my dream career. I'm not looking to get serious. I never want to get married and all that nonsense. But..." She paused.

"But what?"

She let out a frustrated sigh. "I have a family event coming up and it's expected that I bring a date. If I don't, my parents will set me up and that's usually a disaster. The last man they set me up with brought an engagement ring to our first date. I was eighteen!"

"No!"

"And he was thirty-five!" She shuddered violently.

"Dang. That's crazy." He wanted to reach out to her and pull her close, but he was sweaty, and so was she. The heck with it.

He pulled her close, wrapping her in a hug. She shivered again. She didn't put her arms around him, but she seemed to slump forward just a little, resting her cheek on the middle of his chest. He noted that the top of her head came just to his pectoral muscles. She was the shortest girl he'd ever held.

He held her for a few seconds more, then stepped back, giving her upper arms a quick squeeze.

"Hey," he said. "If you're just looking for a handsome date for a family party, forget Javier. I'll go!" He said it jokingly, but he sort of hoped she'd take him up on it.

"I'm not that desperate!" she said, tilting her head up slightly. "I've got several weeks, I'll figure something out." She pulled her keys out of her bag. "Thanks for letting me join you at the gym. Now that it's getting dark earlier…" She paused and peered around. Outside of the bright parking lot lights, the sun had set and it was dark. "I'll have to plan my runs for earlier in the day."

She opened the car door. Grady wanted to push the door closed so they could continue talking. Turning to him again, she said, "I've got some ideas for the lobby and will be ready by noon on Saturday. I'll text you."

"Great. See you Saturday."

She climbed in and left. Grady leaned against his car and watched her go.

NICA WORKED LATE Friday night. She had gotten home at six, drank a protein shake and settled down at her desk. She had uploaded the pictures of the lobby from her camera to her PC, and she displayed them on her large monitor screen as she designed and drafted renderings of what the lobby could look like on her sketchpad.

She was crafting two unique designs. One was a take on country-chic. It displayed a blue-gray shiplap feature wall. Flooring would be dark gray with knotty details. There were two easy chairs refinished in a tan and cream check pattern. She would take the existing wall sconces and spray paint them a dark bronze color. They had clean lines which would work with her design, but the brass color would not. Her design also called for additional can lights to make the lobby brighter, but they would have to hire an electrician to install them.

For extra oomph, she put two simple swing seats into the design. She knew that college students would love the chance to sit and swing and burn nervous energy waiting for a date or taking a break from studying.

She sketched out proposed artwork. The sketches were rough, but she envisioned paintings of the Midwest countryside—she would love to see large renderings of corn and beanfields, as long as she could find the right colors to fit the rest of the decor.

The second design was based on the building's proximity to the ISU campus. She could keep the chairs that were in the lobby and refinish them. Or she could make benches that looked like they came out of a locker room. She knew where to find a faux-terrazzo flooring material that would withstand wear and tear and look amazing. Like in the first design, she would keep the wall sconces, but repaint them in a glossy white paint. She would paint all of the walls a bright white color and add bold artwork.

She was excited about both designs and hoped one of them would please Grady. She had been at her desk for hours, so she stood up and rolled her shoulders back several times. She checked the time on her phone. Just after 10 p.m. She thought about texting Grady to give him a progress report. No, he was probably out on a date. She couldn't imagine that he spent many Friday or Saturday nights alone.

He was incredibly good-looking, with his dark hair and bright green eyes that reminded her of her mother's emerald engagement ring. As a kid, on the rare occasions when her mother would have time to sit and relax, Nica would sit on her lap and spin the ring around her mother's finger. She loved the bright color of the ring and even more, she loved that this was the ring her father proposed to her mother with, after saving for a whole year. When all her friends talked about the diamond engagement rings that they hoped to receive one day, Nica thought about the uniqueness of her mother's ring and wondered why more women didn't want colored gems.

She walked to the kitchen to refill her water bottle. Both Izzy and Paige were out, and the apartment was quiet. She snagged a banana and went back to her room.

She picked up her phone and thought of Grady again. She remembered how it felt to lean against his chest when he'd pulled her to him last night. She was shocked at how comfortable and natural his hug had felt. It had taken every bit of self-control not to throw her arms around his waist and never let go. Her face flushed again thinking about the way her body reacted to his touch. Her heart had raced like she'd been sprinting, and butterflies suddenly took flight in her stomach. She'd never felt so comfortable and safe with a man's touch before, outside of her family. Worrying about how she'd react to a man's touch usually kept her from second, or even, first dates.

She couldn't let herself become infatuated with him. First of all, she was going to work for him. Mixing work and pleasure was never a good idea; she'd learned that the hard way. She had worked in a local *taqueria* in high school and briefly dated one of the cooks. Things were great until they broke up and still had to see each other at work.

Second of all, Grady seemed to be everything that she disliked about a guy. Aggressively driven. Money-focused. Arrogant. Handsome, warm, huggable.

Wait, where did that come from? Sure, he was handsome, she wouldn't even call him cute; that didn't do him justice. But looks may be the only thing going for him. Well, that and the great body, that gave the greatest hug she'd ever felt. Of course she'd noticed the fullness of his biceps and his legs as he lifted weights. He kept himself in shape. She could appreciate that about him. Probably part of his aggressively-driven personality.

And the ultimate reason was, she didn't want to date and get serious about ANYONE. She wanted her independence. She didn't want to have to dim herself for someone else. She didn't want kids—she'd had enough of child-raising with her younger siblings and cousins. And her siblings and cousins would have plenty of kids. She'd be a wonderful aunt. Love 'em and send 'em home.

There was a knock on her door and she called, "Come in".

Paige entered. "You're still up. I heard you walking around." Paige flopped across Nica's bed.

"I didn't hear you come in. How was the date with Trevor?"

"Great," Paige said. "We went to his sister's house and had pizza with her and the boys. It was a blast. How are the designs coming along?"

Nica had told Paige about Grady's project and briefed her on the design concepts while they worked at In Bloom that afternoon.

"Good," Nica answered. "I'm happy with them. I hope Grady likes them, or at least one of them."

"Did you write up costs and what you personally would do, like we discussed?"

"I've started to. I'll have to finish that up in the morning. Then I'll text him to let him know I'm ready to discuss."

"You are amazingly amazing!" Paige exclaimed. "You're going to do so great on this assignment. I can see the social media posts now."

"I hope so. I talked to Lauren about building a website. She has a lot of ideas about building a brand and marketing. I'm envious of her business education."

"Definitely pick her brain. She will not lead you astray."

"Hey," Nica said, "change of subject. Do you think Anna Lee has seemed really tired lately? I'm starting to worry."

"Hmm," Paige's brow wrinkled, "now that you mention it, yes. But I thought it was because of the Pumpkin Festival last weekend. Maybe it's just taking her a little longer to recover. Maybe we should ask if we can do more for her."

"She did say that she may need some help with fall yard cleanup. You're working tomorrow—why don't you ask her about it and see when we can help her out. I'm busy Sunday helping Trevor, but open the next two weekends. Assuming Grady doesn't need me to start on this lobby pronto. Of course, if he hires me at all!"

"Oh, he'll hire you. I'm sure of it. He'd be a fool not to."

Nica thought about working for Grady. The obvious reason to do it was to get the experience. She'd be building a portfolio of work that she could highlight for other potential clients. That was a given. But the thought of getting to spend a little more time with Grady, getting to know him better and to figure out the hot and cold feelings he was stirring in her would be beneficial too.

There was something about Grady that intrigued her. She wanted to figure out why he prompted such quick feelings of irritation in her. If she was being honest with herself, sometimes that irritation felt a little like attraction. And that just didn't make any sense.

CHAPTER FOURTEEN

NICA FINISHED HER designs, plans, and estimates Saturday morning. Pleased with the quality and thoroughness of her work, she was excited to share them with Grady, even if it meant enduring his arrogant attitude and handsome face.

She considered calling him but quickly dismissed the idea. Who did that anymore? She texted instead.

NICA: Hi! I have two design options ready to share!

GRADY: 2? I like options. When can we meet?

NICA: I'm open today.

GRADY: I have a family thing this afternoon. How about dinner?

Nica paused. Dinner? That seemed too relationship-y. This was just a business thing. Why didn't he suggest meeting over coffee? Dinner was a thing. Then again, businesspeople had dinners all the time. Maybe that was just part of his business school training. But on a Saturday? Ugh, she had to reply.

> **NICA:** OK, I guess. People gotta eat.

> **GRADY:** And people have to get work done. Best of both worlds.

Nica groaned. He's so buttoned-down and *t's* crossed, and all that. He seriously needs to lighten up.

> **NICA:** Where should I meet you?

No way was he going to pick her up. That would be too much like a date.

> **GRADY:** Potters. Do you know it?

Seriously? He probably thought she couldn't afford the nice steakhouse and had never been there. She hadn't, but he shouldn't assume that.

> **NICA:** I know it. What time?

> **GRADY:** 6

> **NICA:** I'll be there.

Nica spent several hours reading and studying and tried to get the upcoming dinner with Grady out of her mind. At four she went for a run and showered afterwards.

Izzy walked into Nica's room and looked around. "What are you going to wear?"

Leave it to Izzy to be on her case. "I don't know. Jeans and a sweater?"

"What?! No, no, no! You said you're going to Potters. That's not acceptable."

"You've been there?" Nica asked.

"Yes, I've been there on a couple of dates, and you cannot—must not—wear jeans! Besides, you are presenting yourself. If this is a business meeting, dress accordingly."

"What if Grady shows up in jeans? He said he had a family thing this afternoon. I don't imagine he'll be showing up in a suit!" Nica wondered if she should text Grady and ask about dress etiquette. She didn't want to be over or underdressed. That would prove to him she'd never been there, wouldn't it?

"Much better to be overdressed than underdressed. You could play it off by saying you have a date afterwards. That would make him think."

"Why in the world would I want to tell him that I have a date? The only thing I want him to *think* is that I'm right for this job."

Izzy tilted her head and gave Nica a playful grin, "It's good to keep a man on his toes."

"I don't want to do that. I'm not interested in Grady in a romantic way. This is just a work thing."

"You say you're not interested, but I don't know. I am getting a heart vibration from you when you talk about him."

"A heart what?"

"Vibration. It's like I know when a guy is interested in me. I sense his interest in another dimension. I can pick it up from others too. And *chica*, I'm picking it up from you."

"Have you ever picked this up from me before?" Now she was curious.

"No, not ever." Izzy replied.

Hmm, she was afraid that Izzy was onto something. Nica had never been in love before. But wait, she wasn't into Grady, either. How could Izzy be picking up something?

Nica shook her head vigorously. "Your juju senses must be off.

Can't be a heart vibration. I can barely stand the guy. I'm not over our initial run-in and his assumption that I couldn't do the plumbing repair. Which I did successfully! He's a chauvinistic, pig-headed jerk."

"Well, you know what they say about those strong emotions."

"No. What?"

"The flip side of hate or dislike is like and often one masks the other."

"You're wrong. I don't want to date Grady. You know I don't date."

"Which is a problem. You have to find a date for Evie's party. Or the moms will, and you know what a disaster that can be."

"Don't remind me." Which reminded her of Grady. He said he would go, but did he just say that in the moment to distract her from Javier? The only way to find out was to ask him. She had no other potential date on the horizon, real or fake.

Grady sounded like he had her best interest at heart when he warned her off the "player", Javier. But was that enough to pull off a fake date at the party? Could they pretend to be in a relationship? Would they have enough chemistry to fool her family? There was so much to consider and what to wear tonight was just a start.

NICA'S TRUCK PULLED into the parking lot ten minutes early. She wanted a few minutes to compose herself and make sure the form-fitting dress she was wearing was not bunched up or caught in her underwear. She couldn't believe she'd let Izzy talk her into wearing a dress. She hated dresses. It was a simple sheath dress in a turquoise color that accented her skin tone perfectly. She had bought it for her brother's wedding in the spring.

Since the weather was turning colder, she had a wrap that she could throw around her shoulders if needed.

Sliding carefully out of the truck, she grabbed the wrap, her portfolio with the designs, and a small handbag holding her "MILK" essentials: Money, I.D., Lipstick, and Keys. And also her phone. She hadn't figured out how to work "phone" into Izzy's acronym before she'd exited the house. Well, Nica rarely wore lipstick either, and it was usually a debit card, not money. Whatever, it still helped.

She tossed the wrap over her forearm, tucked the portfolio under her arm, and held onto the purse. She paused for a moment after shutting the truck door. Taking a deep breath, she closed her eyes and envisioned what success would look like. Grady would review the plans, make a decision, raise no objections to the plans or cost, they'd eat dinner, she wouldn't spill anything, and maybe, if there were no warning signs, she'd ask him to be her date for Evie's party. She squared her shoulders and told herself, "You got this!"

Entering the restaurant lobby, she smiled as other customers waiting to be seated turned towards her. Entering places alone sometimes caused trepidation, but tonight she had her shoulders squared and was ready for anything.

But she wasn't ready for the look Grady gave her as he slowly stood, his eyes meeting hers, filled with appreciation. She wondered why—had he been worried that she wouldn't show? Worried that she'd wear sweatpants? She gave herself and Izzy an imaginary high-five for the dress when she saw Grady was wearing a suit. What kind of family thing had required him to wear a suit? Or did he change before meeting her for dinner?

"Good evening," he said, moving towards her and holding out his hand. Nica panicked briefly. Was he going to lean in for a kiss, too? She shook his hand and was happy that he didn't.

"Hello. Have you been waiting long?" she asked.

"Just a few minutes. Let me tell the hostess we're both here."

The hostess smiled at Grady and tilted her head to indicate they should follow her. Grady waited for Nica to step forward and followed her to the table. Nica was pleased to see that they were put at a table and not a booth. It would be easier to share the designs with Grady while sitting next to him. He held out a chair for her, she placed the portfolio on an empty chair, and sat down.

Once the hostess left, Grady smiled and said, "I'm excited to see what you have, but are you all right if we eat first? I'm extremely hungry—very busy day and no time for lunch."

Nica nodded and took a drink of water. As his attention focused on the menu, she took a moment to study him. His expression was calm, but she could tell he was jostling his leg. Nervous energy? Why would he be nervous? She was the one with designs waiting to be judged. If she were lucky enough to get this job, it could be a fabulous opportunity to improve and show off her design and rebuild skills. The extra money was a huge win, too. She could help her Tía Maria out with the cost of Evie's *quinceañera*.

Grady looked up quickly and caught her watching him. "Have you decided what you're having?" he asked. She was thankful he didn't tease her about staring at him.

"Not yet." She opened her menu and scanned the choices. Salmon. Good. Decision made. She closed the menu and put it down. "Now I have."

Grady chuckled. "Decisive. I like that. If you've decided, then I've decided. Hopefully, the server will be here quickly. Would you like some wine?" He paused and asked with an impish grin, "Wait, are you old enough to drink?"

Nica was taken aback by his charming smile, she felt butterflies in her stomach that had nothing to do with her designs or the potential job. Grady's face was one she yearned to study and sketch. She wanted to draw the layers of complexity that she saw—determination, mischievousness, seriousness, energy, and contemplation.

"Yes, Mr. Litwiller," she teased in return. "Do you want to see my ID?"

"No, I'm not carding you. Now, if the server does, I won't stand in their way. Was that a yes to wine?"

"No, thank you. I'll stick to iced tea tonight." She wanted to be in full control of herself tonight. It might look like a date, but this was a business meeting, and she wasn't going to forget that fact.

The server arrived and took their orders. Nica appreciated that Grady didn't try to speak for her or poke fun at her in front of the server. So many dates had done that in the past, and it frustrated her. She was all for laughing and having fun, but not when it could hurt someone's feelings.

"What had you so busy today that you missed lunch?" she asked once the server had left the table.

"A couple things. I helped my younger brother, Cooper, move this morning. Then I watched Lucas's rugby game this afternoon."

"Did you wear the suit to help with moving?" she asked with a smile.

"No, I changed into the suit for dinner. Had just enough time to shower and change."

Wow, glad I went with the dress. This IS a business dinner. "There was no time to eat? No food at the rugby match?"

"No, unfortunately. Someone was selling soft drinks and bags of chips. That was it. I've been telling Lucas I'd get to a game but I have had a hard time scheduling it, and they only have a couple left."

"I've never seen a rugby game in person. I've heard it's pretty brutal."

"It's a tough game, I'll give you that. I wouldn't say brutal. There's another game next Saturday. Would you like to go? I could explain what's happening."

Nica wondered if he would talk down to her, like a know-it-all, as though she were a dummy who wouldn't understand. She'd leave after five minutes if he tried that. But it would be interesting to see a game. She loved sports. Spending more time with Grady would help her figure out why her emotions always ran amok when she was around him. "I work Saturday morning. What time is the game?"

"Two."

"Sounds fun. I'm in."

They were interrupted by the server bringing drinks and salads. Grady stared longingly at the salad and Nica wanted to laugh. He looked so pitiful, his eyebrows knitted together and his eyes appeared to glass over.

As soon as the server walked away, Grady asked about her family and shoveled a forkful of lettuce and cheese into his mouth.

Nica began cutting her salad into smaller chunks as she explained about her chaotic upbringing.

"Wait. How many lived in your house?"

"Fourteen, for five years or so, then the older kids started moving out or going to college."

"Sounds crazy!"

"What about you?" Nica asked. "You mentioned a brother, Cooper. Any others?"

"Yes, I have an older brother, too. Matt. He's married to Julie, and they just had their first baby, a little boy named Charlie. He's not very cool now, but I have hope."

"How old?"

"Five months. He just eats and sleeps."

"Babies do that I hear."

"What about you? Any nieces or nephews?"

"Not yet, but with four brothers and sisters and six cousins that are like siblings, I probably will have. Once they start, I'm sure I'll have a ton."

"I didn't think of it that way. Wow. Eleven kids in one household. That sounds wild. I thought three boys in one house was a lot," he smiled before taking a drink of his wine.

"It wasn't as bad as it sounds. We're a tight family. We had our issues, but we learned to work things out. We are all better negotiators for it."

"So I'd better watch out when we get to the plans for Linden."

Nica laughed. "You should. Hey, this may be too personal, and you don't have to answer if you don't want to, but I'm curious. About your drive for success. Most guys I know in their twenties are focused on having fun and living life. Why are you so focused on increasing your property holdings?"

Grady nodded his head as she spoke, listening intently. He paused a moment before answering. "It's a fine question, I don't mind answering. I've always been serious and focused. Once I latch onto a goal, I strive to make it.

"You might assume," he continued, "that I come from a poor background with my focus on financial stability, but that's not true. We never lacked for anything. My dad worked hard and made enough that my mom didn't have to work, and she got to do what she wanted to do the most—be a full-time mom. That was great, though sometimes I wish we had a babysitter once in a while." He laughed, softly. "We took vacations, but dad always seemed preoccupied by work even when we were on a trip. That bugged me. We could be touring the Grand Canyon and he wouldn't really see it, you know?"

Grady paused again and swirled the wine in this glass. "He's fifty-two now and still works just as hard. He says he's happy, but I don't know. In high school I started reading a lot about building wealth and heard about this retire early movement. Sounded pretty good to me. My plan is to work as hard as I can to build wealth so I can hopefully retire well before I'm fifty."

Nica waited to see if he had any more to add. When he didn't speak for several moments she asked, "And then, what? What will you do when you retire?"

His eyes lit up. "I'm going to travel the world. I would like to set foot on every continent. I might even try to check every country off the list. Wouldn't that be something?"

It was Nica's turn to nod. "Yes, I think that would be pretty cool."

She was relaxed and ready to show Grady her designs. The conversation through dinner had been easy and comfortable. She hadn't expected it; she'd expected Grady to be all business, stuffy, but he wasn't. She could see his drive as he spoke. He was proud of the work he did, both for the bank and for his investment property business. He spoke of his assistant, Linda, with respect and appreciation. He credited Linda for saving his skin on several occasions.

And he wasn't all business. He spoke highly of his family, sharing stories of the trouble he and his brothers got into growing up, frequently pushing the boundaries with their parents. And he also told her about the great memories he had of his grandparents and of the weeks spent on their farm, where the boys would run and play in the yard, fields, barn, and woods for hours at a time.

They were interrupted by the server who cleared away their dinner plates. Nica wanted to get back to the travel conversation, but she reminded herself that they were here on business, and she needed to move along.

"Well. Are you ready to see the designs?" Nica asked, reaching for her portfolio.

"Absolutely! Can't wait!" They began moving the objects in the middle of the table to the side to make room for her portfolio. They both reached for the salt shaker and their hands brushed. Grady laughed and squeezed her hand quickly. "I got this," he said.

His warm hand caused her skin to tingle. She felt the warmth spread up her arm and permeate through her body. She wished briefly that their hands could stay clasped through her presentation, she could take comfort from his warmth and strength. She took a deep breath before speaking. "Great! Here we go!" She unlaced the thick string that tied the portfolio together. "First up is a design I am calling "Midwest Modern". It has a shiplap feature wall with a faux fireplace."

"Faux fireplace?"

"Yes, it's really a PC monitor running a soothing fireplace scene, like you watch on TV at Christmas. It looks cool and there's no fire risk."

"Oh, interesting. Go on."

"I'll add a rough-hewn wood mantel with iron brackets holding it in place. There will be a large round mirror with an iron frame above the mantel. The mirror will help brighten the space, reflecting light from the new ceiling fixtures. I included six new can lights in this design. This will help provide residents with a nice, bright, secure entryway. We will have a sitting area with armchairs placed in front of the fireplace—"

"Faux fireplace."

"Yes. And a large area rug to anchor the sitting area. In this drawing here, you can see I've designed a light tan and cream check pattern on the armchairs, with a medium brown rug. The flooring would be a rich-looking wood laminate in this deep hickory color. Near the hallway I would hang two simple wooden swings. I think it would be a fun detail."

"Wow! Swings!" He smiled broadly.

She grinned back. "Glad you like that idea."

"I love it! So, no coffee table or side tables?" he asked.

"No. I worry your residents will use those as a dumping ground for empty soda cans or coffee cups. This isn't their living room."

"Right. Got it. That's smart."

"Rounding out the design, on the wall facing the front door, we will have a series of pictures in keeping with the Midwest Modern theme. I'm thinking a series of three paintings, depicting corn fields or barns. If I can't find what I'm looking for, I could paint them."

"Wow. You're an artist to boot."

"Well, hold your judgment until you actually see what I can do." She paused. "Any questions about this design? What are your thoughts so far?"

"I like it. It's clean, yet homey. Comfortable. What about design number two?"

"All right. Design two. "Campus Cool". This one is bolder and brighter. Assuming the residents would be ISU students, not Illinois Wesleyan, based on location, I would paint the walls white with a bold red stripe at eye level all around the room. Within the stripe would be pictures of the ISU campus, students at events, sports teams, etc. The feature wall would have a large monitor which would display key dates for Bloomington/Normal and for the college. Someone would have to be responsible for the data feed, maybe your assistant, Linda could take care of it."

Her throat was dry, so she took a sip of water before continuing. "For seating, I have two options. The first is two long benches, kind of like a locker room. People can sit while waiting, but it won't encourage hanging out. The flooring would be this cool terrazzo tile with red flecks. It's durable and easy to clean. The second seating option would be arm chairs, like you find in a doctor's office. Clean lines, red upholstered seats in a tough faux-leather material, easy to clean."

Nica pulled two sheets of paper from the back of the portfolio. "Here is the budget breakdown of both options. I have placeholders for the artwork; these may go up or down a bit based on what I actually find."

"These are great designs, Nica. Well done. Of course, I'm very interested to see the numbers." He put the two design budgets side by side and studied them, asking a few questions about the particulars. Nica answered every question quickly and decisively. She knew she could not let herself get rattled while this numbers man reviewed the numbers. She had spent the afternoon reviewing, checking and double checking all the estimates.

After several minutes studying the estimates, Grady looked up and smiled. Nica waited, wondering what he would say. She hoped he would make a decision tonight, but knew that he might need some time.

"I'm very impressed. And—I'm surprising myself, my business instinct is always to go with the cheaper option—I really like the Midwest Modern design. I think it will attract both college students and others. Right now, the residents are about a fifty percent mix. The Midwest Modern may have a broader appeal. Plus, my grandfather farms, and I love the idea of the farmland paintings or photos in the lobby. I need to talk to Linda on Monday to get the ball rolling, but start planning. I need this quickly. Linda can help with the permits. I hope you can complete everything by the end of the month. That would give us the month of November to get renters on leases to move in by December first. That's the goal, anyway."

Nica took a deep breath. With her class schedule and work schedule at In Bloom, it was going to be tight. But she would make it happen. She might have to call in reinforcements. Luckily for her, her brother Julián and cousin Gabriel were both skilled contractors. They worked with her father, Arturo, and he was the best. If only he had taken her under his wing, like he had the young men in her family. But Arturo could not stomach the idea of her working in the same industry. He was adamant that she become a teacher or an office worker. He did not like to see his daughters or nieces roll up their sleeves and get their hands dirty.

"I'll make sure it is completed by the end of the month. Besides, two of my favorite holidays are coming up, and I don't want to miss out on the fun."

"Which two?" Grady asked.

"Halloween and the Day of the Dead."

"Interesting. I can't wait to hear more about your plans for both. We'll be in frequent contact with this Linden project."

"Won't I work with Linda primarily?"

"Normally, I would say yes, but this is really important to me, and I want to stay involved."

"Involved? Are you going to jump in and help?"

Grady laughed. "That's the last thing you want me to do. I'm all thumbs when it comes to demolition and installation. I'm much better behind the desk, doing the paperwork."

His eyes crinkled as he laughed at himself. Nica appreciated his honesty and his self-deprecation. She thought about how their different strengths complimented each other. He obviously had great business acumen and she had both design and construction skills. Together, they could make an incredible team.

As far as the Linden remodel job went, she had it under control. She was born to do this work, and she was going to throw herself into this project with all the energy and enthusiasm she could give. There was no way she was going to let this project fail.

Besides, being around Grady was starting to stir feelings in her that she wasn't expecting and certainly wasn't prepared for. His size and confidence gave her a sense of security and comfort that was brand new to her. It was like being wrapped up in a cozy blanket, next to a fireplace, with a cup of hot chocolate in hand. If they spent much more time together, she might find herself falling for him.

CHAPTER FIFTEEN

GRADY BOUGHT HIS favorite matcha tea from the Mean Green Caffeine Machine drive-up shop on University Street, then he drove past Nica's apartment building. The work on the rickety stairs would begin today. He hoped it would be done quickly and the young ladies would not be too inconvenienced.

His phone buzzed in his pocket. Linda. He hit the answer button on the car console.

"What's up, Linda Lou?"

"Good Monday morning, boss," she replied. "So, tell me how the dinner date went with the spunky renter. I'm dying to hear all about it."

Grady smiled. He'd spent most of Sunday thinking about the evening with Nica. He'd loved getting to know her. It didn't hurt that she was funny, enthusiastic, and a knockout in her pretty blue dress that had made her deep brown eyes seem like portals to an amazing secret society.

"It wasn't a date."

"Yeah, sure."

"It wasn't. It was a business meeting."

"And?"

"We went over her designs. She's good." He paused as he turned into the bank parking lot. "She brought two options to the table. I want to go forward, so I'll send you the key points when I get to the office today. I want you to send a down payment to her as well—there's no time to lose. We have to get the work done in the next few weeks, so we can try to get the units rented before December first. Then we can get Tom and Marty moving forward with the next building."

"Well, sounds like it was a productive meeting. Can you send me the designs so I can look them over?"

"Yes, I will send them with the bullet points. By the way, is everything on target to start the stair replacement on University?"

"You're awfully concerned about what's going on with Miss Mendoza's apartment. You sure Saturday wasn't a date?"

"She's a tenant. It's a big deal that we're putting her and her roommates through this. They're in school, they work, and we're removing their ability to get in and out of their apartment without looking like burglars. I wish they'd taken us up on the offer to stay in a hotel for a couple of days instead of using the fire escape to get in and out. But anyway, are things on track?"

"I haven't heard anything. I'll reach out to the crew to check in and have them keep me apprised if anything runs off the rails, as usual."

"Thanks, Linda. I appreciate you."

"You should. I am your Wizard of Oz."

"Pulling all the levers that make my little enterprise run smoothly. Keep in touch."

He hung up and thought about the work at Nica's apartment. There would be a bonus payment if the contractors got the work done in two days. He hated to part with the extra cash, but it would be worth it if Nica wasn't inconvenienced. He needed her attention on Linden, after all.

Before leaving his car and starting his workday, he took a few moments to indulge in thoughts of Nica. He loved how her spirit sparkled with a vibrancy that was like the best fireworks show. She should come with a "contents under pressure" warning—ready to blow at any moment. She was unlike anyone he'd dated before.

Sure, he had dated other pretty ladies but none of them caused him to recalculate his future and reconsider the FIRE dream as Nica did. For the first time ever, he thought about marriage. Until now, he felt like he would be a lifelong bachelor. He would leave marriage and kids up to his brothers. He'd be the perfect uncle, but his future did not include the care and feeding of a family. Or so he'd thought. Now that he'd met Nica, he thought about marriage in a new light.

He was surprised at how she'd talked about her family on Saturday night. She was passionate about them and had so many stories to tell about her immediate family and the cousins that she grew up with. He couldn't imagine the chaos a household of eleven kids would entail. His own family with three active boys had been crazy enough. His mom often said she'd wanted to pull her hair out, and as a child he'd fretted about his mom going bald.

Nica's deep brown hair appeared to be silky smooth; his hand clenched thinking about running his fingers through it. Oh boy, this was not where his mind needed to go now. He had a full day of work ahead at the bank. There were two important meetings with high-equity clients, and he needed to be on top of his game.

There was no time to daydream about a future with Nica. He needed to let her do her work at Linden, and he needed to focus on his own work. He needed to get those apartments rented so his investors would come through and he could buy the apartment building on Chestnut.

If he could just accumulate a little more property for his portfolio in the next year, he would be on track for his financial goals.

Unfortunately, now was probably not the time to get distracted by a spunky brunette with an infectious smile and feisty personality.

Though it had been years since he'd been burned by a "sure thing" bet, he still remembered the sting of losing. That caused him to be practical, methodical, and safe in all his business matters. But matters of the heart could not be managed in the same way.

He thought work would be enough to sustain him. He'd put his nose down and pursue success and wealth. Perhaps when he was in his forties, he could bask in the outcomes of success and then enjoy the benefits.

He could begin to pursue his dream of traveling the world and perhaps he'd look for love. Nica was beginning to upend all of those plans. She was starting to occupy a lot of space in his head and if he wasn't careful, she was going to worm her way down into his heart too.

STEPPING ONTO THE stairs of the escape ladder, her backpack caught on one of the handrails and Nica was jerked backward suddenly. She gripped the handrails to keep from falling backwards.

"Drats! That was close," she muttered.

At the landing, she slid the window open cautiously. She knew she was the first one home; Paige and Izzy would be in class for a couple more hours. "Hello?" she called, lifting one leg over the windowsill.

There was no answer, but of course an attacker would not call out a cheerful "hi" in return. She would have to search the apartment before she'd feel comfortable. She left the window open as she began the search. The cool fall breeze brought fresh air and the smell of a bonfire. Someone must be burning leaves and yard debris.

Nica glanced behind every door and under every bed. She quickly shoved back the shower curtain to ensure that no one was hiding in the tub. Once she was confident the apartment was clear, she dropped her backpack in her room and pulled out her laptop. Settling into a comfy position on the couch, she decided to complete the online quiz for history class and review the essay she'd written for her Environment, Resources, and Sustainability class before the others got home.

An hour later, both tasks completed, she stood and stretched. She leaned over into a downward-facing dog pose and had been holding the move for twenty seconds when her phone pinged with a text message.

> **GRADY:** Hi there! Did the workers get started on your stairs today?

Nica studied the text. Shouldn't he know that?

> **NICA:** Yes. Operation Climb Through the Window has begun.

> **GRADY:** Ha! Well, glad they started. Sorry for the inconvenience. I'll have Linda check on their progress at the end of the day. Hopefully, they'll complete it tomorrow.

> **NICA:** Fingers crossed. Scary having to leave the window unlocked when we're not here.

> **GRADY:** Dang! I didn't think of that. Wish you'd taken up the offer to go to a hotel.

NICA: We'll be fine. We're only all gone this morning and Wed morning. Otherwise, we have a plan. I had to search the apt when I got in an hour ago for a serial killer. Luckily, they didn't get the open apt memo.

GRADY: Whew!

NICA: Progress on contract for Linden?

GRADY: Linda's working on it. You should have the first draft by 5 p.m.

NICA: OK. Anything else?

Nica couldn't imagine he really had time to be texting with her during the work day. He was a bank branch manager and it was Monday. He'd said at dinner that his days were packed and stressful. She admired his hard work ethic, but she didn't understand the focus on becoming financially independent. Sure, who doesn't appreciate what money can do for you? She wanted to be able to support herself but she wasn't interested in accumulating non-essential things. She wanted to be free to do what she wanted. She didn't want a lot of furnishings to clean if there was a chance to travel for fun.

GRADY: No. Let me know if you have any problems with the workers or need anything while they're working. Take care.

NICA: Will do.

It was a nice offer and he seemed to be going out of his way to apologize for the inconvenience they were under. Her first instinct was to bristle at the offer. Was he thinking she was a damsel in distress? She wasn't. She wondered if his offer was coming from alpha male vibes.

Her musings were interrupted when the window rose. She glanced around to see Izzy climbing through, holding her high heel shoes in her hand.

"What's wrong with your shoes, Iz?" Nica asked.

"Nothing, but they slide through the metal grates on the stairs. Easier to come up without them."

Nica rolled her eyes. "Why didn't you put sensible shoes on when you left this morning?"

"Uh, no. Class is not the gym."

"But it's not a nightclub, either! Maybe you should carry a sensible pair in your bag for the stairs."

"Now, that I can do. I'll be glad when the stairs are done. But did you check out the guys working? There is a real hottie out there. I'm going to see if they need any refreshments." Izzy dropped her bag on the couch. "As soon as I freshen up."

Nica shook her head and settled back on the couch. She was itching to go for a run, but she wanted to finish homework first. Maybe by the time she got back, the contract would be in her inbox, and she could review it this evening. It would be a great idea to have Paige look it over as well; two sets of eyes and all.

CHAPTER SIXTEEN

NICA AND PAIGE drove home together after work on Wednesday. Grady had called her at lunch time to apologize for the stairs not being done. He asked her to pass his apologies along to her roommates.

He said he wanted to bring dinner over for all of them as part of his apology. Nica couldn't imagine any other landlord doing this and she told him so. He laughed and said they all needed to eat and besides, he enjoyed her company.

Nica was beginning to enjoy Grady's company as well and it made her smile to hear that he felt the same way.

She went to her room and reviewed her design again. She was glad Grady chose the Midwest design. She searched for photographs of Illinois, Ohio, and Indiana landscapes and saved a few favorites to a file on her computer. She would use these as inspiration for the paintings that she would make for the lobby. She created a list of the supplies she would need. She planned to start right away. They would take a while to complete, and she didn't need to wait for a signed contract to begin. She was already worried about the timeline with her busy class schedule.

If that wasn't stressful enough, her mom had called on Tuesday night to say that she had found a date for Nica for Evie's *quinceañera*. Nica had frantically claimed that she already had a date when she didn't, but drastic times called for drastic measures.

Her mom wanted to set her up with a neighbor that had moved in recently. Nica had not met him yet, but had waved at him once the last time she was home. Her mother's description of a "nice young man with hardly any tattoos" was not the ringing endorsement that Nica was willing to trust. After three disastrous blind dates, she was not up for another one.

With Grady coming over tonight to bring them dinner, now was the time to put on her big girl panties and ask him to be her date. They could put aside their business relationship for one night and pretend to be a couple, right?

She couldn't muster up the courage to ask him on Saturday night when the focus had been on the designs for Linden. It would have been too awkward to bring up the *quinceañera* during a business meeting. Even if it was over a nice dinner.

She worried how she was going to manage the growing attraction that she was feeling for Grady. Could she pretend their date at Evie's party was a business arrangement amongst a candlelit dinner, slow dances, beautiful dresses, sharp suits, and party music?

How could she pretend it was only business when the meaning behind a *quinceañera* was a young woman being old enough that she could begin to date and fall in love? Nica had refused her own *quinceañera* because at the time she couldn't imagine getting close enough to someone to fall in love.

At fifteen, the memory of being beaten up was still fresh and she hated thinking about slow dancing with a young man in front of everyone. It had been easy enough to tell her family that she didn't want a coming-of-age party because Izzy had just celebrated hers. She used the pragmatic excuse to save money and she didn't have to confess her history and the real reasons.

Being around Grady was causing Nica to think about letting her guard down and getting close to someone, emotionally and physically. Could she? And could Grady be the one to free her from those painful memories?

Nica followed Paige up the metal escape ladder and hoped that the work on the front stairs would be done tomorrow. Crawling through the window was starting to get annoying.

"What time did Grady say he'd be here?" Paige asked over her shoulder.

"Six thirty-ish."

"What's he bringing?"

"He didn't say."

"Color me intrigued."

They climbed through the window and Paige went to her room. Nica tossed her backpack on a dining chair and went in search of Izzy, finding her in her bedroom. Izzy was lying on the bed with earphones in, tossing a Hello Kitty stuffed toy into the air.

Nica sat on her cousin's fuzzy pink bedspread and waited for Izzy to pull out her earphones. She glanced at the three paintings hanging above Izzy's headboard and felt a surge of happiness and confidence. She had painted them herself as a gift for Izzy on her fifteenth birthday.

There was a single dahlia flower on each canvas. They were ball dahlias, the kind that were perfectly round with petals that were slightly curved. The flower in each painting was a vibrant orange, Nica's favorite color. The canvas backgrounds were in three different shades of pink, Izzy's favorite color.

Dahlias were often used in their family's celebrations. Since the flowers symbolized joy, love and good wishes, it was a natural choice for Nica to paint them for Izzy's birthday.

Nica was thankful she had a little talent with paint and a brush. It made gift giving a little easier on the wallet.

"*Hola,*" Izzy said, sitting up.

"Hey, how was your day?" Nica wanted to ease into the conversation.

"Great. I got a B on my Latin America Geography midterm. I'm pleased. What about you?"

"Good. But I need some advice."

"Shoot."

"I spoke to Mom last night. She said she has a date for me for Evie's party."

"Ooh! And?" Izzy leaned forward.

"Come on, Iz. You know it can't be good. It's the neighbor, Eddie."

Izzy scrunched her face. "Oh."

"Right. Anyway, I told mom I already have a date—"

"You do?" Izzy's eyes widened and a huge grin spread quickly across her face.

"No. I don't. But I had to say that to get her to back off."

"Okay...so what are you going to do?"

"I was thinking I would ask Grady." Nica held her breath, waiting for Izzy's reaction.

"The landlord?"

"Yes. Do you know of any other Gradys?"

"No. It is an odd name, isn't it?"

"You know he's coming over to bring us dinner tonight. I think I'll ask him then. We still have some open details to iron out on the work I'm doing for him at his other apartment building. I thought I could work this in. Is that too ridiculous?"

"Ridiculous would be going with Eddie. This sounds perfectly normal in comparison. But do you know if he's dating anyone? What is his status?"

Izzy always thought of the right relationship details.

"I don't think so, but I don't know for sure. Can you help feel him out while he's here?"

"*Claro, chica.* I'm on it. I will get the juice out of the coconut."

"I don't think that's a saying. In English or Spanish."

"Well, I'm saying it."

"You do you, Boo."

Paige yelled from the living room, "Grady's here!"

Nica groaned. She had wanted to freshen up before he arrived. Too late now.

NICA WALKED INTO the living room in time to see Grady climb over the windowsill with two plastic bags in his hand. She was relieved when he made it through without snagging his fancy suit on a nail or piece of chipped wood. The aroma of tangy barbeque wafted through the room and her stomach growled.

"Hi there, Lit," she called, thinking of his business name.

Paige turned her head quickly. "Are you talking about literature?"

Nica laughed. "No, his business name is Lit-Up Properties."

"Yes, it is. Didn't think I'd ever get called "Lit" though. Hi," he said, turning to Paige and holding out his hand, "If I remember correctly, you're Paige."

"That's right," she said, shaking the proffered hand. "It's nice of you to bring us dinner."

"It's the least I can do," he said. "I apologize for the delay. I can't believe they actually started the work when they didn't have all the supplies on hand."

Nica worried that he would bad-mouth the workers. It was a father and son duo, Guillermo and Diego Peña who were Mexican, and after Izzy had introduced herself to them on Monday, they had been warm and friendly. The girls had even made plans to celebrate All Saints Day with the Peña family.

"We talked to them yesterday," Nica said. "They felt terrible about the mix-up."

"I know," he said, nodding. "I spoke to Guillermo yesterday. It happens, I get it. But I really wanted this job done quickly. I hate that you all need to climb up the escape ladder."

Izzy walked into the room, wearing her high heels. "The stairs are a problem for my shoes!"

Nica shook her head. "I told you, just change for the stairs."

"I know, I have," Izzy agreed. "Learned that lesson the hard way. Why is everyone just standing around while our handsome landlord is standing there with bags of food in his hands?"

Nica was aghast. "Sorry. Let me take those."

Paige asked Izzy for help in her room and Nica wondered if her roommates had conspired to give her some alone time with Grady. Now would be a good time to ask him to the *quinceañera* but she chickened out. He'd only been in the apartment for five minutes. She'd wait until after dinner.

"No," Grady replied quickly. "I got them. Just lead the way."

He followed her through the living room and around the corner into the kitchen-dining room combo.

"You can put the bags on the table, and I'll grab plates and stuff. What would you like to drink? We have iced tea, beer, and diet cola. And water of course."

"Water is fine. Thank you."

Nica gathered plates, napkins, silverware and serving utensils. Not knowing what he'd brought made her pause, but several large spoons had to be a good start.

Grady asked how classes were going, making small talk. Nica joked about her scramble to read ahead in a couple of classes because of the work she would soon start doing at Grady's other apartment building.

"Hey, you got this, right?" he asked, holding a food container in the air. "I don't want you too stressed about it."

"It's fine," she assured him, as he put the container on the table. "I do have this. And I'll especially have it by doing some extra school work this week. Assuming we get the contract worked out tonight."

"Right. I have Linda's notes with me; we can go over them after dinner."

Paige and Izzy entered the room. Izzy's eyes sparkled.

Nica began laying plates around the table.

"I'm taking dinner to my room. I have to study for a test tomorrow," Paige announced, picking up a plate.

"Same," Izzy replied.

Nica now knew what the conversation had been about in Paige's room. That was fine; she and Grady could finalize the contract over dinner.

Once Izzy and Paige retreated to their rooms, Nica made a plate. She plopped a large spoonful of pulled pork onto her plate, along with a colorful, delicious-smelling Mexican street corn. If it tasted half as good as it smelled, she was going to be in heaven.

Grady sat next to her. All the food ended up on the other half of the table. If all four of them had eaten at the small round table, they would have had to set the food up on the counter once they'd dished it up.

After hanging his suit coat on the back of the chair, Grady took a small business card out of his shirt pocket. He flipped it over to the back and glanced at the notes he had there.

"Okay, so these are the outstanding items for the contract. First up, start and end dates. Do you think you can start on Monday, the seventeenth?" he asked.

"Without all the materials?" she teased.

"Oh, right. Materials. We can transfer a thousand dollars tomorrow morning so you can start purchasing materials."

"That should work nicely. Thank you. So, yes, I'll start on the seventeenth."

"Great. Now, we talked about completing by the end of the month. Two weeks would be the twenty-eighth. Do you think that's good?"

"Two weeks would actually be the thirty-first, but yes, I'm good with Friday the twenty-eighth."

"Wonderful. All the design details were outlined and you had no problems with that, right?"

"Right."

"Okay, then I think there's just the matter of an on-time bonus."

Nica's ears perked up. She couldn't wait to hear what he had to say. "Yes?"

"If you complete everything by the twenty-eighth, I will throw in a five-hundred-dollar bonus."

"Really?" Nica gulped audibly. That money could help with Evie's party expenses.

Grady nodded. "Yes, on top of your original estimate. I told you, I really need that lobby done so I can get new renters in by December. If I don't, I will lose the backing of my investors on another property."

"I know, but I'm still surprised by the bonus. I promise you I will get it done on time, even if I have to call in backups to help me. I have a back-up plan in the works already."

"Preparing for contingencies. I like the way you think."

"I try. Is there anything else on your little list?"

Grady smiled. "I like using the business cards for quick notes. They're sturdy, they fit in my shirt pocket easily, and I can only write a few things down, so I get them done and feel like I've accomplished something. And besides, I hold a lot of business meetings with Linda while I'm in the car driving, and it's easy to put my little list of notes on the dashboard and refer to it while driving."

"Is that safe?"

"Safe enough. I just use them for reference, I don't jot additional notes down. If I need to be reminded of something, I ask Linda to shoot me a text or an email.”

“Sounds like a legit process.”

Nica grabbed a spoonful of the street corn and took a bite. “Oh my, this is amazing. I hate to say it, but it puts my Tía’s recipe to shame. Where did you buy this?”

“The BBQ place by the airport. It’s out of the way, but I love it.”

“Would you text me the address?”

“Of course.” Grady took a bite of his pulled-pork sandwich. He didn’t avoid the bun like she did. “So, anything else to close off on for the contract?”

“No. You covered my questions. Will Linda send me an updated contract tomorrow?”

“Yes, she’ll make the tweaks we talked about and send it over. I’m excited to see what you do with the lobby. Your creativity with the In Bloom booth was incredible. And to see you on TV, that was fantastic. You told me that your career was going to be in teaching. How does that align with the remodeling work?”

“Well, they don’t exactly align. My parents want to see me with a steady job with benefits and pushed me towards the teaching degree. I love sports, and have coached some junior club teams, so I thought I would enjoy being a high school P.E. teacher. And, the nice thing about that, I would have time in the summers to work on flipping houses, which is what I really want to do.”

There, she’d said it, told him her dream. She hardly ever told people about that dream, just her closest friends, like Izzy, Paige, and Lauren. Okay, she’d told Anna Lee, too. She could count on them to encourage her, not poke holes in her dreams and tell her about all the challenges that would stand in her way.

“That’s very interesting. There might be future opportunities for us to work together. With my growing property portfolio, I know there will be more remodeling needs. I have a long list of carpenters and contractors that I work with on jobs. If things go well with this Linden property, and if your schedule allows, maybe I can find more work for you."

Nica smiled. "Let's see how this first job goes before we start planning future partnerships."

"You think I'm going to be a jerk as a boss, don't you?"

"I hope not, but we'll see."

She thought about Evie's party. The discussions were closed on the contract. Now might be the best time to ask. She had brought it up at the gym when she'd eyed Javier. Grady had jokingly said he would go, but she hadn't pursued it then. She took a deep breath.

"Grady…"

"Yes?"

"Remember at the gym when I mentioned the family event that I need a date for?"

"Yes. And remember I warned you off Javier."

"Right." She nodded. "Anyway, my cousin Evie's *quinceañera*…"

"*Quince-* what?"

"*Quinceañera.*" She said it slowly, enunciating each syllable. "For her fifteenth birthday. It's a big deal in our culture; sort of like a débutante ball."

"Thank goodness we don't have those here. High school formals were bad enough."

"I agree."

"So, you had one?"

"No! I passed. Izzy had just had hers, and I didn't think it made sense to have another one. They are a huge deal and expensive. Plus, I hate all the attention. But regardless, I'm trying to be a good sport about Evie's. Actually, this job came at a perfect time. I'm going to use some of the earnings to help my family financially. But the reason I brought it up is that, I really need a date. And I wanted to see if you were serious about going with me."

She paused and watched Grady closely. There was a speck of barbecue sauce at the corner of his lip, and she couldn't take her eyes off it. Her mind filled with ways to wipe it off. She resisted the urge. Instead, she pointed at her own mouth and tapped. He got the message and picked up his napkin. It was killing her that he hadn't responded yet.

She barreled ahead. "It's a Saturday afternoon and evening. In Chicago. Probably best to stay the night, as the party will go late. You probably have obligations. It's okay. Never mind. I can find someone else."

She grabbed her plate and started to stand. Grady put a hand on her arm, lightly. She felt pleasant tingles flit up her arm.

"Wait," he said. "I did not say no. I was processing. I have questions. Will you please stay?"

She sat back down and waited.

"First, how formal is it? Do I need to rent a tuxedo?"

"Oh, no," she responded adamantly. "A suit is fine."

"Okay. Do I need to learn any dances before I go?"

"No, we don't even have to dance. All eyes will be on Evie and her court."

"Court?"

"Yes, she'll have a court. She'll have a *Chambelan de Honor*, her date, and then additional *damas y chambelanes*. Her court."

"Wow. I'm intrigued. When is it?"

"October twenty-second."

"I'm in!"

"Are you sure? You don't have to."

"Hey, you asked me, didn't you? And I told you at the gym that I'd go with you."

"I thought you were just saying that in the moment. I didn't think you meant it." Her shoulders slumped forward slightly. "I'm becoming desperate. My mom wants to set me up with a neighbor. And I don't know him, I've only seen him briefly, but he's not my type. At all."

"Hmm, I would like to hear more about your type."

At that moment, Izzy strolled into the room. "Nica's type? We're still trying to figure that out." She smirked.

Nica wanted to throttle her cousin. Not only had she left her alone after saying she'd help with the conversation, now she had to poke fun at Nica's dating life.

Nica stood quickly and grabbed her empty plate. "I'll do the dishes."

Izzy sat down and looked over the food containers. "Shoot. No more street corn?"

"No," Grady responded, "I had three helpings."

Nica's back was to them and she smiled. She was actually the one that had taken three helpings, but Grady was taking credit, or blame, for it.

She heard a chair scrape along the floor and turned back towards the table. Grady stood with his plate in his hand.

"Where should I put this?" he asked.

"The counter is fine. Do you want to take the leftovers home with you?"

"No, it's for all of you. Hey, would you mind walking out to the car with me, Nica? I have those other papers that I mentioned."

Nica's forehead wrinkled. She didn't remember talking about other papers.

"I'll do the dishes, Nic. Go ahead. Since someone ate all the corn."

Grady looked at Nica and winked. That was super sweet. Maybe he wasn't a stuffy yuppie, after all.

GRADY INSISTED ON walking down the escape ladder first as a safety measure. Nica wanted to protest but decided to let it slide. She didn't want to give him a reason for backing out of being her date for Evie's party. And with years of practice, she was highly skilled at holding her tongue to keep the peace.

Safely on the ground, Nica wished she'd brought a jacket with her. It was a chilly fall evening, and though she appreciated the change in season, she preferred to be properly clothed when the temperature dipped.

Walking towards the street, Grady asked several questions about the location and timing of events for the party.

"Shoot. Hold on a minute, I'll be right back."

Nica raced up the fire escape and rushed to her room to grab the invitation for Evie's party to give to Grady. She could refer to Izzy's invite if needed, but as much as the family was talking and planning for this event, she didn't think she'd need to reference it.

Grady was still standing in the yard, looking over the progress on the main set of stairs to their apartment, when she returned.

"I hope they are done by Friday," he said when she approached.

"Yeah, that would be great. I'm surprised the neighbors haven't called the cops on us yet." She replied.

"That could be interesting. I never should have suggested the fire escape as a means to get in and out. I should have said you had to be out while the work was being done." He looked down at the ground and Nica could see the worry in his face. His forehead was creased and his lips were tightly pinched.

"Don't stress over it, please. We're fine."

"Well, please let me or Linda know if you need anything. I would lose my mind if something happened to you or your roommates."

Wow. That was super sweet. He did care. But was he just worried about being sued and it hurting his bottom line? It was hard for Nica to discern just where his concern came from. There was a tiny part of her that thought maybe he liked her. Like, really liked her, as in they could be a thing. But it was hard to tell. He was professional and didn't flirt with her, so he was hard to read.

"Linda has been great to me on the phone and via email."

"She's my right hand."

"I can tell. I'm happy someone keeps you on your toes. Oh, and here. This is the formal invite for Evie's party; it has all the details, addresses, etc. If you're still willing," she added.

"Of course. Sounds interesting, I'm excited to experience it."

Nica smiled at him. It was fun to see Grady's excitement. She originally pictured him as a buttoned-down control freak but now she was starting to see the adventurous side of him.

"Great. I hope you don't mind driving up yourself. I will go up with Izzy on Friday to help get things ready."

"That's not a problem. I love long car drives—gives me a chance to listen to an audiobook."

"What kind of books do you like?"

Nica thought about Paige. She was an avid reader and wanted to get into publishing in some capacity. Nica liked the occasional cozy mystery, but she didn't like sitting still to read. She preferred to listen to an audiobook while she ran.

"Mostly non-fiction, books about finance, or biographies of famous men who've succeeded. I'm a big fan of Dave Ramsey and read everything his company publishes when it comes to finance or business."

"You just read about successful men, huh?" she teased, with a lifted eyebrow.

"Oh, no! I should have said successful *people*! Women and men! I don't exclusively read about men in business. I've read a couple of books by and about Arianna Huffington, Janice Bryant Howroyd, and Meg Whitman, among many others. It doesn't matter to me who I learn from, I just want to learn."

He'd redeemed himself. Nica gave an inward sigh of relief. "Good to hear. Well, I should let you get on with your evening." She turned towards the road, assuming his car was parked close by.

"Hey, thanks again for the invite to your cousin's party. I'm looking forward to it."

"Thanks for agreeing. If you could just act like we're dating while you're there, that would be great. That will go a long way in getting my family off my back about dating."

"So, you don't date?"

"Well, I have, but it's just not a top priority. I am focusing on school and work. And I don't want to date for dating's sake. I'm not dying to get married or anything. If it happens, great. If not, I'm enough. I'm happy with myself and my interests."

She waited for his reply with trepidation. Would he turn and run at her declaration?

He nodded a few times but there was a sparkle in his eye. He didn't seem mad.

"I like your attitude. I feel the same way, maybe for different reasons. But everyone asks, "Who are you dating?" "Why aren't you engaged?" "Don't you want to settle down?" I guess when you're in your twenties, it's what everyone thinks you should be focused on. I want to build my property management company and my holdings. That, on top of my day job, is all I can handle right now."

Nica nodded. Good. They were on the same page. No relationships were the best relationships, or something like that. "Sounds like we have a lot in common," she said.

CHAPTER SEVENTEEN

IT WAS ALL hands on deck Saturday morning at In Bloom. Paige, Lauren, Tilly, Anna Lee, and Nica were gathered around the worktable, working on arrangements for a large wedding that evening.

Nica enjoyed the work and the camaraderie with her colleagues. Under Anna Lee's guidance and nurturing, they were comfortable sharing their successes, worries, and challenges. At times, the flowers took a backseat to the issues at hand.

Today, the conversation focused on Tilly's recent breakup with Kyle. She had thought the relationship was going well. They had dated for almost two years when Kyle broke up with her over dinner. She was certain the only reason he'd taken her out to eat was so she wouldn't make a scene. She was devastated.

"I'm not dating ever again!" she declared to the group.

"Hogwash!" Anna Lee declared, shaking the bunch of roses in her hand at Tilly. "A beautiful young lady like yourself will have men falling all over themselves once they know you're single."

"That may be so," Tilly replied, "but I don't have to give into the temptation. This broken heart has done me in."

Nica gave Paige a side-eye. When Paige had first started dating her boyfriend, Trevor, she'd felt like Tilly was always flirting with him, even though Tilly was dating Kyle at the time. Paige said she thought Tilly didn't know how NOT to flirt. Nica had to talk Paige off the ledge a few times that summer.

"Anna Lee's right," Paige said. "You'll be dating again in no time."

Tilly sighed dramatically. "Well, any guy that comes along will have to be extra, extra scrumptious for me to consider it. Now, NO setting me up with your friends or cousins or neighbors." She shook her head emphatically, causing her long side braids to flip-flop across her shoulders.

They all laughed at Tilly's outburst. "I'll second that, Tilly. No setups, PLEASE!" Nica called.

Paige wrapped a silver ribbon around the bridesmaid bouquet in her hand. "Nica, come on. Of course you don't need a setup, you're dating the landlord!"

Lauren exclaimed, "What?! You've been holding out on us, Nica! Spill! Spill!"

"I'm not dating the landlord. He hired me to do a remodel for him. It's professional only." Nica hoped Paige wouldn't bring up the fake date for the *quinceañera*.

"Not dating?" Paige said. "You've been to the gym together, dinner together, he brought all of us dinner, and—"

"Don't say it," Nica pleaded. "It sounds worse than it is."

"Okay, then you explain it," Paige said, seeing the curiosity on the others' faces.

Nica took a deep breath and looked around at her friends. She trusted this group of ladies. She could do this.

"I asked him to go to my cousin's *quinceañera* with me. It's an important occasion, and my mom was threatening to set me up with a neighbor I'm sort of turned off by, to be honest. So, since I'm already working with Grady, I thought he might be willing to attend with me as my guest."

"You mean date, right?" Anna Lee asked.

"Well, sure. Date. Guest. Same thing."

"Not really, but I get your point. It's not a romantic thing," Lauren said. Her comments eased the tension Nica was holding in her shoulders.

"Totally not romantic. We're on the same page about that. I told him I'm not interested in a serious relationship. Ever."

"Ever?" Tilly asked.

"Ever. And he said the same thing. He went on and on about how there's all this pressure to marry in your twenties and how he's not interested in that. He wants to focus on his career and accumulating wealth."

"Oh?" Tilly asked, her voice rising.

Nica's stomach twinged. Now she really knew how Paige felt about Tilly flirting with Trevor.

Of course, Tilly perked up at wealth. She came from money, and Kyle had come from money. A match made in stocks and bonds.

Paige jumped in. "Well, I think it's great that you're both on the same page. It will make the pretend date easier. No expectations. No disappointments."

Anna Lee misted the centerpiece she was working on with water. "Pretend date? What's that? Either it's a date or it's not."

Nica felt a tension headache coming on. She rolled her shoulders and took a deep breath before answering. "It's not an 'I might be interested in him, he might be interested in me' date. It's more like a business arrangement between us. We'll pretend it's a real date to throw my family off. This way they won't ask a bunch of questions, or set me up."

Anna Lee grunted. "Fake date. I'll be."

Nica mostly felt the same way. What a ridiculous premise. It was embarrassing.

Lauren, who stood next to Nica, leaned sideways and gave Nica a half-hug. "Hey, I've done the fake date thing too, Nica. Sometimes it's just easier than going alone—and so much better than not going at all!"

"It sounds good to me," Tilly chimed in. "Better than dating a jerky jerk and getting your heart broken." She sniffled.

Nica wanted to relate to that. But honestly, she'd never had her heart broken. Not like that. She'd dated occasionally, but always called things off before they got serious. She was uncomfortable with physical contact and didn't want to have to explain that to a boyfriend. That's why this was ideal—a fake date to important events, no setups by her mom or other family members—life would be just fine!

NICA AND GRADY had decided to meet at the park where Lucas's rugby match was taking place, since Nica would be coming directly from In Bloom and might be a few minutes late. Luckily, she finished work with plenty of time, and Lauren and Tilly volunteered to transport everything to the venue, so Nica was free to leave.

She arrived at the park a few minutes early and searched the crowd for Grady. According to his text message, he was already there, hanging around talking to Lucas and a few other friends.

Nica eyed the field carefully. It wasn't well marked, and she didn't want to stroll onto the field accidentally. The two teams were warming up and seemed to be running around haphazardly. Of course, Nica knew nothing about the rules, moves, or strategy in rugby, so they could have been running plays.

She sensed Grady before she actually saw him. There was a large group of people huddled near the sideline, shouting at the players. She paused about fifteen feet behind the group and looked for Grady. She couldn't hear or see him, but she was confident that he was in that group.

A whistle blew, and the players began to run toward the sideline. The large group in front of her started to disperse, and there he was. He was talking to his friend Truman, whom she recognized from the night at the gym. Grady laughed and threw his head back, causing Nica to smile though she couldn't hear what had made him laugh.

Grady checked his watch and began looking around. One corner of her mouth perked up as she watched him. He was dressed appropriately. He wore black track pants, running shoes, and a gray hoodie. Other than at the gym, she'd never seen him dressed so casually. It was a nice look for him. Not so stuffy. She liked it. It was more in line with her normal attire.

Since it was fall and the weather was turning, she was in jeans, lined boots, a sweater, and an oversized jacket. If they were going to sit on bleachers, she wanted to make sure her bum wasn't too close to a metal seat. After years of participating in sports herself and cheering on family members, she knew to be prepared for any possible weather. She had two duffel bags stashed behind the seat in her truck with emergency clothing, outerwear, and first aid kits.

Grady finally spotted her in the crowd. He patted Truman on the shoulder and said something Nica couldn't hear. Truman turned and gave her a wave. Grady left him standing with the others and approached her, with a big smile. She felt as though the sun had come out, though it was just as cloudy and gray as it had been all morning.

"Hey! So glad you made it before the start of the match," he said as he approached. He held out his hand for her to shake, and she did, a little disappointed that it wasn't a hug.

"I did. I'm looking forward to watching and learning about rugby. Does everyone stand by the side?" she asked.

"A lot of people do, but I thought we could sit in the stands—easier to see. Would you like something before we sit down? There's a better concession situation this week than there was last week."

"Sure. Coffee or hot chocolate sounds good."

They walked to the concession stand. Nica noticed a large banner stating that the stand was being run by volunteers from a non-profit and that all proceeds would be donated to the organization.

"Two hot chocolates, please," Grady said to a cute redhead with glasses.

He turned to Nica as they waited for their drinks. "How was work this morning?"

Nica told him about the arrangements, bouquets, and boutonnières they'd created under Anna Lee's watchful eye.

When the young woman brought their hot drinks, Nica watched Grady pay her the exact change for the drinks, then slyly drop a hundred-dollar bill in their "Donation Tip Jar" when the woman turned away. Based on the way Grady moved, he didn't want Nica to see what he'd done either, so she didn't say anything about it.

The action took her by surprise. Grady seemed so fixated on acquiring wealth that it took her a moment to convince herself that he really did leave a big tip. Maybe he wasn't a complete tightwad, after all.

As they made their way to the bleachers, Nica thought about how her first impressions of Grady were being turned upside down. He'd seemed so uptight and cold when she'd first met him, but now she was seeing a different side of him. He obviously hadn't wanted to draw attention to himself when he'd slipped the money into the jar. That action spoke to a generous spirit and a humble attitude. If he were someone she would consider dating, that would be two checkmarks in the plus column.

As they settled on the bleachers, Nica took a sip of her hot chocolate and hummed audibly.

"Is it good?" Grady asked.

"Delicious!" she answered. "Oh, I wanted to thank you for having the stairs replaced. I didn't think it would be noticeable, but I do feel safer going up and down them. The additional landing is a perk too. Thanks again. I appreciate that you did that without raising our rent."

"Hey, it needed to be done," he nudged her lightly with his shoulder, but he had to lean over several inches to bump her. "Those old stairs were a safety hazard. And, I got the pleasure of meeting you and your roommates, too. I'm glad you're no longer climbing through the window."

"You and me both!"

Their location in the bleachers gave them a good view of the action on the field. Grady explained the basic terms and plays for rugby, and she started to get clear on knock-ons, rucks, line-outs, and tries. She had some familiarity with scrum just from hearing about rugby. Grady was honest about his limited knowledge of the rules, but he was an entertaining commentator and kept her in stitches. They rooted enthusiastically for Lucas and his team, cheering and yelling with the other spectators in the stand.

During one particularly dramatic play on the field, one of the men on Lucas's team yelped in pain in the middle of a scrum as the players were jostling for position. There was more pushing and shoving, then the group broke apart to reveal the man writhing on the ground as the other players continued the play down the field.

Watching him, Nica shivered violently. She normally didn't have a problem with roughhousing in sports. It was part of the game, but seeing someone in intense physical pain took her back to the terrible incident that had occurred when she was twelve years old and got jumped by three bigger boys who had been teasing her about her dominance on the soccer field in P.E. class. Their teasing had turned physical when she'd spoken her mind about their lack of ability. She was used to teases and taunts from her siblings and cousins, and it had never turned physical at home. She'd been shocked when that time, it had.

Seeing her shiver, Grady reached out and put his hand on her shoulder. "Hey, are you okay?" he asked, leaning closer.

His touch caused another shudder to wrack her body, and she leaned away. "Yes, I'm fine," she said, though her voice broke.

"Okay," Grady said, slowly. "I don't believe you, but I won't push you, Nica. If I said something that offended you, please tell me."

"No, you didn't. It was that play on the field when the guy got hurt. It sort of triggered something. Don't worry about it, I'm fine."

She wasn't fine, but she was glad when Grady didn't press for more details. There were a few tense minutes before Lucas's team scored. Everyone stood to cheer, and Nica was finally able to shake off most of the unease that the memory had stirred.

Later, as they waited out the half-time break, Grady asked for more details about Nica's family, especially her siblings and cousins. He was still amazed at the idea of a houseful of eleven kids.

He shook his head when Nica talked about the bathroom routines: they'd just had two and a half baths for their family of fourteen!

"There were times when I thought having two brothers was too much," he said. "Getting attention from the parents, being heard in a fight, that sort of thing. I don't know, maybe my issues boil down to being the middle kid. The oldest gets all the praise and the youngest gets all the spoils. Or so they say."

She nodded.

"What about you," he asked. "Do you want lots of kids?"

"Whoa. I'm not sure I want *any* kids. I feel like I've done my share of child-raising. I mean, I love kids but don't feel the need to have my own. Besides, I can't wait to have niblings. With four siblings, I expect to have a bunch."

"Niblings?"

"Nieces and nephews—my siblings' kids. Niblings."

"That's a funny word."

"Maybe, but I like it. Besides, I don't know if it's a non-conforming streak or what, but I reject the standard expectations of being a woman. Especially the kids thing, but also the idea that I have to marry to be whole. I hate that."

"You're still young. That could change."

"Sure, anything is possible, but I don't know. I don't want to have a man to 'take care of me.' I can take care of myself."

He turned away from her, and she wondered if he was mad or disappointed in her response.

"I respect that," he said. "I know what you mean. Marriage isn't for everyone. I have an uncle who has a serious, committed relationship with a woman but neither of them wants to get married. It's been interesting watching the family perspectives around it. For years, it seemed so scandalous. Now, no one talks about it. So odd."

"To each their own, right?"

"Right. Speaking of my family, tomorrow is my nephew's baby dedication at church, and afterwards, we're having lunch at my grandfather's farm. I don't suppose you would be interested in attending. As my fake date, of course," he teased.

She rolled her eyes. "Why do we even have to call it a fake date? Can't I just attend as your friend and someone who's doing work for you?"

"Hmm. You're right. Why conform to the societal expectations of dating? Would you like to come as my friend?"

His green eyes held a mischievous look. She liked how easy it was to be honest with him. She was able to speak her mind and not worry about his reaction. If they were in a relationship or considering a relationship, she might have to hold her tongue and conform to his expectations of her. Speaking her mind was not something she was comfortable doing when talking to her own family, let alone new friends or strangers.

"Yes, that sounds fun. I like that we're exchanging cultural experiences. You'll go to your first *quinceañera* with me, and I'll go to a baby dedication with you. We're expanding our horizons, Mr. Litwiller."

"Please don't ever call me Mr. Litwiller. Makes me feel old and our relationship seem formal. Just Grady, please. And I agree—I like the exchange of cultures. There's always more to learn about others. I'm excited to know more about you and your family."

Funny he mentioned their relationship. He didn't want it to be formal. What did he want it to be? She tried not to read into his comment.

"One family at a time. Tomorrow, I get to meet your family and learn more about you. Believe me, I'm going to be asking questions. And in a couple of weeks, you get to meet my family and learn more about me. Just remember, we'll be pretend dating then, so you'll have to ask appropriate questions. Got it, Grady?" She dragged out his name, playfully.

He smiled, and she noted the perfect symmetry of his smile—his straight teeth and full lips surrounded by a no-shave Saturday kind of shadow. She already admitted to herself that he was handsome. Seeing his generosity today and hearing his desire to learn about others? If she didn't watch it, she might actually start to care for this stuffy guy in a suit.

NICA WAS CURLED up on the couch under her comforter when Paige got home from her date with Trevor that evening.

The TV was on, and Nica was trying to watch *Monster-in-Law*, but minutes went by and she couldn't remember what had happened on the screen. When Paige came in, she sat up and clicked the remote to turn off the TV.

"How was the date?" Nica asked as Paige sat by her on the couch.

"Dreamy," Paige responded. "Trevor took me to that tapas restaurant that Izzy recommended for dinner. It was a cute place and very romantic. Then, we went to the Castle Theater to see Leah Marlene in concert. It was awesome!" Leah Marlene had been a recent American Idol contestant, and everyone was thrilled to cheer her on.

Nica shifted, her back against the armrest of the couch, and faced Paige. "I think it was romantic because you were with Trevor. It wouldn't have mattered where you went."

"Maybe you're right. Regardless, it was great." Paige sighed. "How was the rugby match? Did you enjoy it?"

Nica looked down at the comforter and noticed a loose thread. She began pulling on it lightly, not wanting to cause a large snag.

"It was okay."

"Just okay? Wait, what happened?" Paige leaned over and reached for Nica's hand. "Did Grady do something stupid?"

Nica squeezed Paige's hand. "It wasn't anything like that. Grady was cool. No, there was a rough play on the field, someone got hurt, and it triggered a memory that I haven't thought about in a long, long time."

"What? Nica, you're scaring me. What happened?"

"I got beat up by a couple of boys when I was in junior high. Fortunately, or unfortunately, all the bruises were under my clothes, so no one else saw them. I was too embarrassed to tell anyone, so I didn't. You're the first person I've told."

Nica felt a little weight lift at sharing this story. She continued, "When I saw this guy lying on the ground, hurt, it triggered the memory. It caused a physical reaction in me; my body shook, and Grady noticed it. He was concerned and leaned towards me, putting his hand on my shoulder, which caused another tremor. He backed off and gave me some space. I didn't tell him what was wrong. He seemed cautious with me, and after a while, we fell back into normal conversation. My anxiety lifted, and it was fine."

"That doesn't sound fine. It sounds like you've repressed this issue. Have you ever seen a therapist for this?"

"No, I haven't. I got over it and took some self-defense classes, so I know what to do if it happens again. I'm fine. It's just weird that the memory popped up today at the match. I'm happy Grady didn't push."

"Nica, honey," Paige had tears in her eyes, which made Nica look away. "If seeing someone hurt caused a reaction in your body, a reaction that someone else noticed, then I don't think it's fine. I think you should see someone and talk this through. What usually happens when someone touches you?"

Nica was quiet, processing Paige's question. She tried to think back to the last time someone had touched her, besides Grady's hug at the gym. More specifically, to when a man had touched her. She usually found a reason not to date a guy a second time, and it was rare for a first date to get physical, so it wasn't easy to remember. There were several first dates that had ended in a kiss, and she had no memories of those causing a reaction.

"You just touched me, and it was fine."

"I squeezed your hand. You know and trust me. What about if a guy holds your hand, or hugs you, or goes further?"

Nica sighed. "I don't do a lot of second dates. I've kissed guys and never had a problem. Kissing is different than getting punched in the stomach, though."

"You're right. But maybe if things progress with Grady and you have issues with him touching you, you should consider counseling."

"If things progress with Grady? What are you talking about? We're just friends!"

"Just friends who seem to be spending a lot of time together." Paige raised her eyebrows. "And not just working together."

They both heard a key in the lock. Izzy was home. Paige looked at Nica. "Does Izzy know that you got beat up?"

"No, and don't tell her. Like I said, it's not a big deal—it happened a long time ago. I just got reminded today."

"Well, it concerned you enough to talk to me about it, so it must mean something. Just remember what I suggested. If issues come up with Grady, or whoever," she stressed, "then consider counseling. Please. It's nothing to be ashamed or embarrassed about. Mental health is just as important as physical health."

"I will. Thanks for listening to me. It means a lot."

"I'm here for you, friend."

Nica put her game face on, waiting for Izzy to walk in and tell them all about her date. It was great to see her cousin and her roommate going out and dating. She was excited about Paige's relationship with Trevor, they really seemed to be meant for each other. Izzy loved to date. She said it was like having a big box of mixed chocolates—it was exciting to try out all the different flavors. Nica was partial to chocolate-covered caramels, rich and creamy with complementary flavors. This made her think of Grady and her. Could they be complementary, or were they too different? Would they always clash?

Grady could be overbearing, but was he just being protective? Nica appreciated his drive and ambition. She was that way too, but she'd have to work harder than Grady to get what she wanted. It had surely come easier for Grady with his background, his connections, and his good looks. Doors must open easily for him.

But he'd offered her the work at Linden, and if she did a good job, she was certain it would lead to other doors opening for her. Grady would put in a good word for her, she was sure of it. As long as she executed her ideas well, and there were no major issues—and of course, as long as she didn't blow the budget. She knew Grady's priorities.

CHAPTER EIGHTEEN

NICA CHECKED THE time on her phone. Only twenty minutes until Grady picked her up. She was ready, but she wanted to put one more coat of paint on the candlesticks that she'd found at a secondhand store. The tall, rectangular shape would look great on the mantle in the Linden lobby, but the silver color had to go. She had cleaned the metal. Now she just needed to apply the two coats of spray paint evenly and thoroughly.

Her painting station was set up on the landing of the fire escape. A drop cloth was draped over the railing, covering the landing. The cool fall breeze would ensure a faster drying time, but she worried about leaves landing on the candlesticks and sticking to the wet paint.

Her favorite playlist was on, and she shimmied her shoulders in time to the JLo beat. The music helped settle her nerves about this outing with Grady. It wasn't a date—it was their second non-date in as many days. She reminded herself that he was a business partner, nothing more. She was going to this baby dedication and family luncheon to help him out.

It was only fair since he'd agreed to go to her family event. And it would be advantageous to get to know more about the non-work side of Grady.

It would be a fun day, as long as Grady didn't place his hand on her lower back as he introduced her to the people he was closest to in this world. If he did that, she might not be prepared for the way his touch was beginning to be something she welcomed. Something she longed for. Something she might miss when it was taken away.

And as long as he didn't hold her gaze with his green, earnest eyes. Eyes that spoke even when his mouth didn't. Eyes that said "I see you, all of you."

Why was she even thinking about his eyes? She needed to concentrate on the task at hand. Not think about his hands. His hand that had shaken hers every time he saw her. Was it five times now? Six? Now she was thinking about his hands and his warm, comforting handshake.

She pulled herself from her reverie. This was not helpful. She needed to put a stop to these pleasant thoughts about Grady and focus on the negatives. They didn't have a lot in common. On paper, they were complete opposites. Their cultural, religious, economic, social, and political backgrounds would be at odds, and they would argue about everything. What kind of relationship would that be? Couples that shared these things argued and disagreed. What would it be like when they disagreed on everything?

A gust of wind blew up. The tarp rippled beneath her, its corner whipping around and landing on a candlestick.

"Drats," she muttered, pulling the plastic off the wet paint. She assessed the damage. Nothing a third coat wouldn't fix.

The window rose and Izzy poked her head out. "Got a strawberry-banana protein shake for you," she said, handing Nica a large tumbler through the open window. "You didn't eat breakfast."

Sometimes Izzy acted like one of the moms. She'd make a great mom one day. Unlike Nica, who couldn't imagine trying to keep a baby, then a toddler, then a child, and then a teenager alive.

"Thanks, Iz," she said, taking a long sip of the cold, creamy drink. "I'd better start putting things away. Grady will be here soon."

"Where are you two going again? A christening?" Izzy's hair was in a shower cap, a deep-conditioning treatment in progress, and her face was covered with a mint green facial mask. Nica secretly hoped Grady would get to see Izzy during her Sunday morning beauty routine. Then he would know that even a natural beauty like Izzy utilized treatments and products to enhance her looks.

"No," she responded to Izzy's question. "A baby dedication. It's different. It's not Catholic."

"Oh," Izzy said, raising a perfectly plucked eyebrow. "That's interesting. Will you know what you're supposed to do?"

Nica thought about their experiences in church. Years of repetition had taught them when to stand, when to kneel, when to pray, what to pray. She didn't feel prepared for this ceremony, but she trusted that Grady would explain things to her, like he had at the rugby game. He wouldn't let her flounder in front of his family. She was not certain about a lot of things in life, but she was certain of that.

"Probably not, but I'll follow along," she answered, leaving no opening for further questioning by handing the protein shake back to Izzy. "Thanks for this, but will you take it in, please? I need to grab everything out here."

Izzy took the tumbler and vacated the window. Nica put the can of spray paint into the back pocket of her baggy overalls and gingerly moved the candlesticks off the drop cloth, setting them aside for a moment. She folded the drop cloth in on itself to prevent smearing the wet paint somewhere it didn't belong.

Carefully, she navigated the climb into the living room, careful not to touch the candlesticks or the drop cloth to the window frame. She dropped the items off in her room and changed her clothes. She put on a pair of black pants, black flats, and a blue blouse. She brushed her short dark hair, which had gotten slightly tangled in the wind, and took extra time applying her makeup.

Normally, she swiped on mascara and called it a day. Going to church and to a party with Grady and meeting his family called for more effort. Applying lipstick, she reminded herself that this was definitely not a date. She would wear makeup for a job interview. Meeting a friend's family was sort of the same thing.

NICA WAS BRIEFLY introduced to Grady's family at the church, but there was no time to remember their names, let alone get to know any of them.

In Grady's car after the service, she asked for more information on his family members: what they did for a living, liked, and didn't like. She wanted to be better prepared when she met them again at the party.

"Don't worry too much about it. They are going to like you. What's not to like? You are smart and spicy and—"

"Spicy?" she asked. "I'm not food."

"No, of course not," he replied. "But you *are* witty with a side of sass."

"I still don't see how you get spicy out of that."

"Just how my brain works."

"Weird."

"Yeah," Grady laughed. "You could say that."

Grady put on his turn signal and slowed. Nica looked around. All she saw were fields. Some of them had been harvested already, but many still had rows and rows of dried corn stalks.

They turned onto a gravel road. "Wow, these country roads are rough," she said.

"Technically, it's not a road. This is my grandpa's driveway."

"Really? I can't even see a house."

"It's a long driveway."

Grady wasn't driving fast, just a few miles an hour. Nica wondered if he was trying to keep rocks from shooting up and scratching the car's paint.

She felt a tremor of nervousness; she wanted to make a good impression on Grady's family. Not that she would be seeing them often—this was a special occasion.

Finally, the driveway curved, they passed the corn fields flanking the drive, and a large farmhouse came into view. It was two-story, with a wide porch that ran along the front, lined with rocking chairs. It reminded her a little bit of Trevor's house, an old farmhouse that he was restoring. She had helped him with a few projects; most recently they had refinished the hardwood floors. They were beautiful when finished, but a tough job to do.

Grady stopped the car and they climbed out. The sun was shining, and it warmed Nica's skin through her clothes.

"Are you ready?" he asked.

"Doesn't look like anyone is here," she replied.

"My grandpa is here. His truck is in the garage."

Nica saw the garage just around the corner of the house. Past it, she could see a large white barn.

"Wow, a barn! I've never been in one before."

"What?" Grady exclaimed. "You're kidding me, right?"

"No. City girl. Never had the opportunity to go inside one."

"Well, that's changing today. First, let's go in, so you can meet my Grandpa Fred."

They walked up the steps to the house, and Nica smiled, seeing all of the pillows on the rocking chairs. Each of the pillows had an embroidered animal on it—a chicken, a pig, a cow, a horse, a duck, a lamb, a rabbit, and a goat—eight chairs and eight pillows. Nica wondered if they were handmade.

Before they reached the front door, it opened and a short older man walked out. This must be Grady's grandfather.

Grady stopped and waited for his grandfather to come out onto the porch. "Hi, Grandpa!" he called.

"Hello, Grady. Who's this pretty young lady?"

Nica blushed. She worried that his grandfather thought she was Grady's girlfriend, not just a friend.

"This is my friend, Nica Mendoza. Nica, this is my grandfather, Fred Olsson."

"Hello, Mr. Olsson," she said, holding out her hand. "It's very nice to meet you."

"Oh, no. Call me Fred. There's no formality here on the farm." Fred shook her hand and held on to it for a moment, studying her. "Grady wasn't wrong. You are a beautiful young lady."

Now Grady's face turned pink. "Grandpa, some things we don't share."

Nica laughed like she was sharing a joke with the older man.

Several cars parked in front of the house. "Ah, here's the rest of the group," Fred said. "We can get on with lunch soon."

The next couple of hours were filled with family stories and good-natured kidding from Grady's family. Nica enjoyed getting to know Grady's family and loved seeing how often everyone asked for, and seemed genuinely appreciative of, Grady's advice.

No one, other than Fred, hinted at any sort of relationship between the two of them, which eased Nica's mind. It was possible to be accepted as a friend, not a girlfriend!

When Julie said they needed to get home to get baby Charlie down for a nap, Grandpa Fred wholeheartedly agreed. Everyone jumped in and cleaned up the food and washed dishes quickly. Grady's parents left after Matt and Julie. His younger brother, Cooper, said he needed to see a guy about a thing.

As everyone was leaving, Grady told his grandpa that he wanted to show Nica around the farm and not to be surprised if his car was still there when Fred got up from his nap.

They waved everyone off and Grady led the way to the metal

building first. Inside, he showed her the tractors and other large equipment. He told her that several of the combines were in the field, already harvesting.

Nica asked questions and laughed when she was able to stump Grady. He may have been around the farm growing up, but he was not an expert on farming implements.

Next, they walked towards the old wooden barn. It was a big white building. On the side facing the road, a large quilt square was painted red, white, and blue in a star pattern.

"Wow, that's super cool. What's the significance of the painting?" she asked.

Grady paused and nodded briefly. "We did that a few years ago, after my Grandma Miriam died, as a way to honor her. She loved to quilt, and that pattern was taken from one of the quilts that she made, my mom's favorite quilt. It still covers my parents' bed."

"What a beautiful way to honor her. What was she like?"

Grady led the way into the barn and clicked on a light switch. Several hanging lights flickered on in the middle of the barn. There were windows that needed cleaning on each side, not letting in much light.

Grady pointed out the empty horse stalls as he answered her. "Grandma Miriam was amazing, a tough lady who loved her family ferociously. She worked hard and laughed harder. And she made the very best peanut butter cookies, my absolute favorite."

Nica noted that little nugget of information for later use. "She sounds wonderful. You're lucky you had a grandma like that."

"What about your grandparents?"

"My mom's parents live in the Chicago area too. We're close, and we're lucky to have them here. They did a lot to help out, especially once my uncle died. My dad's parents still live in Mexico. I've only met them a few times. I plan to go for a long visit when I graduate from college. I'd like to meet more of my extended family."

They reached the end of the row of horse stalls. Grady pointed out some of the farm equipment stored there. At the end of the row, he pointed out the built-in ladder that led up into the loft area. "Want to check it out?" he asked.

"Oh, yes," she said. "After you." She didn't want to climb up first and have him watching her butt.

Grady climbed the ladder steps and pushed open a small, square door. He looked down at her. "Come on up."

Nica climbed quickly. Grady held out his hand as she reached the upper portion. She grabbed it and stepped off the ladder.

Looking around, she let out a soft sound of surprise. It was a large, open room, filled with mounds of hay.

"If there are no horses, why all the hay?" she asked.

"The hay is used for mulching the garden and flower beds. Want to try something fun?" he asked teasingly.

"What?"

He pointed further up the ladder. "See the rope that's tucked behind the ladder rung? We can climb up, grab the rope, swing out into the stacks of hay, and drop. It's a lot of fun."

"Grady, we're dressed in nice clothes. That doesn't sound like a good idea. Besides, couldn't there be bugs and small animals in the hay?" She shivered.

"There could be, but you won't notice."

"The clothes?"

"It's hay, you can dust it off. Watch." He climbed back on the ladder and started up. About ten feet up, he pushed open a large door that let in lots of light. As Nica looked around, she saw that the stacks of hay were five to ten feet tall. She still wasn't sure about jumping into it.

"Watching?" he asked.

"Watching you break a leg," she called.

"No way." He grabbed the rope and shook it. Nica noticed that the rope was on a pulley system in the pitch of the barn roof, not static. "Grady—" she started.

Too late, he was off. He kicked off the ladder with a strong push and the pulley started rolling. It took him about fifteen feet into the barn and stopped. Grady's body jerked and he went flying, twisted in the air, and spread out his arms and legs, landing on the hay in a Superman position.

He rose up, laughing. "That does not get old! Your turn." He stood and started to dust hay from his clothes. "I'll bring the rope back in a second. Are you ready?"

Nica smiled. "Yes!"

Grady brought the rope to her. It creaked loudly as it traversed the pulley system. Nica started climbing the ladder before he even reached her.

Once she had climbed several rungs, she paused and looked down as Grady approached. He was still smiling broadly, and she noted the lines around his eyes. He looked more relaxed and happier at this moment than ever before. It was as though being at his grandfather's farm helped him forget the responsibilities and pressures of his work life. Here it was about fun and family. She liked seeing this side of him. It was the complete opposite of what she'd seen in him when they'd first met.

"Ready?" he asked, looking up.

"Definitely." She turned around on the rung and held onto the ladder's side. Grady pulled the rope toward her, and she grabbed on. She looked down briefly at the hole in the floor, where the trap door stood open to the lower level. *Don't fall straight down,* she told herself.

She climbed up one more step and gripped the rope higher. Pulling her shoulders back, she pushed off with her feet, thrusting power through her legs. She let go of the ladder and let herself be carried with the pulley. As with Grady, the pulley hit a stop in the ceiling, and her body's momentum swung her forward. Unlike Grady, she didn't twist her body so she'd fall face first. She let go of the rope as she stared at the ceiling and let herself fall on her back. Landing in the hay, she fell inwards a couple of feet.

What a rush! It was like jumping into a pool from the diving board—the free fall and feeling of relinquishing control was intoxicating.

She sputtered as the hay got in her mouth and eyes. Shoot, she should have closed her eyes! She pushed up into a sitting position and tried not to think about little critters hiding in the hay.

"Are you all right?" Grady called.

"Yep! Should have shut my mouth," she said, spitting hay out and laughing.

"Oh, yes, I should have warned you about that."

She could hear him moving toward her. "I'm okay, Grady. I'll get up in a second."

"No broken bones, then?" he asked, and she could tell he was just a couple of steps behind her.

She brushed the hair and hay out of her face as she shifted around towards him. "No broken bones, but I'm having a hard time getting my feet under me. Help me up?"

"Of course." He reached towards her and she grabbed his hand. "One, two," he counted off, "three!" He pulled her up with a jerk, and she crashed into him, her free hand landing in the middle of his chest. "Whoa."

"Oomph," she said as her body followed her hand. He let go of her hand and put both arms around her as he swayed slightly to his left.

"Steady now," he said, continuing to hold her.

Grady's arms around her were not bothering her at all. It felt safe, not threatening. She could smell the woodsy scent of either his body wash or his aftershave and it was comforting. She wanted to inhale deeply and savor the smell. She didn't, but she wanted to.

She felt woozy for a second and rested her head on his chest, closing her eyes.

"You okay?" he asked, rubbing her back lightly.

"Yes, I think so. Felt a little dizzy for a second." She let out a sigh. "The swing and then standing up too quickly, I guess." She wouldn't admit that his closeness was what was making her heart race and her breath become shallow.

"Take your time." He pulled her closer. Her arms started to feel trapped, so she shimmied to free them. Grady did not let her go, so she relaxed and put her arms around him.

He didn't say anything, he just held her. Nica thought about the agreement that they were just friends. Friends hugged each other. This was fine. Just fine.

After a few more moments, Grady leaned back and looked down at her. "How are you doing, Spicy?"

Physically, she was fine. Emotionally, she was riding the biggest roller coaster of her life. She smiled at the nickname; he wasn't letting it go. "I'm fine."

"Ready to go again?" he asked, smiling.

"As fun as that was, I think I'll pass." The air around them was too thick, she needed air. "Swinging was a blast. Next time, I would like to be better dressed for the activity. Like maybe in a wetsuit and a swim cap! Keep the hay from getting in everything."

"Next time, huh? Then you did like it. I'm glad." He squeezed her lightly and stepped back. "Well, let's get downstairs and shake the hay off."

Nica giggled. That sounded like a weird euphemism.

# CHAPTER NINETEEN

GRADY GOT OFF work a little early on Tuesday to run some errands, so he was home by the time he needed to call Linda for their end-of-day check-in. He planned to lift weights in his home gym after the phone call and was already in a t-shirt and shorts when she called. He was in his office, laptop open, a notebook under his wrist, and a pen in hand when the phone rang.

"Linda," he said.

"Grady. How was the day?"

"Good. Errands are done. Already home. Ready to work out and hit the skins."

She laughed. "I assume you mean the drums..."

"Yes, of course. So, did the contract with Nica get signed today?"

"Yep. All good there. I'm just waiting for her bank info so I can transfer the down payment, then she can purchase supplies. If all goes well, she'll get started on Monday."

Grady sighed. "This has to go well. We have a tight deadline and I have to get more units rented. Hey, I have another challenge that I would like your input on."

"Oh, girl trouble?" she teased.

"No. No trouble there. It's my grandpa's farm. He wants to sell and I don't want to see it leave the family."

"You're going to turn into a farmer?" she asked, the doubt clear in her tone.

"That's a negative. We'll look for someone to lease the land to farm it."

"Oh, so a business opportunity."

"It's more than that. It's our family legacy—our heritage." Grady thought about Nica describing the tradition of the *quinceañera*. "I had hoped Cooper would become a farmer and buy the place, but that's not going to work out."

"Good thing. I couldn't imagine Cooper living the country life."

Grady tried to decide if there was a hidden message in her tone. Had he missed something? Did Linda have a little crush on Coop?

"I couldn't either, now, but as a kid, he said that's what he wanted." He wondered how he could ask her about her feelings for Cooper. No, better not. He'd talk to Cooper first. Feel him out.

"What do you need me to do?"

"Do some research into farm acreage in the area. What do trending sales look like? How much property is available? Recent sales and price per acre, that sort of thing."

"Got it. I should be able to compile a report for you by Friday. Sound good?"

Grady shifted gears. "Perfect. And would you look into freeing up funds for a down payment? I know that's going to be tough with the Chestnut property coming up. Assuming Tom and Marty don't pull out of that deal."

"Is your grandfather in a hurry to sell?"

"No, he didn't talk about a timeline, but I doubt that he wants to farm next year. Maybe I can talk him into leasing the land for next year. To buy me the time to get past the Chestnut deal. I should be in a better position by next summer...at least if you tell me I will be," he chuckled.

"I think I should research farmers that are looking to lease more land. Are you sure there is a market for it?"

"Good point. We would need to lease it. And Linda, be sure to look for working farmers, not corporate farming companies."

"You got it. Anything else?"

"No. That's it for tonight."

Linda changed the subject. "Hey, I wanted to ask about the baby dedication on Sunday. How did that go? Did you take Nica with you?"

"I did. It was great. Everyone liked her, and my family didn't scare her off."

"So, is this going beyond the professional, working relationship?"

"We're friends. Nothing more."

He thought back to their time in the barn. He'd come so close to kissing her when he pulled her out of the hay, and she stumbled into his arms. When she'd looked up at him while standing in his embrace, he thought he'd seen a flicker of desire. He'd come so close to leaning in and kissing her, but he remembered her comment about being just friends. He'd agreed to the friends label. Staying in the friend zone was the smart thing to do. The right thing to do. He didn't want a serious relationship. He wasn't the marrying kind, and she didn't seem to be, either. Ironically, they were a great match—two single people who didn't want to get married. Didn't want to have kids.

It almost seemed perfect. Just being friends would be fine. But then he remembered how he felt when his brother Cooper flirted with Nica. Cooper had leaned down and bumped her shoulder with his, causing Nica to laugh and practically bat her eyes at him. Grady couldn't tell what they were talking about; he was too far away. He fought an urge to growl at his brother. He'd never felt the need to growl at anyone or anything ever before, the sensation was completely foreign to him.

"You still there, Grady?" Linda asked.

"What?"

"I think you zoned out on me. I bet you were daydreaming about your renter again." She giggled. "Anyway, I was asking if you got the email that Marty sent today? He copied me on it. He wants to know how confident you are about getting the Linden apartments rented by December first. I could reply to him if you want to give me your answer."

Grady shook his head though he knew Linda couldn't see him. "No, I haven't seen it yet, and no, I don't need you to reply. I'll do it later tonight. I'd better blow off some steam lifting weights and drumming before I reply to him. I'm frustrated that they've thrown this wrench into the mix. But I'm confident that Nica will do a great job with the remodel, and we'll have no problem getting it rented. The dominoes will fall in their proper sequence. I gotta go if you don't have anything else."

"No, nothing else. I'll wait for another day when you're ready to talk about your growing infatuation with Miss Nica. Night!" She hung up, and Grady pushed back from his desk. He grabbed the drumsticks from the cup holder and began tapping on the leather desk blotter.

I can't fire Linda, she's my right hand. But it's like working with a family member. She knows which buttons to push.

He had to come up with a way to pay her back for her mouthy assumptions.

Well, in a couple of weeks, Nica's work would be done, he'd pay her, and then he'd never have to talk to Linda about her again. He could continue to see Nica, if she was game, but then his personal life could be out of Linda's purview. Well, as much as he could keep it out, with her eagle eye. How many times had that failed in the past?

All he knew was that his feelings for Nica were growing. He loved her energetic spirit and her independence. The fact that she had similar goals to his—no marriage and no kids—was a plus, like the interest earned on money sitting in the bank.

CHAPTER TWENTY

LAUREN POPPED INTO the retail space where Nica was restocking single stem roses. "Hey, Anna Lee asked for you in the back, she's working on the schedule."

Nica put the bucket of flowers on the counter before following Lauren to the consultant room where Anna Lee was working.

Lauren took a seat. Anna Lee looked up, pulling her reading glasses off her nose. "Remind me. You said you had a special project starting. What are the dates again?"

Nica walked towards the desk and put her hands on the back of one of the guest chairs. "I start Monday and have to be done in two weeks. With being out of town for my cousin's party, I won't be available to work here until the twenty-ninth. Is that okay? Do you have enough coverage? I might be able to swing a shift during that time if you need me to."

Anna Lee scribbled a note. "I'll put you down for the twenty-ninth, we should be fine until then. What are you doing again?"

"I'm remodeling the lobby of an apartment building near the ISU campus. I'm super excited about the job, and the cool thing is that the opportunity came from the TV segment that highlighted your booth at the Pumpkin Festival."

"That's wonderful. I'm proud of you, Cricket."

"Thanks, Anna Lee."

Lauren smiled at Nica. "Paige says your landlord and now, boss, is extremely handsome. That's got to make the job more interesting."

"Oh, yeah?" Anna Lee questioned, a grin on her face.

"Sure, Paige may think he's handsome. I think he's okay.'"

"Just, okay?" Lauren prodded.

"Fine," Nica relented, regretting the words before they were out of her mouth. "He's good-looking. But he's not my type. He's too uptight and too much of a Type A personality."

"Hey!" Lauren protested, "What's wrong with a Type A personality?"

"Nothing! Nothing!" Nica held up her hands in surrender. "Type A personalities get things done. They have drive and determination—nothing wrong with that."

Anna Lee stood and stretched. "You've got drive and determination, Nica, even if you don't consider yourself an A personality. You're a B plus on your worst day."

Salty, Anna Lee's orange tabby cat, jumped on her desk and perched near the edge, giving Nica a hard stare. *Darn, that cat was nosy.*

"I hope you're right." Nica said, petting Salty. "I'm going to need a lot of drive and determination to get this job done on time and on budget. Grady is counting on me. There's a bigger investment deal riding on the success of this remodel, so, I have to pull it off, even if it means calling in reinforcements or pulling a few all-nighters. I hope I can keep my grades from slipping, too."

"Sounds like you bit off more than you can chew, my dear," Anna Lee said. "If there's anything I can do to help you, please let me know. I know a thing or two about decorating."

Nica smiled. Of course, she did. She was a genius at flower design, and she rehabbed old furniture and found objects into up-cycled pieces that sold for good money in her shop. Maybe

Anna Lee could help her brainstorm a couple of extra surprise touches for the Linden lobby.

"Thanks, Anna Lee. I may take you up on that. I have all of the design basics covered, and I have a strong vision for the end result, but I may come back to you for some ideas on unique pieces to take it over the top. I'd love to really make Grady's eyes pop when he sees the final reveal."

Anna Lee nodded. "You got it. Now, I've got to get this schedule done so I can get home before dark. I got payroll and a pinot noir waiting for me when I get home."

They all knew Anna Lee didn't like to drive her scooter (with Salty in a backpack!) after dark. She complained about all the drunks and newbie drivers on the streets.

Nica loved the idea of soliciting her help on a couple of custom pieces for Grady's lobby—maybe a funky art piece for the faux mantel, or an artificial floral arrangement in a large pot that could be put on a stand across from the front door. So many cool ideas were flitting through her mind. She couldn't wait to get started.

NICA WAS SITTING on her bed with a drawing pad on her knees, sketching a few ideas for the farming landscapes that she wanted to create for the Linden lobby, when Paige walked in and sat on the edge of the bed.

"What are you working on?" Paige asked, picking a piece of lint off her black leggings. She had on an oversized Pontiac High School sweatshirt, and her auburn hair was pulled up into a ponytail holder.

"Planning the artwork for Grady's lobby."

"When do you start again?"

"Monday. I have a detailed plan on my desk if you want to check it out."

"Thanks, but that's okay. Let me know if you need help. I'm not handy, but maybe I could recruit Trevor to help out if you need it."

"I may take you both up on that offer. It's going to be tight to finish everything in two weeks and keep up with schoolwork. I don't want to let Grady down." Nica paused. "It would be bad for my reputation."

"Yes, there's that. But does it have anything to do with Grady himself? I'm starting to think you might have a little thing going for him. Do you?"

"He's a friend." Nica shrugged.

"Who happens to be going to an important family event with you." Paige gave her a quizzical look. "And you went to an important family event with him. People usually just do that when they like each other."

"Well, it started as a favor to me. But I think we can be good friends. We have a lot in common and we have similar goals: to stay unmarried and not have kids."

"Interesting. Fine. Put that aside for a moment. Those shared goals, I mean. Actually, close your eyes. This will be fun." Paige bounced a little on the bed.

Nica groaned. "Fine. Eyes are closed."

Paige spoke in a soft voice. "Imagine Grady standing in front of you. Look him up and down. Take in his clothes, his shoes. Is he carrying anything? Now, look at his face. Is he smiling? Is he laughing? Okay. Do you have a strong picture in your mind?"

Nica nodded. The image she conjured was of him in the barn as he held her in his arms. There was a piece of hay stuck to the back of his head, and she wanted to reach up to brush it off him.

"All right, good," Paige continued. "Now, how do you feel? What emotions are coursing through your body? Are you tingling?

Are you worried? Are you happy? Now is the part where you respond. Take your time. Quietly, tell me what you are feeling as you continue to keep this image in your mind."

Nica let out a slow breath. "I feel secure. And content. A little bit silly. Happy. And excited. Can I open my eyes now?"

"No. Hold on. Keep this image in your mind. Now, I want you to describe Grady to me. Not how you feel about him. Just describe him."

Nica paused. Describe him? Now? She had to let go of her early impressions of the stuffy guy in a suit. She'd learned so much more about him since their initial meeting.

"Well," she began. "He's smart and determined and goal-oriented. Maybe a little too money-focused. He's driven to accumulate wealth, but not necessarily material goods. He dresses nicely but isn't flashy with his clothes or his car. He cares about family but doesn't want one of his own. He is a great listener. And he doesn't speak for me; he doesn't butt in if I'm talking to someone. He doesn't tease me. And I suppose he's handsome."

The image in her mind started playing tricks with her. She still pictured herself in his arms, just like they'd been in his grandfather's barn. She was panting slightly from the exhilaration of swinging from the rope and jumping into the hay. Then the image began to move, and Grady lowered his head while his eyes stayed on hers. His lips parted slightly as they moved ever closer.

"Whoa!" Nica exclaimed, opening her eyes.

"What's wrong?"

"Uh…" Nica looked at Paige and shook her head. "Nothing. The image moved. Spooked me."

Paige smiled. "Well, that's interesting. What happened?"

"Nothing. Got a little carried away, I guess. So, that was fun. Did you get what you wanted?"

"The question is, did *you*?" Paige raised her eyebrows and gave

Nica a pointed look. "You spoke very highly of Grady. I think you've warmed up to him."

"Did you get what you came for?"

Paige laughed. "Are you telling me I wore out my welcome?"

"Yes! Time for you to leave. I want to finish these sketches before I go to bed."

Paige left her in peace and Nica turned back to her sketch pad. The image of Grady came to mind again and she flipped over a sheet in her pad. She started to sketch out Grady's grandfather's barn. She drew in the row of trees to the right of the barn and a hint of the house to the left. It wasn't to scale, but she was more interested in the idea than the actual image. The barn itself, she tried to draw as it was. The colorful barn quilt on the side, the windows, the scale, she wanted them all perfect. She drafted the hayloft door open and penciled in some hay floating out of the window. In her imagination, she could hear their laughter from that day in the loft.

Once completed, this painting would not hang in the lobby of the Linden building. She'd give it to Grady himself, as a thank you gift for his trusting her to do the work at Linden, and a memento of their time in the barn.

She finished the sketch and put her materials on the floor beside her bed. Picking up her phone to set the alarm, she noticed a missed text message.

> **GRADY:** Hey, since you seemed to enjoy climbing in Grandpa's barn, would you like to go indoor rock climbing with me on Sat?

For someone that seemed busy and focused, it was surprising that he'd take time for something like this. Even more surprising? The fact that he'd ask *her* and not friends like Lucas and Truman. Could he want to be more than friends?

NICA: Indoor rock climbing? That's a thing?

GRADY: Yes! Upper Limits–Google it. I've heard good things.

Nica took a moment to look it up. It was a thing, and looked fun and challenging.

NICA: I'm in.

GRADY: I'll pick you up at two.

NICA: That's fine. Am I ever going to find out where YOU live?

GRADY: Sure. Saturday. I'll grill dinner at my place after we climb.

NICA: Hope I don't break a bone–I've got an important job starting on Mon.

GRADY: I won't let you get hurt–I'm invested in that job, too!

Nica smiled. Of course he was.

NICA: Good night, Grady.

GRADY: Night, Spicy.

CHAPTER TWENTY-ONE

NICA PUT THE package of peanut butter cookies she made for Grady on the floor between her feet. She buckled her seat belt and sat back in the leather seat. A moment later, Grady climbed into the driver's side and pushed the ignition button.

"I'm really excited to try this place out," he said as he pulled away from the curb.

"Me, too. Looks fun. I've never been rock climbing. This should be cool. I may find a new favorite pastime."

"They have a membership option if we like it enough."

Nica mused at his use of 'we'. 'We' sounded like a relationship, a romantic relationship, not just a friendship. Didn't it?

"I guess it could become a recurring thing. After I finish the remodel at Linden, of course," she said with a teasing tone in her voice.

"Right. No more fun and games until that work is done. Speaking of, I spoke to Linda yesterday. She said the permits have been approved, so you're good to start."

"Anytime?"

"Yes."

"Should we cancel this excursion so I can go and start?"

"Heck no," he said, glancing her way. "I have the afternoon planned out. We'll do indoor rock climbing until we get tired, or they kick us out. Then we'll go to my place for hamburgers on the grill."

"Neat. I can't wait to see your place. I have all these assumptions in my head. I want to see how far off I am."

"Oh? Tell me more."

"Okay. You have a one-bedroom place, because why take care of more than you need?" Nica was getting warmed up. "It would interfere with your work life. And you live in a ground-floor apartment in a three-unit walk-up. The other two apartments pay for the building so effectively you live rent-free. Oh! And you have a green pet snake. A long, gross one. How am I doing so far?" She grinned, waiting for Grady's response.

"Wrong on all three counts. My snake is black," he said dryly, but he winked, so she knew he was teasing. "See, you thought you had me pegged, but you are so wrong."

Nica laughed as Grady pulled into the parking lot of Upper Limits. She leaned forward to look up at the tall structures.

"Wow. I haven't seen buildings this large since I left Chicago," she said.

Grady laughed. "There are a few other buildings in town as tall as this."

"This" was a series of old grain silos more than six stories tall. The upper half of each silo was lit up by the sun shining on the concrete exteriors.

Grady continued. "It's cool that they turned these old grain towers into indoor rock climbing. I love the inventive reuse of older structures—so much better than tearing them down and building something new."

They started walking towards the entrance. Nica nudged him with her shoulder. "Are you sure about that? Couldn't you have torn these down and built three apartment buildings on the site? Think of all that revenue!"

"A lot of investors would do that. But I don't like to. There's only so much farmland available, and if we keep expanding suburbs and industrial parks onto the farmland, I don't know what will happen. That's why I've focused on buying existing buildings. I would prefer to reuse and rehab rather than build fresh."

"That's my feeling, too!" Nica said, surprised to share this outlook with Grady. "I like looking at something that's there and figuring out what I can do to improve it. I don't mind a blank slate—I have that all the time when I'm drawing or painting, but when it comes to houses and rooms, I like the do-over. I don't think I'd be good with new builds and coming up with designs from scratch."

"Oh, come on, Spicy. You'd be good at anything you did. I'm confident about that."

Grady's words warmed her. It was incredible to hear someone say that about her. Her parents were so cautious. They felt they were doing the right thing by stressing all the challenges that could come from her dreams, and instead they encouraged her to do what was safe in their minds—teach.

Inside, they reviewed their options. They could boulder: climb with no ropes but only go so far off the ground. They could also top rope, which would require someone to belay the climber. That option required a class, and they decided they didn't have time for that. They settled on the option to auto belay, which only required a short orientation.

Once they completed the orientation and were strapped into their gear, they began to climb. They raced, teased, and laughed the entire time they were climbing in the silo. The two-hour excursion passed by too quickly.

They laughed all the way to Grady's house after the climbing adventure, reliving their joy in the sport and their camaraderie. Nica marveled at the good fortune of having met Grady. Their friendship today, was a long way from their first disastrous encounter.

NICA WAS SURPRISED when Grady finally pulled into a driveway and declared, "We're here."

The house was a modest brick ranch duplex. Grady told her he owned both sides of the duplex and rented the second unit out. That did not surprise Nica, of course. But she'd expected a more modern home for the man who was always impeccably dressed and drove a nice car with only a few years on it.

Following Grady to the front door, she noticed some evergreen shrubs surrounding the small front porch. "No flowers?" she asked.

"No time to weed or care for much plant life. These bushes are easy to care for and presentable."

"I would have said sterile or bland, not presentable."

"Hey, now. Be nice, or I won't let you see the rest of my boring, presentable home," he said, punching a passcode on the keypad lock.

Entering the house, they stepped into the living room. There was a light gray couch and matching loveseat with pillows that had obviously come with the set. The love seat was in front of the picture window, and lying on the back of the love seat, on top of a gray throw blanket, was a fat gray cat. There was no artwork on the walls. On the wall opposite the couch was a large TV on a stand. A plain candle sat on the small wooden coffee table.

"Is your cat friendly?" she asked.

"Yes, he's chill. His name is Chad."

Nica's eyes continued to rove over every surface. Seeing the blank wall above the couch, she decided that the painting of his grandfather's barn could be much larger than she'd originally planned. If she wanted to, she could make it three feet tall and four feet wide.

The living room was separated from the kitchen by a counter. There wasn't enough room for barstools on the living room side. The kitchen was simple and masculine. The cabinets were all white, the appliances were black. Nica thought about how hard it was to keep the black appliances in her family home clean. She felt for Grady and wondered if he did his own cleaning.

"Grady, here, I brought you some peanut butter cookies," she held the container out. "Dessert?"

"Oh, wow! They're my favorite kind!"

"I remembered."

"That is so thoughtful of you. Thank you! I know I should wait until after dinner, but do you mind if I try one?"

She laughed. "Not at all. I am anxious to hear what you think."

He opened the container and quickly grabbed a cookie. Taking a bite, he moaned. "Delicious. I'm tempted to skip the dinner and just eat these!"

"As many calories as we burned climbing today, i think we need something more substantial for dinner."

Grady closed the container and set it on the counter. "You're right. Would you like something to drink?" He asked, opening the door to the refrigerator.

"Cold water?"

"Sure." He closed the door, reached into a cabinet for two glasses, and got water from the dispenser in the refrigerator door. "Here."

She took the glass, looking around the efficient kitchen. The only touch of color came from two small pots of herbs in the window over the sink, facing the side yard and a neighbor's house.

"You grow your own herbs?"

"My sister-in-law brought those over. I think it's a test to see if I can keep them alive. If they continue to survive, I think she'll eventually let me babysit my nephew."

"You haven't yet?"

"Not yet. Again, I think I'm being tested."

"Your nephew was adorable. And I can see her hesitation to trust her baby to just anyone."

"Just anyone? I'm his uncle! But I know what you're saying. Well, how hungry are you?"

"I could eat."

"Great. Let me show you the rest of the place, then I'll get the grill going."

Leading the way out of the kitchen, he turned left, walked down a short hallway past the only bathroom, and showed her his office. A large executive-style L-shaped desk in the corner faced the back window, with a nice view of the yard. Through it, Nica could see a few trees displaying their fall leaves. In the opposite corner was a treadmill.

Next, Grady showed her his bedroom. There was a common theme: simple, utilitarian. She saw a large bed with a gray comforter and a dresser holding a TV. "Nice," she said.

"Kind of boring, huh?" he responded. "Let me show you the basement. More of my personality comes out there."

She was intrigued by his words. *He has a personality?* She smiled to herself.

He led her down a narrow stairway to the basement. Now, here was some personality! There was a large drum set, a futon couch, and a couple of comfy chairs. The walls were bright white, and someone had painted a Red Hot Chili Peppers logo on the wall above the couch. Flanking the logo were two large, framed posters featuring the band.

"You're a Chili Peppers fan, huh?"

"Yes," he said with a smile. "Remember I said the cat's name is Chad? He was named for the drummer, Chad Smith."

"Wow, I had not taken you for a geek until now," she teased.

"Geek?"

"Not for listening to the Chili Peppers, but for naming a pet after a drummer. That is top geek behavior."

She went to the far wall to look at the albums and DVDs on the shelf. She pulled out the first album. "What's this?"

"Vinyl. The best way to listen to great music."

"Oh, if you say so."

"I do and I'll show you. Have a seat and listen. You will not regret it."

"Hey, I thought you were going to cook, I'm hungry."

"Fine. I'll put an album on. You sit here and listen to at least two songs, and I'll go start on dinner."

He put on an album that Nica didn't recognize. She sat back and relaxed on the futon as the music filled the room. Leaning back, she looked at the ceiling. There was a funky array of what she assumed were acoustic tiles lining the ceiling. They must muffle the sound of the music from the stereo and the drums, she surmised.

Satisfied that she'd listened long enough, she went upstairs. She didn't attempt to turn off the record, afraid she'd damage it. Music and his album collection seemed important to Grady.

Upstairs, she returned to the kitchen where there was a sliding glass door leading out to a small sitting area and the grill. She found Grady outside with a spatula in hand.

"What can I do to help?" she asked.

"Nothing. I got it under control."

"I bet you always do."

"What?" His eyes locked on her.

"Have things under control. You seem to be the type of person who never gets out of control."

"Well, I would normally agree, but the situation with the investors has me feeling a bit out of control."

"Right! No pressure on me!"

"Hey, you got this. I know you do."

Nica warmed at his words. He was confident in her ability, unlike her parents. Maybe with a few more big projects behind her, they would start to understand that this was where her passion lay. And that she was good at it.

Nica took a seat at the small metal table and looked around. The area was neat but plain. The table and chairs and the grill were the only items on the concrete patio. There were no pots of mums or decorative accessories.

Grady flipped the burgers and lowered the lid on the grill. As he did so, a man walked towards them, coming from behind the house.

"I smelled the grill goin' so I came over," the man said. As he drew closer, he noticed Nica. "Oh! Didn't realize you had company, Grady. Didn't mean to interrupt."

"Not an interruption, neighbor." Grady said, waving the spatula. "Come on. Have a seat." Turning to Nica, he said, "Nica, I'd like you to meet my neighbor, Lionel. Lionel, this is Nica."

"Pleased to meet you," Lionel said, holding his hand out.

Nica shook his hand. "Pleasure is mine."

"So, how was the climb today?" Lionel asked, pulling out a seat.

"Amazing!" Nica said.

Grady agreed. "Yes, Lionel. Thanks for the recommendation. It was fantastic. Are you going to stay for dinner?"

"Oh, no. I don't want to interrupt your date. Just wanted to say hello. Oh, and to thank you for what you did."

Grady looked embarrassed. "Oh, please. Don't mention it. Hey, I'm going to grab some onions to throw on the grill. Can I get either of you a beer?"

"No," Lionel answered, "Not for me. Like I said, I'm not staying."

Nica asked for another water. After Grady went indoors, she turned to Lionel. "You embarrassed Grady. What'd he do?"

Lionel glanced towards the slider. "He returned my rent check uncashed. I told him I'd had an unexpected car repair, just making conversation, you know. Didn't expect him to return my rent. But that's Grady. He's a good man."

"Wow. That's," she paused. She wanted to say, "shocking" but worried that it would sound like a put-down. Instead, she said "cool". It was surprising, Grady spoke about his financial concerns and goals, but here was another example of his generosity.

Grady stepped through the door with an aluminum foil pouch and Nica's glass of water. He put the pouch on the grill as Lionel stood up.

"I'll catch you later, Grady. Nice meeting you, Nica," he said as he left the patio.

Grady manned the grill and answered Nica's questions about the house and neighborhood. She didn't bring up what Lionel had told her about the rent. She didn't want to embarrass him, but she put the information away. If she had a score card, she'd put another check in the 'plus' column for Grady. Maybe two checks—generous and humble. Grady could have taken credit for what he'd done in front of her, but he hushed Lionel before it could come out. So, either he didn't want her to know, or he worried Lionel might be embarrassed about the bind he'd been in. Either way, it showed that sweet side of Grady that was taking up more and more space in her daydreams. And her heart.

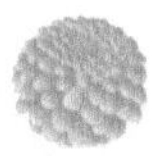

AFTER TAKING NICA home, Grady pulled into his drive and walked over to his neighbor's door. He knocked, and when Lionel opened the door, he asked, "Got a beer?"

"Of course! Come on in, Grady. Want to sit out back?"

Though they were in two sides of the same duplex, their floor plans were different. Lionel's unit was a one-bedroom, which was in the middle of the unit, the kitchen in the back, so his sliding door led out to the back yard, while Grady's led out to the side. Grady had liked the separation when he saw the units. In his opinion, it was better than duplexes with similar layouts that practically shared a back patio, with just a small wooden wall separating them.

"Out back would be nice. We won't be able to do it much longer. It'll be too cold before we know it," he said, following Lionel through the house.

"It's chilly. I can get a small fire going."

"I hope I'm not interrupting anything."

"Just watching some b'ball. Not invested in the game."

Lionel stopped at the fridge and grabbed a couple of bottles. He handed one to Grady and opened the sliding door. "Got your gal home safely?"

"I wouldn't call her my gal. We're friends."

"Mm, hmm," Lionel said, clearly not believing him.

"Neither of us is interested in anything serious. We're just having fun."

"You could have rock climbing fun with male friends, yet you took a girl."

"She's athletic, I thought she would enjoy it. She did."

Lionel pointed Grady to an Adirondack chair in the yard, near the fire pit. "She's a pretty little thing. I could see why you'd like hanging around her."

Grady watched Lionel stack logs and add kindling. "She is. But she's more than that. She's fun to be around. She helps me loosen up and think about things other than work and properties and investments. She makes me want to be a better brother, uncle, and son. And grandson. In a weird way, she's made me think even harder about buying my grandfather's farm. Her passion for her family, her heritage, makes me appreciate mine a little more."

"That's quite the speech, Grady. I think you may see her as more than a friend."

Grady leaned back in the chair and looked towards the sky. It was a crisp, clear fall night and he could see a few stars in the sky. The streetlights prevented a good show. He had to go to his grandfather's farm for a good view of the stars. As kids, he and his brothers would climb into the barn loft, open the large door that was used to lift bales of hay into the loft, and dangle their legs over the edge as they tried to identify the constellations in the sky. Cooper was fascinated with astronomy and would be the one to point them out to his older brothers. Matt and Grady learned quickly and loved spending the time star-gazing, especially if it got them out of doing supper dishes.

Coming out of his star gazing, Grady said, "Now's not the best time for a relationship. Besides, she's going to start working for me come Monday."

"What's that?" Lionel asked.

"She's remodeling the lobby of one of my apartment buildings. It needs to be done on the cheap because money's tight. The building is old, and the lobby is an eyesore. I saw Nica on the local news when they highlighted a cool setup she did for her boss at the Morton Pumpkin Festival. Nica designed these lightweight panels that created the illusion of a building, not just a tent shelter. So unique! Kind of like her. Unique."

Lionel poked the now steady fire. "I got that from my brief introduction. Have to say I was surprised to see a cute Hispanic girl. Of course, never seen you bring home any girl before, so guess I didn't know what your type was."

Grady thought about the comment. If someone had asked him a month or two ago, he would have said he was too busy to date. But he was enjoying getting to know Nica and he wanted to learn more about her heritage. He'd get to continue his education at her cousin's *quinceañera* in a week.

"I don't know about types, Lionel. But I know I like her."

Lionel nodded and sipped his beer.

Grady thought about how compatible he was with Nica. They had similar interests. They were both driven. Neither one of them was worried about getting married and having babies. Maybe they could work long-term. She could rehab the houses he purchased and still flip houses on her own. They would just have to coordinate timing.

He liked the idea of seeing someone who wasn't rushing to get to the altar. Someone who said she would be happy with "niblings." He smiled to himself, thinking of that term again. He felt the same way. He'd be an involved uncle and hoped his brothers had several kids each.

Thinking of his brothers made him think about his grandfather's farm again. If only there was a way to come up with the money to put a down payment on it. If he could someone to lease the land for farming in the spring, the finances might work. There had to be a way. As soon as Nica finished Linden, he'd focus on getting renters. Then he'd have time to come up with a plan to buy his grandfather's farm.

CHAPTER TWENTY-TWO

A S SOON AS Nica got out of class on Monday, she drove to Grady's apartment building on Linden. She'd spent Sunday going over her plans and buying supplies. She was thankful that everything she needed to get started fit in her truck. She'd have to go back to the supply store later in the week to pick up the flooring and shiplap. First, she had to tackle demolition and the battered seagull hanging by the front door would be the first to go.

Inside the building, she was pleased to see that the old furniture had been removed. She'd have to thank Grady for that later. There was a large notice taped to the wall as well. "Attention, residents! A lobby remodel will begin on Monday, October 17th, and continue for two weeks. We apologize for the mess and noise. Please let us know if you have any concerns during the remodel. Thank you!–Lit-Up Property Mgmt."

She assumed Grady's assistant, Linda, had written and hung the sign. She hoped she'd get to meet Linda someday. She seemed like an in-charge kind of person. She'd have to be, to keep up with Grady.

There was a utility room off the lobby, with a sink and a few cleaning products. Nica filled a bucket of water to clean the wallpaper scraper as she worked. Then she started steaming and scraping the old wallpaper off the walls. To stay on schedule, she needed to remove the wallpaper and pull up the carpeting today.

Thirty minutes into the job, a woman walked in the front door and spoke to Nica.

"I see they got the cleaning lady starting before the men get to work," she said.

Nica bristled. "I'm the one doing the work, and the cleaning," she said to the woman. "I may request some assistance if I get crunched on time, but I'm capable of doing it all myself."

"Well, my, my. I'm pleased to hear that. In my youth, no one would have hired a woman to do a remodel like this. Proud of you, girl."

"Thank you, ma'am." Nica was proud of herself for holding her tongue and not getting snippy with the lady.

Hours later the walls were free of the old wallpaper and Nica started pulling up the dirty and smelly shag carpeting. She stopped when her phone pinged.

GRADY: How's it going on the remodel? Any issues?

NICA: No issues. Under control.

GRADY: Good. Can I bring you anything when I get off work?

Nica paused. Was he offering to bring dinner? Supplies? Both?

NICA: No. I'm good.

GRADY: OK. Let me know if that changes.

Nica returned to the flooring and had to stop when her phone pinged again.

PAIGE: Need help?

NICA: No. Thx!

Her text message went off just as soon as she put her phone in her back pocket. *I'm good, Paige,* she thought.

GRADY: I'm looking forward to Sat.

Nica smiled at the screen. She was too, if she was being honest. She was nervous about him meeting her parents. They might expect to hear engagement news before the end of the year. Ugh.

NICA: Hope you know what you're getting into.

GRADY: I have full faith and trust in you to guide the way.

Grady's words sent all the feels zipping through her chest. Someone once told her the word for the feeling was *kama muta.* She couldn't remember if a man had ever told her he had faith and trust in her. She didn't know she longed to hear that until Grady said it. The feeling gave her a further bolt of conviction that she would succeed in this remodel. It was time to get back to work. She'd have to wait and sort through her feelings for Grady later.

BY FRIDAY AFTERNOON, Nica was giving herself a high-five. Everything was under control and running smoothly. She was keeping up with class work *and* was on schedule at Linden.

While exchanging text messages with Grady on Thursday night, she mentioned that Friday was International Nacho Day. He promised to bring her an order of nachos from her favorite restaurant for lunch. He had originally asked to take her out to dinner to celebrate a productive week, but she'd reminded him that she and Izzy had to drive to Chicago on Friday night to help get ready for Evie's *quinceañera*.

The door opened and Nica turned quickly, automatic nail gun in her hand.

"Whoa," Grady said, holding up his hands, a bag of food in his grip. "Watch where you point that thing."

"Ha. Ha. I know what I'm doing." She turned back to the ship-lap wall and finished nailing up the last board. "Perfect timing, I'm ready for a break."

"Great! I brought nourishment." He looked around for a place to sit and Nica pointed at the five-gallon buckets near the entrance.

"I have a lid for those. They make great seats in a pinch."

"If you say so. Where do we put the food?"

"I'll grab something. Hold on."

Returning from the utility closet with a gallon of paint, Nica set it between their makeshift stools. "So, what do you think?"

"It's looking great. I can see your vision coming to life. Well done! Any chance you'll finish before next Friday?"

Nica shook her head. "If you just jinxed me, you are going to be in big trouble."

"Oh, boy. You're right. Sorry. Kind of like saying good luck to someone going onstage, huh. Sorry about that. What time are you and Izzy leaving for Chicago?"

"I'll meet her at our apartment at three and we'll head out. My bag is already packed. The family is holding dinner until we get there, so hopefully we have no issues with traffic."

"I'll meet you at the reception hall at four tomorrow, right?"

"Yes, with your fancy suit on, Mr. Litwiller."

"You've got it. And we get to pretend we're in love. Should be fun."

Nica did not miss the sparkle in his eye. She spooned another serving of nachos onto her plate before responding. "Something like that. My family should be easy to fool, so we don't have to push it too far."

Grady leaned forward. "And what would be not too far, but far enough? Do we hold hands? Dance slow dances? Whisper sweet nothings to each other?"

Nica groaned. "I've made a big mistake, haven't I?"

"No mistake. I like teasing you. It'll be great. We'll fool everyone perfectly. I'll follow your lead, and if things don't seem to be going well, I may have to surprise you with my devotion."

Nica started choking on a tortilla chip.

"You okay?" Grady asked, standing quickly to his feet.

"Yes!" Nica managed to shout. "I'm fine!"

"My devotion got to you already." He sat back down, smiling.

Nica looked at the self-satisfied look on his face and wanted to flick the gooey cheese, sour cream, black bean, and jalapeño nacho topping at him. But there was a risk a food fight would start, and they might get food on the freshly painted walls. She did NOT want to clean up that mess.

"You are getting to me; I'll give you that. Don't you need to get back to work? I do." She stood and walked her paper plate to the large garbage bag in the corner.

"Yes, I do. I have a meeting at two-thirty and I need a little time to prep. Thanks for letting me hang out and eat with you."

"And thank you for bringing lunch. Those nachos were great."

"I'll see you tomorrow, *girlfriend*." He stressed the last word.

"Go, Grady. I'll see you tomorrow."

Nica was pleased that she and Grady could tease each other now. So much better than the mean things she'd wanted to say to him when they'd first met. If they managed to pull off the appearance of a relationship tomorrow, she'd be thrilled.

She just needed to remind herself that it was a pretend date, not a real date. If Grady did lean into her tomorrow and whisper in her ear, she just might forget the fake date part of the whole thing. She really needed to keep her heart under lock and key.

CHAPTER TWENTY-THREE

GRADY LEFT HOME at noon, four hours before he needed to arrive. GPS said it was a three-hour drive, so he had a one-hour contingency buffer. Perfect. He would park, walk around, get his bearings, and be waiting at the reception hall twenty minutes early, if all went well.

He pushed play on the audiobook he'd downloaded from the library the day before. It was a Spanish language manual for beginners, and he hoped he'd be able to use a few words to impress Nica's family.

Twenty minutes into the book, his phone rang with a call from his brother Cooper.

"Hey, Coop. What's up?"

"Hi. Can you help me move a couch this afternoon for Andrea?"

"Sorry, bro. No. I'm on my way to Chicago right now."

"Chicago?"

"Yes. I'm going to a family thing with Nica."

"Oh, right, you mentioned that. I forgot. Things seem to be going well with you and your new girlfriend."

"We're friends, Cooper. Just friends."

The tone of his voice must have been a clue to Cooper. "You sure about that, big brother? You sound tense, or a bit pissed off."

"I would probably change the label, but she seems content with 'just friends.' Maybe that will change when she finishes the remodel in Linden. Maybe if she's not working for me, we can move the relationship forward."

"That sounds hopeful. I like your positive energy," Cooper snickered softly. "Okay, since you can't help me with the couch, I'm going to let you go. Drive safe."

"Later."

Nothing like a brother to make you deal with what's really going on. If he was being honest, Grady wanted to take this relationship further. Much further.

NICA SAT IN the back of the limo that carried her mother, her aunt, Izzy, Evie, and her *damas*. The men were in a separate limo.

The mass at church was over, and they were on their way to the reception hall. Nica was nervous, both from caring about Evie enjoying her special day and about Grady meeting her family. She wasn't sure she could pull off this fake date situation.

What if her family asked all sorts of questions about their relationship: *How long have you been dating? How did you meet?* (She did not want to tell that story!) Who was interested first? When will you get engaged? Will there be a marriage in the new year? How many babies do you plan to have?

These were real concerns. Her mom and Tía Maria could be relentless when they were on the hunt for information. Nica's best hope was that they would both be focused on Evie's *quinceañera* and wouldn't give Nica and her date a thought.

Those hopes were dashed when the limo pulled up in front of the hall and she saw Grady standing by the front door.

"OOOOH, who is the handsome man in the black suit standing by the door?" Tía Maria asked, gawking at Grady. Nica was thankful the windows were rolled up-a defense against the chill in the air and from embarrassingly loud aunts.

Izzy leaned forward to look. "Oh, that's Grady, Nica's boyfriend!"

Nica wanted to groan. Why did Izzy say "boyfriend"? Why not just date?

"It is?" Nica's mother, Juanita, asked.

"Yes! It is. I can't wait for you all to meet him." Was she pretending to be excited, or were the butterflies in her stomach indicative of her very real excitement at seeing Grady?

Nica watched as Grady turned towards the street. He saw the limo pull up and straightened his shoulders. There was no denying how handsome he was. He had a slight five o'clock shadow, and his dark hair was neatly combed into place. He'd asked Nica what she was wearing so he could coordinate with her. She smoothed down the skirt of her rose-colored dress as she noticed his matching pocket square.

The back door opened, and Tía Maria jumped out first, her phone in hand so she could take pictures of Evie emerging from the limo. Evie was told to wait patiently for the limo carrying the men to arrive. Tía Maria wanted a picture with Evie's escort taking her hand as she stepped out.

"Is it all right if the rest of us get out, Tía?" Nica asked. She wanted to say hello to Grady as soon as she could.

"Yes, you and Izzy can. I want the rest of the girls to wait for their dates."

Izzy looked at Nica. "I guess we're the old maids in this situation." She stepped out of the limo before Nica.

"Fine with me if it means less posing for pictures. Let's go."

Grady had approached the limo and he held out his hand as Izzy exited. Izzy stepped out of the way quickly and Nica exited.

As Grady took her hand, she felt the butterflies take flight in her stomach. She knew she could trust him to be a respectable date, fake or not. He wouldn't do anything to embarrass her or himself. They could pretend to be dating for the next few hours and then go right back to being just friends. Well, employer and employee, then just friends.

"Nica. You look absolutely stunning!" he said, helping her from the car. His comment was loud enough that she heard several gasps from the girls and her mother, still in the limo behind her.

Nica smiled at him just as she heard her aunt shout, "Smile!" Nica knew her aunt was taking a picture of them. Good. They'd have proof she'd brought a date!

"Hi. Thank you. How was the drive up?" Nica asked.

"Good."

"Are you ready for the craziness?"

"Absolutely." Dropping his voice, he asked, "Can I kiss you?"

"Sure. Make it look good," she whispered back.

Grady put one hand on her waist and gently pulled her forward. He cupped her cheek with his other hand and Nica thought she was going to faint with anticipation. Maybe her dress was too tight.

Grady leaned down to her and his lips touched hers, hesitantly at first. *What's he waiting for*, she wondered. His lips pressed softly, and Nica knew she'd faint. It was not supposed to feel like this! She wasn't supposed to feel so *delighted* at the kiss. It should just feel like a friendly kiss, not a romantic kiss. She felt warm and adored. She would never forget this kiss.

Grady pulled away and she wanted to grab him by his tie and drag him back. Whoa! They were much better actors than she'd expected. That felt like a REAL kiss.

He smiled at her and whispered, "Are you okay?"

"Hmm? Oh yes, I'm fine. I'm so happy you made it!" she added in a voice loud enough for her mom and aunt to hear.

Playing her part, she grabbed his hand and pulled him towards her aunt. "Tía Maria, I would like you to meet Grady Litwiller. My date. I mean, boyfriend."

Her aunt's eyes shot to Nica. Joy and excitement were written all over her face. "Hello, Grady. It is wonderful to meet Nica's boyfriend. We are so happy you were able to make it to our celebration."

"*El gusto es mio*," Grady said. He smiled widely, showing his perfectly straight teeth.

Her aunt looked like she was going to swoon. "I look forward to talking to you more inside. Please enjoy yourselves." She gave Nica a wink.

The second limo had arrived, and the men were getting out. "I'll introduce you to everyone inside. Let's get out of the way so they can get pictures," Nica said, taking Grady's hand and leading him up the stairs to stand by Izzy.

She surprised herself by grabbing his hand. *It's all for show*, she thought. She liked it though, maybe too much.

Izzy tapped her foot. "It's too cold to wait out here. If we step inside, we can see all the action from the foyer."

"And be out of sight of all the prying eyes," Nica murmured.

It took thirty minutes for Evie and her court to disembark from the cars, be photographed, and get inside. While they waited for Evie's court to enter, Nica took Grady around to meet her family. There were polite handshakes, friendly hugs, and a couple of threatening handshakes from Nica's protective brothers, Julián and Marcos.

During this time, Nica explained to Grady what had happened during the mass prior to the reception. She explained that Evie was gifted a rosary and a tiara. The tiara symbolizes that she is always a princess to her family and before God. Nica was pleased that Grady asked considerate and respectful questions.

The lights dimmed twice, and Nica told Grady they needed to take their seats for the formal toasts. They made their way to their assigned table and sat. Nica's father, standing in for Evie's deceased father, made his way to the front with a microphone. Tía Maria and Evie joined him. Arturo started with a beautiful prayer and followed it with an equally beautiful toast for Evie. He ended by thanking the guests for their presence. Next, Tía Maria said a few words and finally, Evie, thanked the guests as well.

Nica whispered in Grady's ear what would happen next, "Next is the Changing of the Shoes ceremony. Tía Maria will present Evie with her first *official* pair of high heels. This is one of the symbols of her transitioning to adulthood."

"Adulthood?" Grady whisper-exclaimed, "She's only fifteen."

"I know," Nica said, "but looking back a few generations, girls married young. Not so much now. After that, Evie will be presented with her last doll, it's called *ceremonia de la ultima muñeca* in Spanish. After that, there will be a dance with Evie and my dad, then the rest of Evie's party will join in. Sort of like the progression of dances at a wedding."

Nica sighed. "Times like these, the ache of my uncle's passing is especially sharp. I wish he was here."

"I bet you do." Grady put his hand on her knee and squeezed lightly. The gesture warmed her heart and she blinked rapidly to keep the tears from falling.

As the formal dances ended and everyone took their seats, the servers began delivering salads. As everyone else at their table was focused on their dates, Nica and Grady had a chance to strategize about the rest of the evening. Grady asked questions about her family members, trying to keep all the names straight.

"It's expected that it will take you a while to learn the names, so don't worry too much about it," she said.

He leaned over and put his arm around her shoulder. "I like that you assume I'll be around your family some more."

She was aware of his aftershave, with its hints of cedar wood and vanilla. She had the urge to rest her head on his shoulder and just breathe. She closed her eyes briefly to block the over-stimulation of colors and people and decorations and all the things around her.

Grady picked up the dinner roll basket and held it out for her. "Roll?"

"No, thanks," she shook her head. "So, you're going back tonight, right? You didn't get a hotel?"

"That's right. It's why I'm not drinking. I figured if I leave by 10:30, I'll be home by one. There won't be a lot of traffic."

"Would you mind if I rode back with you?"

"Of course not, but I thought you were riding back with Izzy tomorrow."

"I was, but Paige texted me today. She's going to Anna Lee's house to help with yard work and asked if I could help. I agreed. I don't think it will take too long and I should be able to get over to Linden to do a little work. I would like to paint the shiplap tomorrow, then Monday I can start to put down the new flooring."

"Your family won't miss you tomorrow?" he asked.

"I'll ask for forgiveness, not permission. We can sneak out. I'll ask Izzy to bring my stuff tomorrow."

"All right. Do you want some help tomorrow with the flooring?"

"Are you offering your help, Mr. Litwiller?" she teased. "I didn't think you did physical labor."

"I don't, but I don't mind helping out. Just let me know when you are heading over and I'll join you."

Izzy leaned across Grady. "They're getting ready to start dancing. We are all supposed to join in to get the guests dancing. Do not sit this out! I won't answer to the moms for you."

Grady lifted a brow. "Sounds serious. Good thing I got my dancing shoes on. But what about dessert?"

Nica laughed. "That will be out in a little while don't worry, there will be plenty of desserts."

"Desserts? Plural?"

"Yes, Grady."

"My kind of party! Let's shake a leg!"

They joined the others on the dance floor for several upbeat songs, then took a break and were talking to Nica's parents when the first slow song came on.

"May I have this dance?" Grady asked her, holding out his hand.

Nica hesitated. Her mom blurted out, "Go on and dance!"

Grady led her on to the dance floor and turned to her in the midst of a number of couples. "Trying to stay away from prying eyes," he said as he pulled her in close to him.

Their height difference was helped in the moment by the high heels she'd worn at Izzy's insistence. The heels which had made it easier to kiss him outside.

She had to snap out of that line of thinking. "Thank you again for coming and being my fake date."

"This doesn't feel like a fake date," he replied, squeezing her a little closer.

She agreed. It felt right being in his arms and swaying slowly to the music.

She didn't want to kill the mood. She wouldn't split hairs about fake or real dates. She was just going to enjoy the calm moment. She turned her head to the side and rested on Grady's chest. She felt him let out a breath, like he was as content as she was.

The sweet moment was broken a few seconds later when her younger brother Marcos danced a little closer with his date. "Hey, Nic. Let's see you kiss your boyfriend!" he taunted.

Her eyes widened as she looked up to Grady. A second kiss on a fake date? He nodded towards her brother and gave her a sly smile. He leaned down and put his soft lips on hers and she melted. She heard her brother whoop behind her, but she didn't care. Everyone could step off this dance floor right now and shine a spotlight on her and Grady. She would not mind. As long as Grady was kissing her and had his strong arms wrapped around her, she wasn't going anywhere.

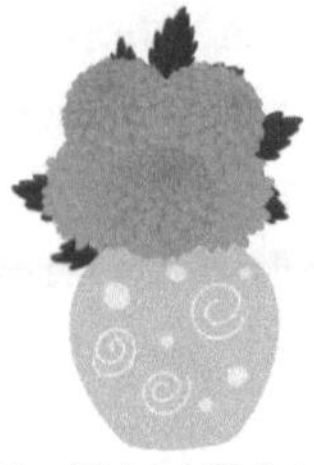

CHAPTER TWENTY-FOUR

OURS LATER, GRADY looked at Nica and asked, "Ready to run?"

She laughed. "Yes."

He insisted on saying goodbye to her parents and aunt. He thanked them for a beautiful evening and said he hoped to see them again soon.

Nica thought there was a slim chance of that happening. As far as she knew, there were no big events coming up—no weddings, no baptisms, no birthday parties where she would be expected to bring another date. This was a one and done deal with Grady.

Outside, the sun had gone down and so had the temperature. Nica regretted not wearing a coat. She folded her arms across her chest as she followed Grady. She hoped his car wasn't far. It wasn't. Being early had allowed Grady to grab a spot in the first row.

"Brr, good thing your car is so close," she said, beginning to climb in.

"Here take my jacket," Grady said, pulling it off.

"I'll warm up quickly as soon as I get in the car."

"Take it," he insisted.

Thanking him, she pulled it on. She took a moment to enjoy the scent of his aftershave again, then put on her seat belt. "So, what did you think?"

"It was fantastic. I enjoyed myself even more than I expected. It was fun getting to know your family, and therefore getting to know you better. I can't tell you how many stories I heard about you when I went for refreshments or to use the restroom. Your family loves to talk!"

Nica groaned. "Please, if there was anything that troubled you, ask me to get my side of it. Who knows what nonsense they were filling your head with. It's a big family, sometimes people misremember. They may say I did something when really it was Izzy."

"Sure, sure. I heard great stories, nothing alarming. So, I guess we pulled it off then."

"The fake date? Yeah, we did." She smiled, though she knew Grady couldn't see it while navigating the narrow street with cars parked on either side.

Grady swallowed audibly. "I was thinking. Maybe it wasn't really a fake date. It didn't feel fake to me."

Nica turned in her seat to face him squarely. "Not even when you were forced to kiss me?"

"Especially not then." He swiped his hand away from the wheel like a baseball umpire calling a runner out at home.

"Then that was a real, legitimate kiss?" she asked, hesitantly.

"Yes, it was. They were. Both of the kisses were real to me."

She gasped softly and thought about the evening. At first, it had seemed fake to her because she was so worried they would be found out. But as the evening wore on, she'd forgotten it was fake, too. When they'd danced, she'd floated across the floor in his arms like they were the only people in the room. "I know what you're saying. It felt real to me too."

"Good. So, I was thinking…"

"Yeah?"

Grady paused like he was considering his words carefully. "What if we invested in our friendship a bit more? Take it from friendship and bump it up a few percentage points?"

Nica grinned, conveying the warmth and joy she felt. "That's maybe the *least* romantic thing that any guy asking me out has ever said to me."

His fingers tapped a rhythmic pattern on the wheel. "Well? Did it work?"

"Can I finish the job at Linden this week, and then we can revisit the conversation? I don't want anyone thinking I'm dating my boss."

"Logical. I like logic. Fine. But can we plan for a real date now, for after you finish the remodel? Just schedule a day to go on a date?"

She tried to suppress a yawn. The late night and long day were catching up to her and she was feeling warm from his jacket, the seat warmer, and the heat blowing through the vents. "Absolutely not! Ask me out for a real date *after* Friday. I'll be done on Friday, then you'll no longer be my boss."

"Fine." Grady gave her a sweet grin, illuminated by the dashboard lights. He turned on his blinker and glanced over his shoulder to merge onto the interstate. "I'll ask you out after Friday. Now, you're tired. Close your eyes and rest. I've got this drive. I'll stop and get a coffee if I start to feel drowsy, but I'm feeling amped up right now. You don't mind if I turn on an audiobook softly, do you?"

"Of course not. You shouldn't drive late at night in complete silence."

Nica leaned her head back to rest on the seat. She closed her eyes and smiled when she heard the beginning of the Spanish instruction audiobook begin to teach the verb tenses of the verb "to be"–I am, *soy*; you are, *eres*; he is, *es*; we are, *somos*; they are, *son*. She drifted off thinking about teaching Grady more informal Spanish in the future.

TWENTY MINUTES LATER, Nica was breathing softly and steadily. If she wasn't asleep, Grady assumed she would be soon. The GPS said they had ninety more minutes to reach her apartment in Bloomington.

Though the audiobook still played, and the narrator still conjugated verbs and introduced new vocabulary, Grady was no longer listening to learn. It was a pleasant backdrop as he rehashed the events of the day in his mind. He was surprised at how comfortable he'd felt meeting so many members of Nica's family all at once. He had anticipated needing to put on a game face and just get through it. But instead, he'd enjoyed every minute of it.

His apprehension had melted when Nica had stepped out of the limo and her eyes locked on his. Seeing the nervousness in her eyes caused a shift inside him. He was no longer worried about what might happen. He knew that no matter what, he wanted to be strong for Nica. He did not want to let her down. He wanted to be whatever she needed him to be. She said that if Grady hadn't come, her mother would have tried to set her up with someone, and he couldn't let that happen.

There was something guarded about Nica. She said coming from a big family had soured her on marriage and raising kids, and he understood that. But he could tell that she was full of love and caring. She would fight you in a heartbeat if you gave Izzy a strange look or said something critical about one of her friends or family members. Her love and loyalty were fierce. She was passionate. And on those occasions when she was comfortable and her joy spilled out of her, lighting up her face and twinkling out of her eyes, it caused Grady's heart to swell.

He started to think about how he'd ask her out for their first official date. It wouldn't be a text. It wouldn't be a phone call. It had to be more meaningful than that. Since she worked in a flower shop, it should probably involve flowers. This was the start of something special. Nica was special, and he was going to show her in any and every way he could how special she was. The first date would be romantic but not over the top; he did not want to scare her away.

He smiled, thinking about trying to catch a goldfinch when he was a child. The bird was tiny and hopping around the yard in search of seeds that had fallen from the feeder. Grady thought he could catch it; he was so much larger, and he assumed, smarter than the bird. But he quickly learned that what the small bird lacked in size, he made up for with his eyesight and wings.

An hour later, Grady pulled into a parking spot not far from Nica's apartment building. Technically, his building, but she lived there.

He gently shook her shoulder. "Hey, Sleepy Spice."

Nica rubbed her eyes. "What did you call me?"

Grady chuckled. "Sleepy Spice. You weren't acting so spicy. We're here. I'll walk you to your door."

They exited the car and walked up the new staircase. Grady was happy to see that the contractor had put down slip-proof strips on the stairs. Winter was coming, and the snow and ice could be a bad situation on the stairs.

At the top, Nica unlocked the door and pushed it open. She shrugged out of Grady's suit jacket. "Here. Thank you again for letting me borrow it."

"Any time," he said. "Can I kiss you good night?"

Grady enjoyed seeing the smile spread slowly across her face.

"Grady, were you even paying attention to the conversation about waiting to date until *after* I'm done working for you? If we're not dating, we shouldn't be kissing," she said, but there was a gleam in her eyes.

"I was listening. But, from the look on your face, I think you like the idea of a kiss." He continued when she didn't react. "All right. Fine. I'll wait." He stuck out his hand.

She shook his hand solemnly. "Thank you, Grady for not making this weird." She raised an eyebrow and Grady laughed heartily.

He stopped shaking her hand and held it. Just holding her hand was enough. It was a connection. He wanted more but he'd agreed to wait as she asked.

He squeezed her hand softly and let go. "Get inside. You must be cold. Text me tomorrow when you head over to Linden, and I'll meet you there."

He wanted to lean over and kiss the tip of her nose at least, but he resisted. "Night, Spicy."

She laughed and stepped inside. "Night, Grady."

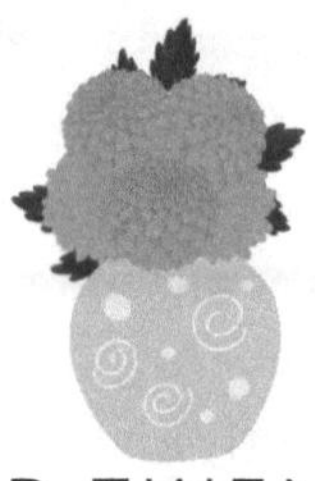

CHAPTER TWENTY-FIVE

PAIGE PULLED UP to the window of the drive-through lane and paid for their coffees.

"I hope Anna Lee likes hazelnut," she said as she handed the drink carrier to Nica.

"We'll find out soon enough. Did she tell you what all she needed help with today?" Nica asked, looking at the time on the dash. If they were done at Anna Lee's by noon, she would be able to get about five hours of work done on the remodel. She needed to get back home early—she had homework that couldn't be put off.

"Digging up some plants, raking leaves, and moving some furniture. So, shifting topics. I'm all ears. Tell me about the party. I want all the juicy details too, don't leave anything out."

Nica wasn't ready to share. "We'll be at Anna Lee's in five minutes. There's no time for all the details. It was great though. I think Evie was happy, and that's the most important thing."

"True. But I want to know what happened with Grady."

"He was the perfect fake date. I think we fooled everyone." Her heart was feeling foolish today. She wasn't ready to tell Paige that Grady had brought up the idea of taking the relationship up a few notches. Or percentage points, as he put it. Such a math guy.

She was still riding high on the thrill of the night. Grady had been the perfect date. He knew the right things to say to her and to her family. He was attentive and flirtatious.

Paige pulled into Anna Lee's brick driveway, and Nica lifted the drink tray to avoid any spills from the bumpy bricks.

They found Anna Lee in the backyard, with a rake in hand. The sun was shining, and Anna Lee wore enormous black sunglasses, the medical kind that Nica's grandma had worn after cataract surgery.

"Mornin' girls," she called as they approached.

"Good morning," they said in unison.

"We brought you a coffee," said Paige. "Do you like hazelnut flavoring?"

"As long as it's not decaf, I'll drink it. Why don't we take a seat, drink our coffee, and make a game plan," she said, leaning the rake against a tree.

Nica didn't want to waste time planning; she wanted to get the work done so she could go, but she didn't want to be rude. "Sounds good."

They followed Anna Lee up the steps and onto the screened-in back porch. Salty, was curled up on a carpet-covered perch by a window, the sun's rays warming him. The porch was furnished with a white wicker loveseat and matching chair. Their stuffed cushions were covered in a white material covered with tiny pink roses. There was a small bookcase along the far wall with a row of blue Mason jars on top, holding various flower cuttings.

"Let's sit here," Anna Lee said, sitting on the loveseat.

Paige joined her as Nica put the drink carrier on the small table between them.

"What do you need us to do, Anna Lee?" Nica asked, jumping to the task at hand.

"If you two could help me rake the leaves and dig up my dahlia bulbs, I can burn the leaves when you go."

"Paige said something about moving furniture..." Nica prompted.

"Yes, I have a recliner that's seen much better days. If you could carry it out to the curb, the garbage truck can pick it up tomorrow. That is, if someone doesn't grab it first. I hope someone does though, better than it going to the landfill. Just because I think it's too worn—Salty's claws have done a number on it over the years—doesn't mean someone else wouldn't find it useful. But John hinted at a new matching set of recliners for Christmas, so I thought I'd make room. Maybe he'll remember the idea then."

John was Anna Lee's recent beau. She didn't give up a lot of details, but the girls had seen him in the flower shop a few times and had pestered her enough to at least admit she was seeing him.

"Oh, that sounds nice!" Paige exclaimed. "I think that's so romantic."

Nica was happy to see the delight in Paige's face. She was in a great place with Trevor. Watching them grow closer and happier had been encouraging for Nica. Seeing her friend happily in love made her more open to the idea.

"Don't know about it being romantic at our age," Anna Lee said, laughing. She leaned back with her coffee cup in hand. "But it's companionable. Now, let's get back to the work. The raking will take the longest, so should we knock off the other two tasks first?"

"That sounds good. Nica has work to do at Grady's apartment building today, so we're going to be fast and efficient." Paige winked at Nica. "As soon as we drink our coffee."

"I appreciate your offer to help today, ladies. I've had a harder time than usual adjusting to the onset of fall. Normally, the seasons come with their own gifts, and I relish each one. But this year, I'm feeling a bit blah. I guess winter came for me sooner than expected. Feeling the need to hibernate, rest, and renew.

But first," she perked up, "let's get the fall work done. Winter will be along soon enough."

"Not too soon, I hope," Nica said, "I want to enjoy the fall season."

"Hey, speaking of fun fall activities," Paige said, setting her coffee cup down, "there's a ghost tour at Duncan Manor in Towanda on Saturday. Would you like to go?"

"Duncan Manor?" Nica asked.

"Yes, you can see it from the interstate. If you're going north on I-55, it's on your right, just before the Towanda exit."

"Oh, I know that place. It's unique. I'm always up for a ghost tour. I'm in. Let's ask Izzy, too." Nica turned toward their boss, "Would you like to go, Anna Lee?"

Anna Lee nodded her head slowly and pursed her lips. "Maybe. Let me see how I'm feeling Saturday. It could be an In Bloom excursion. Maybe Lauren and Tilly could go, too. We should do that more often. I was planning to start with a New Year's party here in January."

"That would be awesome, Anna Lee," Paige exclaimed. "I would love to help you plan it. Remember that I leave for my internship in early January. New Year's is my favorite holiday. Maybe we could all make vision boards for the new year!"

Anna Lee smiled. "At my age, I think about vision boards in terms of months, not years. But I hear what you're saying, and I like that. Ask the other girls their thoughts. If everyone is game, we'll do it."

"Back to *this* time of the year," Nica said. "We've got Halloween and then the Day of the Dead. Speaking of, Anna Lee, will you have marigolds in for next week? I haven't seen any in the shop before."

"Don't get a lot of requests for marigolds. What do you need them for?"

"We use them for the Day of the Dead, to recognize and honor our loved ones that have passed on. Izzy and I take time to remember her dad and other friends and family members we've lost. Marigolds help the spirits find us, and flowers, of course, represent the fragility of life."

"An important thing to remember. I'll work with my suppliers and have some for you, Cricket." Anna Lee stood and ruffled the fur on Salty's neck. "This work isn't going to do itself, let's get busy."

Paige and Nica took the recliner out first, and it was gone when they left two hours later, putting a big smile on Anna Lee's face.

Anna Lee instructed them on how to dig up her dahlia tubers to store for the winter. She talked about the symbolism of the flower, sharing that it was a symbol of commitment, dignity, and elegance.

"I love dahlias," said Nica. "I painted pictures of dahlias for my cousin Izzy for her fifteenth birthday. You've seen them, Paige, they hang above Izzy's bed."

"Right!" Paige said, pulling a tuber from the ground, "They're gorgeous paintings!"

"The dahlia reminds me of you, Nica," Anna Lee said. "Another symbol of the flower is staying graceful under pressure, and you do that well. I've seen it."

Nica put the tuber she'd dug from the ground into the crate of wood shavings that would be the dahlias home for the winter. "That's sweet of you to say. I don't always feel graceful under pressure. I guess I hide my concerns well."

She thought about the pressure she was currently under to finish the remodel for Grady, complete her homework on time, and dodge the phone calls and text messages from her mother, who was already asking for more details about Grady.

Anna Lee shifted the tuber in the crate, adding more wood shavings on top. "If you're hiding them, be careful. Hidden stress is bad for your health. Trust me, I know."

Nica wanted to ask what she meant but didn't want to pry. "I know. That's a big part of my studies. Working out is my favorite way to destress. I run when I'm angry. It helps that toxic energy to drain away. When I'm anxious or stressed, I like to do yoga to calm my busy brain." She dropped the last tuber into the crate. "That's all the dahlias. Time to grab the rakes?" She needed to speed things up.

"Yes. You'll find rakes in the garage. Will you take the crate with ya?" Anna Lee asked, grabbing the rake leaning against the tree.

"Of course."

When they had all of the leaves raked, Anna Lee said she'd burn them after a short rest.

As Paige and Nica started down the drive to the car, Anna Lee stood on the back steps, ready to go in. She called after them, "Girls, be good, and if you can't be good, be careful." She cackled a laugh as she opened the door.

CHAPTER TWENTY-SIX

BACK AT THEIR apartment building, Nica jumped out of Paige's car and into her own. She stopped at the grocery store and grabbed a to-go salad for lunch. She'd eat it as soon as she got to the Linden property. The yard work at Anna Lee's had spurred her appetite.

In the building, she grabbed two empty buckets from the utility room and brought them into the lobby. She hoped there wouldn't be a lot of people going in and out the lobby as she ate lunch or later as she worked on the floors. She wondered if Grady had been serious about stopping by to help. Just in case he was, she shot him a text to let him know she was there.

Grady showed up fifteen minutes later.

"That was fast," Nica said. She'd just thrown out the empty salad container and was clapping her hands together to get rid of crumbs.

"I was ready. Just waiting for the bat signal."

Nica took a moment to look him over. He *looked* ready to work. He had on sturdy-looking brown pants, brown work boots, a long-sleeved t-shirt, and a flannel. "How often have you worn that outfit?"

"Truth?"

She nodded.

"I bought it yesterday. But with you around, I thought it was a good investment. Especially these boots—they have steel toes!"

Nica laughed. "Well, you do seem prepared. I hope you work out okay. I've had to lay off all my other help."

"Ha!" Grady said. "You are your own help."

"I know," she said, grinning. "Ready to get to work?"

An hour later, they were making progress. It took a little while to get the tools set up. The laminate flooring had been in the utility room getting acclimated to the temperature and humidity levels of the building for a few days so it was ready to be installed.

Nica began laying out the floorboards to ensure that identical pieces were not right next to each other. She asked Grady to open the boxes of flooring and sort the pieces into piles that she could grab from. After laying out three rows, she had Grady pause. There was enough to get started.

Working together was surprisingly easy. She had expected Grady to be bossy and act like a know-it-all, but he wasn't, and he didn't. He deferred to her, asked questions, and took direction well. He even cracked jokes and made her laugh.

She snapped the first pieces of flooring together, showing Grady the method. They came up with a procedure, taking turns laying and snapping a piece in place.

After a few false starts, they got into a groove. They had laid the first two rows when the front door opened and Grady's brother, Matt, entered.

Grady looked over to Nica. "I told him I was here. Hey, Matt."

"Hi guys. Can't stay, but Julie made some cookies, and insisted I bring some when she heard Grady was here doing physical labor." He smiled as he held up a plastic container. "How's he doing, Nica? Causing you more grief than help?"

"She just said I was doing great," Grady said before Nica could respond.

She rolled her eyes. "I'm happy he goes back to work tomorrow."

"Hey, now," Grady retorted.

"How was the party last night?" Matt asked, looking at Nica.

But, *again*, Grady answered before she could. "It was fantastic. We had a great time." He changed the subject and Nica wondered why he didn't elaborate more on Evie's party. "Remind me, did you say that Mom and Dad wanted us over for dinner on Friday or Saturday?"

"Friday. Not sure what the occasion is. They're just getting us together, I guess."

Nica listened to the brothers make plans for Friday with a growing irritation. Grady spoke *for* her. Twice! Matt was clearly asking her those questions, but Grady took it upon himself to answer. Did he think she was too shy around his brother to answer? Didn't matter, it wasn't right. She tried to shake her irritation.

She thought about their agreement. She'd told Grady he couldn't ask her out until she was finished with this job. She'd be finished Friday. She wondered if he'd ask her to his family's dinner. It would be nice to spend more time with his family. But it would be fine if he didn't. She'd be ready for a long, hot bath on Friday night. She was going to need it after several more days of remodeling.

Matt left and they resumed installing the flooring. Once they finished, Grady asked what was next.

Nica checked the time. "Nothing for today. I will come in tomorrow and install the baseboards. I need to get home and do homework. It's been a busy weekend."

"Man, homework." Grady was picking up the empty flooring boxes. "I don't envy you. Well, can I take you to dinner first?"

Nica put tools into her toolbox. "That sort of sounds like a date. No."

"Friends go out for dinner."

"I know, but I need to get home. Oh, Grady. While you're here, I wanted to show you something. When I was in here the other day, I got to thinking about the utility room door. Once we're done in the lobby, it's going to stick out, and not in a good way. It will clash with the new colors and the design elements here. I was thinking we should swap out the door. It's a solid door, so not the cheapest. I should be able to replace it for around six hundred dollars. What do you think?"

Grady looked towards the utility door but didn't say anything. Nica began to brace herself for his objections. If he objected, she *could* paint it, but she was worried that the paint would be a sad attempt at improvement because of the years of abuse the door had taken. It really needed to be replaced.

He finally nodded and said, "I see what you mean. Sure, that's fine. Well, if there's nothing else for today, I'll take the trash out with me as I go. See you later." He left.

Nica felt like she'd won a battle but lost a war. She regretted asking to replace the door. Maybe she should have just painted it and let that be good enough. Grady might be worried about what additional oversights she had made which would cost more money. She should have considered that door in her original design. Another lesson learned.

Then there was the issue of Grady speaking for her. That had to be her biggest pet peeve. Coming from a household with eleven kids, it was often a shouting match to get attention. She hated not being heard or allowed to speak for herself.

She really wanted to go for a run to shake off the irritation, but she had to get home to study.

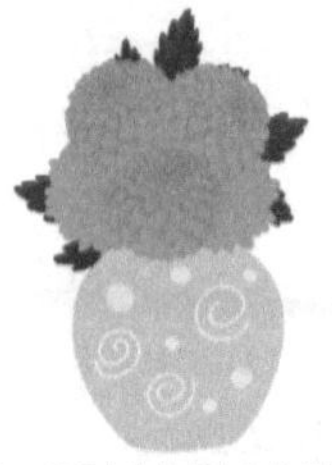

CHAPTER TWENTY-SEVEN

RADY'S FOOT WAS a little heavy on the gas pedal, so he told himself to let up. He was nearing a school zone and didn't want to risk a ticket. Such a waste of money when it was clearly something he could control.

He hit the speaker button on his steering wheel and told the car system to call Linda. When Linda answered, she practically shouted, "Tell me how the weekend went with your *friend*."

"Not now. Got a lot on my mind. First of which, Nica needs another six hundred dollars to replace a door. Can you send her the money?" Grady noticed a patrol car at the next intersection and gave himself a mental high-five for slowing down.

"Of course," she responded. "You, okay? You're sounding a bit cranky. Must not have been a good weekend."

Grady paused before answering her. The trouble with working with a friend you've known for years was the way they could see through the game face you tried to put on. "The weekend was fantastic. We'll talk about it another time, though. What do *you* need to talk to me about this morning?"

He needed to wait before talking to her about Nica and their budding romance. He was still peeved about the extra cost for the door, but he told himself to let it go—it wasn't a big cost, and she was right, it needed to be replaced. It was a learning experience, and he was confident she'd learn from it.

Maybe it was just lack of experience and she'd get better over time. Maybe he needed to let up a bit. He knew this was her dream, and he'd seen what she'd done with her boss's booth at the festival. But he hadn't asked her about her other experience.

He'd begun to think about a long-term partnership with Nica, both romantically and professionally. With her vision and remodeling skills, it was a match made in investment property heaven. He could buy the properties and she could renovate them. He'd need to be more understanding when there were minor oversights and misses.

"Grady? You still there?"

Shoot, Grady had been distracted by thoughts of Nica and missed what Linda was saying. "I'm sorry. What did you say?"

"Do you want me to give Tom and Marty a status update on Linden?" she asked. Grady could hear her tapping something—a pen on her desk, maybe? Had she picked up the drumming habit from him?

"Can we hold off a couple of days? I didn't ask Nica if replacing the utility door would push out the completion date. Let me check with her."

"Okay. I'll put it down to follow up on Wednesday. That's all I had this morning. It's Monday, so we'll see what kind of issues come up today."

"Sounds good." He disconnected the call as he pulled into the bank parking lot. He needed to talk to Nica, but that would have to wait until he was in a better mood.

NICA FINALLY GOT a chance to rehash the weekend with Izzy on Monday evening. It was 9 p.m. and she was tired from a long day of classes, where she'd realized that she was falling behind in her studies, followed by installing the baseboards and crown molding at Grady's apartment building.

Izzy was in Nica's room, sitting cross-legged on her bed. Nica was on a yoga mat, doing some relaxation poses to help with her stiff muscles and prepare her for sleep.

"I want all the details," Izzy said, bouncing on the bed. "Don't leave anything out. You and Grady were the hot gossip at breakfast yesterday. Everyone was trying to pump me for information. Now, I need information," she said with a devilish grin.

Nica stretched forward, reaching for her ankles. This conversation was not going to allow for a restful sleep.

"Saturday was rather surprising. It was completely different than I expected. It quickly turned from a fake date that we were just trying to get through into a rather romantic evening. You know he kissed me on the dance floor when Marcos dared us. We'd kissed once before that too. That's when it started to change and seem like a real date to me. We talked about it, too, on the way home, and we both agreed that it didn't feel like a fake date after all, but a real one. We said we'd see what a real relationship might look like—beyond being friends, I mean."

"I knew what you meant. Go on. What happened when you got home? Did you invite him in?"

"No. We agreed that it was a great evening, but I said I wanted to wait to date until after the remodel. Technically, he's my boss and that's yuck. Maybe that's the issue…"

Nica paused, thinking about what she'd just said. Maybe that's why Grady had grown cold yesterday. Was he just putting his boss hat on?

"What issue?" Izzy prompted.

"I think he's mad at me now. At the apartment building yesterday, I asked him if I could replace the utility room door and told him it'd cost about six hundred dollars. He seemed to get quiet after that. He agreed ultimately, but his mood changed. And he never reached out today. His office manager, Linda, transferred the money to me, but that was it. I'm not sure what to think."

"Do you think he's mad about the additional cost?"

"I do. That's the only thing I can think of that changed. But before that came up, he sort of ticked me off. His brother Matt came in and brought us cookies that his wife made. What ticked me off was that Grady spoke for me. Matt asked me a couple of questions, but Grady answered. I absolutely hate that. It's the worst feeling, like he wanted to control me. Like he was afraid of what my answer would be. It's disrespectful."

Nica thought about how her parents did that. Someone would ask Nica a question, and her mother or father would jump in to answer it. They had done it since she was a child, and it still made her feel like a child when it happened now.

"Agreed. So, what's next?"

Nica sat back on her heels. "I don't know. I need to finish the remodel and then see if he asks me out. Maybe he's changed his mind already. Maybe he got caught up in the romance of Evie's *quince*. Now, back in the real world, he's back to business and back to no serious relationships. That's probably what I should be focused on, too. I didn't want a serious relationship before Grady anyway."

"But see, *chica*? Finding the right man can change everything you planned. It's nature."

Nica considered her cousin's words. Had she found the right man, or had she just fallen under the spell of the magic of the *quinceañera*?

She didn't know. She shooed Izzy out of her room and climbed into bed. She decided she was going to focus on the remodel for now. Tomorrow, she was going to cut the holes in the ceiling for the new can lights so the electrician could come on Thursday to install them. And she would scrape and paint the front door. If she didn't hear from Grady until Friday, when it was done, that was fine with her. She didn't have time to get distracted by her handsome boss.

CHAPTER TWENTY-EIGHT

THE RINGING OF his cell phone caused Grady to sit straight up in bed. *What the heck?*

He reached for the phone and noticed that his cat Chad had not moved from his spot on the other pillow. *That cat can sleep through anything*, he thought, reaching for his phone.

He saw that it was Linda. *Why was she calling at four in the morning?*

"Yes?" he grunted into the phone.

"We got a problem, boss."

"What?"

"Bad news. A pipe burst at Linden. It was in the lobby ceiling, and it flooded the lobby. The good news is that a resident heard the water rushing, investigated, and called an emergency plumbing company. They are there already and shut the water off. But the resident said it's bad—several inches of water in the lobby. He mentioned that the new flooring just went in this week. He was bummed."

Grady mumbled a few curse words as she spoke. "You've got to be kidding me."

"Would I?" she asked, and Grady heard the irritation in her voice. It was too early, neither of them had had their coffee so tempers flared. "I know you better than to tease at a time like this. What do you want to do?"

"I'll get dressed and head over there now." His mind was racing. "Nica said she was planning to cut the ceiling for can lights yesterday so the electrician can install the new fixtures. That must have caused the leak."

"Um, are you sure you're not jumping to conclusions? See what the plumber says first, Grady."

He grunted again. "I'll call you if I need anything."

"Sure." She hung up.

Grady flipped the covers back roughly. He wouldn't waste time taking a shower. He'd have to come home and do that after he saw the damage for himself. He thought about the extra time and expense. This was going to be nothing like the $600 amount that Nica asked for the other day. If he were to guess, this could even double the original estimate.

He pulled on a pair of heavy sweatpants, a long-sleeved t-shirt, and old tennis shoes. If there were inches of water in the lobby, he wouldn't care that these got wet.

On the drive to the apartment building, Grady debated calling Nica to get her out of bed and over to survey the damage too. No, he'd check it out first and then call her to let her know.

Grady arrived twenty-five minutes after Linda's phone call. Linda must have told the plumber to wait for Grady to arrive, because he was pacing in the lobby when Grady got there.

The front door was propped open, and water was still running out onto the walkway. Entering the building, Grady introduced himself to the plumber. He recognized the resident, who was still hanging out, talking to the plumber.

Grady's eyes searched the ceiling. It was easy to see that water was still dripping out of one of the newly cut holes.

"Hello. I'm Grady Litwiller," he said, shaking the plumber's hand. "Do you know what happened?"

"Not sure yet. I got the water turned off. Luckily, it's the pipe that goes into that utility closet over there, so it's not impacting your residents. I had to cut a few more holes, as you can see, to find the leak. I need to get a few parts before I can fix it. Since it's not causing an issue for the residents, I'll come back to fix the pipe in a couple days. My schedule is booked right now. I'll also patch the drywall on the ceiling where I had to cut, but I won't paint it. You'll have to call in a painter or contractor for that. Looks like you're working with a contractor already. They could do it."

The resident—Bob? Grady couldn't remember his name—chimed in. "I was just telling him about the remodel that's been happening. I can't believe that poor woman's work has been ruined. I talked to her Monday when she was installing the baseboards. I told her the floor looked great."

Grady thought about telling Bob that he had helped install the floor under Nica's watchful guidance. "It is bad timing."

Nica was going to be devastated. So much of her hard work would need to be redone. And with her school schedule, this was not good. He wondered if he should take a couple vacation days off from the bank to help. At least, he had some experience now in laying the wood laminate flooring.

Turning to the plumber, Grady continued. "Can you tell if the new holes in the ceiling for lighting caused this?"

"I should be able to tell on Friday when I get a closer look. I'll let you know."

Grady thanked him and he left. Surveying the lobby, he decided it would need to be closed off for a couple days. He went to his car to get paper to make a sign for the front door directing residents and visitors to the back door. He was grateful that was an option. He found a rope in the utility room and loosely roped off the lobby from the short hallway and stairwell.

Then he grabbed a mop and attempted to push the rest of the water out the front door.

Climbing into his car after the work was done, he picked up the drumsticks and tapped out a fast beat on the steering wheel. It was nearly 6 a.m. Time to reach out to Nica. It was still early so he sent a text.

> **GRADY:** Burst pipe at Linden. Lobby flooded. We'll need to replace the flooring. I'm going to see if I can take off work to help but I don't expect it to be done by Friday.

He put his phone down. He wouldn't wait for a reply.

NICA REACHED FOR her phone to turn off the alarm. It was 7 a.m., and she was looking forward to a run before her day got busy.

She noticed the text message indicator was on. She read Grady's text and panicked. He'd texted an hour ago. She hadn't heard it.

"No, no, no, this can't be happening," she mumbled, her fingers shaking as she tried to text him back.

> **NICA:** Oh no, what happened?

> **GRADY:** Not sure yet. Linda can fill you in.

Whoa. That felt like a brush off. She pulled on a sweatshirt and jeans. She needed to rush over to see the damage and assess what needed to be done.

In her rush, she parked on the street in front of the building. The lobby door was locked, but just peeping in the window, she could tell it was bad. A few of the floorboards were already warping. She jogged around the side of the building and entered through the back door. She lifted the rope that was preventing residents from walking through the mess. When she stepped into the lobby, the floor made a squishing sound.

"What happened?" she muttered to herself. She flipped on the overhead lights and heard a pop.

She looked up at the ceiling and saw water stains around one of the fixtures. Then she noticed the jagged holes in the ceiling, separate from the ones she cut for the new can lights.

She called Linda who explained what she knew and said that the plumber would be back on Friday to fix the pipe. Nica couldn't use the sink in the utility room until he'd repaired the pipe, but she could work around it at this point. But if the pipe wasn't fixed until Friday, getting the ceiling patched and repainted would be a problem for the timeline.

"Is Grady pissed?" she asked.

"He didn't say he was, but knowing Grady, he's not happy," Linda said.

"And he assumes it's my fault, right?"

"Well, he didn't say that, specifically. But he did point out that you cut new holes in the ceiling yesterday for lights. So that's probably his conclusion. But I talked to the plumber myself and he said he won't know until he investigates further and repairs the pipe. Give Grady time to cool off. That's my recommendation."

"And he said to send you the bill for the additional materials, right?"

"That's my understanding, yes," Linda said. "Since you've seen the damage, can you give me an estimate of when you'll be able to finish? I know it won't be Friday now."

Nica considered the question. Her reputation was on the line. This was terrible. She'd promised Grady she'd have the lobby done by Friday, no matter what. She hadn't anticipated this catastrophe; how could she? Grady must realize that. Her schedule was now torn apart. She'd have to pull up the flooring and baseboards and possibly replace parts of the drywall. She tried to calculate the time and expense.

"I need some time to think. Let me get back to you on both counts." She hung up.

She thought about Grady's reaction on Sunday to the additional expense of replacing the utility room door. And now this! She knew he was stressed about getting this place rented so he could buy another rental building. He might even lose his investors. She wasn't going to add to his stress. She would bite the bullet and pay for the cost of the additional materials out of her profit.

That would help his financial situation, but how to address the timeline? This was the painful part. She was going to have to call her dad for help. If she asked, she thought he would come. But he'd have to give up his work commitments to do so. Maybe her dad could send her brother or cousins. She hated to ask but that's what families were for. This was her backup plan after all.

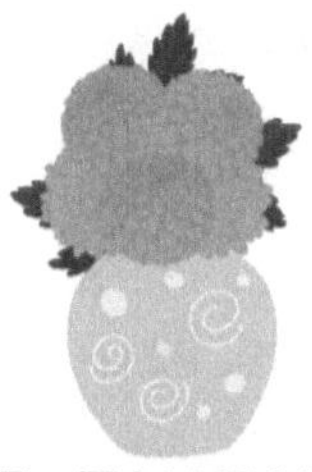

CHAPTER TWENTY-NINE

THE PHONE CALL with her dad was short but not sweet. She hated asking for help. She feared that her parents would never support her desire to flip houses now. They would point to this incident as the reason she couldn't do it, and they'd continue to advocate that she become a teacher.

But, as painful as it was to ask him for assistance, he was going to come through and he was bringing her brothers and one of her cousins. They would be here in a couple of hours.

She had run to the equipment rental center to rent large industrial fans. She needed to get them into the lobby to start the drying process.

When her reinforcements arrived, they would rip out the damaged materials quickly and reassess. She called Izzy for logistic support. "Hey Izzy," she said, pulling out of the parking lot.

"What's up? Why did you leave so early this morning?" Izzy asked.

"A pipe burst in the ceiling of Grady's lobby. Water was everywhere. It's damaged the floors and baseboards I just installed. Now, it all has to be ripped out."

"Oh no! I'm so sorry, Nica."

"I'm working on it. I even called Dad for help."

"You did?" The shock was evident in Izzy's voice.

"Yes, that's why I'm calling you. Can you make dinner for all of us? Dad, Julián, Marcos, and Gabriel are coming."

"Whoa. It's that bad?"

"Yes. One more favor. I can't afford to pay for hotel rooms for them, and they'll need to stay at least one night, if not two. Can you let Paige know, and then figure out how we can sleep four more people?"

"Of course. I got all that. Food, sleeping, check and check. I'll plan to make breakfast tomorrow, too. What else can I do to help?"

"That's enough for now."

"Oh, *prima,* I'm so sorry. What about classes? Are you going today?"

"I can't. I have to fix this."

"Was it your fault?"

Nica sighed, "I don't think so. I was careful and I reviewed the building blueprints to see where the electrical and plumbing lines ran. I thought I drilled in the right spots. The plumber will assess and let us know on Friday. Regardless, I have to fix it. I told Grady I would be done on time, and I'm not going to let this setback stop me. I'm keeping my commitment."

"I'm sure it wasn't your fault, Nica," Izzy quickly put in.

"We'll see. I've got to go. I'm pulling back into the apartment parking lot, and I have to set up fans to dry it out. I'll keep in touch. Thanks, Iz."

"You got it!"

NICA SURVEYED THE lobby again. The fans were starting to work; the floor was looking drier. She'd been to the hardware store and bought new flooring, which was in the back of her truck. No sense in bringing it in now, there was nowhere dry enough to put it.

She checked the time. Her dad and the rest of the rescue crew should arrive in thirty minutes. She had enough time to call Grady to update him on her plan. It was close enough to the lunch hour; she hoped he'd have time to talk to her.

When he answered, she jumped right in with her update. "I wanted to give you an update. I've got a plan. I've called in extra help. I rented commercial fans to dry out the floors, and I've bought the new materials. We'll get the new flooring and baseboards in tomorrow. With the extra help, I'll still make the Friday due date."

"Do you need my help? I can take some time off work at the bank."

Wow, she couldn't believe he offered! He must be desperate for this project to complete on time.

"No, Grady. I've got my dad and a few others coming to help. We'll get it done."

She waited anxiously for his response.

"It would be great if you could pull it off," he said, a hint of uncertainty in his voice.

"I got this." She paused, garnering the courage to continue. "Grady, I had the blueprints, so I knew where that water pipe was, and I took the appropriate measurements for the ceiling fixtures. I'm almost certain I didn't cut into that pipe."

Grady didn't say anything for several seconds. "Hey, it's okay. People make mistakes. The plumber will confirm on Friday."

He didn't believe her. Wouldn't believe her. Wouldn't *listen* to her. He heard her words but not her conviction. It was a blow.

"I know you're worried and disappointed. Please don't be. It's going to be all right." She sounded much more confident than she felt. "You'll see."

"Okay. I have to go. Keep us posted on progress, and let us know if you need anything else." He hung up without saying goodbye.

Keep *us* posted. Meaning *work through Linda, not me.*

He wants to know how much more it's going to cost him. That mattered more to him than the impact on her.

She was going to be happy when this was over. She was thankful they had decided to not date during the remodel. She needed to remind herself that he was a client, a tough client, but a client. She had several lessons to take away from this situation, and only a few were about remodeling.

CHAPTER THIRTY

TWO DAYS OF working non-stop. Her dad, brothers, and cousin helped until midnight on Wednesday. They stayed the night and then headed home to Chicago early on Thursday to be back in time for work. Missing one day of work was hard enough; they couldn't miss two.

But that one day helping Nica made the difference. They'd ripped out the floors, baseboards, and parts of the walls that were damaged. Once everything was dry, they'd installed new flooring and baseboards, and patched the drywall.

On Thursday, Nica installed the fake fireplace, including the monitor set up to run a looped fireplace scene.

Friday morning, she had to work around the plumber, who was replacing the broken section of pipe. She had worked with Linda to reschedule the electrician to come Friday afternoon. Once the plumber finished his repairs in the morning, Nica was able to start painting over the holes that the plumber had made and patched, while the electrician installed the can lights.

Once the electrician left, she gave the entire ceiling a final coat of paint. Then she was finally ready to add the furniture, hang the swings and the landscapes she had painted, and add in the decorative touches.

The plumber confirmed that she had not caused the pipe to burst. The break was nowhere near where she'd cut holes for the new light fixtures. What Grady had seen was just the way the water traveled above the ceiling. It had made its way to the opening and dripped out.

She felt vindicated but was not going to boast about it to Grady. She trusted that the plumber would get the information to Linda and Grady, then maybe Grady would apologize to her for jumping to conclusions.

By 7 p.m. she had completed everything. She took pictures and video of the finished project. She was going to highlight this project on her social media and in her portfolio. She was proud of what she accomplished—not only the design and the execution, but dealing with the consequences of the burst pipe. She hadn't freaked out; she'd managed it. She had called in help, got to work, and got it done.

She hoped that when Grady cooled down and was told that it wasn't her fault, he would give her a great testimonial. Despite the burst pipe, she was going to finish on time and within Grady's budget! She would not charge him for the additional materials; she would take that out of her profit and chalk it up as the cost of experience. Going forward, she would build more contingency time into her proposed schedules and budget.

She wasn't sure what the hardest part of this had been for her— having to call her dad for help, or the damage it had done to her new, tentative relationship with Grady. She had been beginning to see how a relationship between them could work. Not just work but be great for both of them. She had seen what love could be like with someone who had similar goals and sentiments. It could be a true partnership, not a power play. But she didn't want to be with someone who doubted her, and apparently Grady did.

Once she was finished and ready to leave, she called Linda to tell her that the work was done.

"Wow!" Linda exclaimed. "You did it! You pulled it off! Grady is going to be so impressed."

"I'm not so sure about that. He seemed to put the blame squarely on me when I talked to him on Wednesday. Did the plumber call you and explain the issue?"

"Yes, he did. I can't wait to tell Grady."

"He doesn't know?"

"No. He said he had a packed day today at the bank—lots of meetings. As soon as he got off, he was going to a family dinner. He asked to touch base with me tomorrow morning. I'll tell him then."

"I see. Well, it was nice working with you, Linda," Nica said, ready to hang up and be done with this project.

"Wait. Do you have the additional invoice ready to send to me?"

"There is no additional invoice."

"But you had to get more flooring, right? Grady was expecting an invoice for the materials and the extra work that you had to do."

"There's no additional invoice," Nica repeated.

Linda paused, almost like she was calculating. "Okay...." She drawled. "I'll be sure to let Grady know. Take care."

Nica hung up the phone. She hoped Grady would be pleased, but she didn't expect that to change the trajectory of their now defunct relationship.

She grabbed her toolbox and left. She was going home, drinking a glass of wine, and finishing the painting of Grady's grandfather's barn. She had hoped she'd be giving it to him under better circumstances, like when they were celebrating the lobby completion. Now she wasn't sure Grady would want to see her again.

AS GRADY PUSHED the last piece of steak around on his plate, he realized he hadn't tasted anything. Not the steak, not the green beans, and not the mashed potatoes. This was usually his favorite meal that his parents cooked, but it was not doing anything for him tonight.

"Grady don't play with your food," his mother admonished.

"Yikes!" Cooper teased. "Haven't heard that in years. Didn't think we'd hear it again until baby Charlie got a little bit bigger."

Grady set his fork down. "Sorry, Mom."

Sitting across the table from Grady, Matt nudged his foot under the table and raised an eyebrow, silently asking if he was okay. Grady gave a slight shake of his head, indicating he didn't want to talk about it at the table.

After the table was cleared and everyone moved to the family room, Matt asked Grady to help him get the baby's playpen out of the car.

Outside, Matt turned to Grady before they even got to the car. "All right. What's going on? Is it work or could it possibly be that pretty little brunette?"

Grady shoved his hands into his pockets. He would have grabbed his jacket if he had known he was going to get waylaid by his big brother.

"It's both, actually. There was an issue in the lobby this week. A pipe broke, it flooded the room, and Nica's been working to fix it. She said she was still going to complete the job on time. Which was today. I haven't heard if she's done or not yet. And I don't know what the additional cost is going to be. It's stressful. And," Grady continued, "with that stress, I've been sort of aloof with Nica. Things were great over the weekend. The party, working together on Sunday. I was excited. Ready to move the relationship further. But she wanted to wait until after she finished the work on the lobby—not mix business with pleasure. But when the flooding happened, I freaked out. I assumed it was her fault.

She told me she'd been extremely careful, and she didn't think it was. Like an idiot, I didn't give her the benefit of the doubt. I shut down. I was under stress, thinking about buying the Chestnut building. I spread myself way, way too thin. I know she's working hard trying to rip out what got ruined and redo the work that had already been completed, and I wasn't very supportive." He took a deep breath. "I'm feeling like a jerk."

Matt nodded slowly. "That's heavy. If you don't trust her, that's not a good start to a relationship, and I know you said you wanted to pursue a relationship with her once this project was done. If you mean that, you are going to have to apologize, and I mean a big apology. You're going to need to grovel. Maybe even send flowers. Even if it was her fault, Grady."

"That would be taking the high road."

Matt started walking to the car. "It sounds like you acted like a jerk. She may not forgive you. You'll have to prepare for that."

Grady followed, grabbing the playpen once Matt opened the trunk. "I'm also frustrated with myself for getting into such a tight financial situation. I told you that I've been planning to buy another apartment building but needed investors. That pushed the remodel forward so I could get Linden rented. And on top of all that, now I'm worried about Grandpa's farm. He keeps getting offers to buy it, and he's ready to retire. I would love to buy it and find a farmer to lease the land so we can keep it in the family. Maybe Charlie would be interested in farming, or one of your future kids, or Cooper's future kids."

Matt nodded as Grady continued. "But if I go through with buying the apartment building, I will be completely tapped. All my cash will be tied up for a while. If things go well, I should start to have cash flow in a couple months. I don't know what the additional repairs for Linden will be—haven't gotten an invoice from Nica yet."

They started walking back to the house.

"That's a lot of moving parts. What can I do to help?"

Grady considered. "Thanks for asking what was wrong and for listening. I could take a few pointers from you."

"You could take a *lot* of pointers from me." Matt chuckled. "You need to step back and figure out what you want out of life, Grady. You could invest in real estate; you can strive to be rich in dollars. But at the end of the day, that won't bring you real happiness. Not like a family will. I know your views on getting married and having kids, but I tell you, brother, my family is the best thing that has ever happened to me. I wake up smiling, knowing I get to try to be the best husband and father I can be. I guess what I'm trying to say is that there's more to life than wealth."

Grady listened to Matt's advice and knew he was right. There was more to life than investing. Nica had opened his mind and heart to the idea of dating and getting serious about someone. He'd even thought earlier in the evening when he was holding Charlie that he'd love it if his kid had Nica's deep brown eyes. The thought had floored him. It had come from out of nowhere. It was definitely time to rethink his priorities.

CHAPTER THIRTY-ONE

GRADY WENT INTO the bank on Saturday morning to catch up on paperwork. He debated checking in with Nica to see how the work was coming along on Linden. It would be good to have a new finish date, so he and Linda could work on the plans to advertise and show the apartments.

Linda had sent him a file of the farming research that he had asked for, and he was itching to look it over, but he would wait until he got home.

He was able to wrap up by eleven and head out, stopping to pick up a burger and fries on his way home.

At home, he put the takeout bag on the table and walked to his office to grab his laptop. He arranged everything on the kitchen table so he could review the report while he ate.

Finishing lunch and the report at the same time, he gave Linda a call.

"Hey, Groovy Grady," she said, answering.

"You're awfully chipper today," he noted.

"It is a glorious fall day in the beautiful city of Bloomington, Illinois. I'm healthy, happy, and thankful to be alive. What can I say?"

Grady wished for a little bit of her enthusiasm, but after the week he'd had, it wasn't there. "You're too much."

"You know it. You love it."

"I don't know about that. I looked over the research that you sent me. Great job. I wondered—"

"Whoa. Stop right there. Are we not going to talk about the elephant in the room?"

"There's an elephant?"

"Linden! You big doof. Don't you want to hear all the news?"

"Sure. Do we have a new completion date?" Grady picked up his pen, ready to take notes.

"There's no new date—"

"Ugh."

"You didn't let me finish! There's no new date because it's done. She finished yesterday."

"What?"

"You heard me. She's all done."

"Wow. I'm shocked. I thought for sure it was going to take several more days to get it done. That's great. Now we can start with some ads and see if we can get new renters."

"And don't you have more questions for me?" Her voice was so full of cheer, it was almost too much.

"Like?" he asked.

"What the plumber found out?"

"Oh, right. What did he say? What caused the leak?" He thought about the several new holes that Nica had drilled.

"The pipe was just old. Corroded. The rupture occurred at least three feet away from anywhere Nica cut."

Grady let her words sink in. It wasn't Nica's fault. He smiled, and then his face quickly dropped. He had jumped to conclusions and acted like a jerk. How would Nica forgive him?

"Well, that's great news," he finally said. "You were right. I did jump to conclusions."

"What did you say?" Linda asked.

"You heard me. You were right."

"I love it when you say that out loud."

"Please don't rub it in. I am going to have to grovel to Nica for this. Guess I can do that when I bring her a check for the additional costs. Did she give you an estimate or invoice for that?"

Linda didn't answer right away, and the skin on Grady's neck prickled.

"No." She finally answered.

"Oh, okay, I can wait.

"No, she didn't give an estimate, said there wouldn't be any additional charges. She covered it out of her own pocket."

"She can't do that."

"She did."

Grady squeezed the pen in his hand so hard that it broke. "Shoot!"

"What happened?"

"Nothing. Sorry."

"You can plan to double your groveling," she said with a laugh.

"I have to go. Thanks for the update," he said, standing.

"Hey, didn't you have questions about the research?"

"They can wait," he said. "I've got some things to do."

He hung up the phone and changed his clothes.

He'd have to run over to see the finished Linden lobby this afternoon. He couldn't believe she finished it on time and didn't submit an additional invoice. It pained him to consider all the costs to her—to her pride, her wallet, and her time. He would reimburse her and make it up to her. He'd think of the right thing to do.

He had a lot to think about: his grandfather's farm, buying the place on Chestnut, Nica. Especially Nica. This kind of thinking required drumming. Lots of drumming. He grabbed a bottle of water and headed to his basement.

NICA THOUGHT ABOUT backing out of the ghost tour at Duncan Manor on Saturday afternoon. She was physically and emotionally exhausted after the disastrous week, but Paige would not let her back out. Izzy and everyone from In Bloom were going. Nica had to be a team player and join in.

Their car caravan pulled into the long drive leading up to Duncan Manor. The house and gardens around it were breathtaking. Nica was thankful that Anna Lee had insisted on the afternoon tour rather than the evening one. It was easier to see the colorful mums and late fall flowers surrounding the three-and-a-half story home.

Despite her initial hesitation, Nica was excited to meet the couple who had bought and were restoring the historical Italianate farmhouse.

Their group browsed the artist and vendor booths set up in the giant pole barn until it was time to go on the tour. There were actors who portrayed the original residents of the house and told their sad and tragic tales.

Nica was amazed at the work that had been done in the building. She was thrilled to see this unique 1866 house being restored. She admired the dedication it must have taken. The house had sat empty for many, many years.

Walking through the house gave her so many ideas for things she could try. She had worried that after the mishap at Linden that she would be scared off construction, but after seeing Duncan Manor, she was revitalized. This she could do! This she wanted to do. Ultimately, she had completed the work at Linden. It had required bringing in her dad, which she had dreaded, but at the end of the day, he'd said he was proud of what she'd done.

He had asked to see the before pictures of the lobby and asked detailed questions about her design and what work she had completed. He told her she had done good work. His praise was going to fulfill her for a long time, and it made her realize it was time to have a serious talk with her parents about her career.

As soon as they were done here at the manor, she was driving home to spend the night with her family and have that heart to heart with her parents.

After the tour, Paige interrupted her mental musings by suggesting that they go for coffee.

"Sorry, I can't," Nica responded. "I'm going home to my parents' now. I'll be back tomorrow afternoon."

"Really? Seems sudden," Paige said.

"I know. But I need to talk to them—to explain my passion is in remodeling and flipping houses, not teaching. Now that my dad has seen my work on the lobby, maybe they'll be more receptive than they have been in the past."

Paige smiled. "You're right. This may be the best time. Are you going to switch majors?"

"No, I'm going to finish it out, and I may teach for a couple of years. Use my degree and continue to grow my portfolio of projects. I'll need time to save up money to buy a house that can be flipped, anyway. I'm going to add some business courses if I can. If not, I'll take some classes at the junior college later."

"You've got it worked out. Your parents will surely get behind you."

Nica shrugged. "I hope so."

She told everyone goodbye and got in her car. Looking at the backseat, she saw the painting of Grady's grandfather's barn. Her plan was to drop it off at his house on her way back home on Sunday. She hoped she might catch him at home. Her newfound hope that her parents may listen to her dreams fueled hope that there was a chance to patch things up with Grady.

CHAPTER THIRTY-TWO

COMING HOME WAS relaxing now that most of her siblings and cousins were out of the house.

Her parents had company Saturday evening, so there was no time for a heart to heart. That was fine; she spent the evening watching movies with her sister Lucia and cousin Evie. It was fun to get to rehash Evie's *quinceañera* with the girls. But the questions that they raised about Grady brought too much pain, so she kept redirecting back to Evie's experience.

Knowing her parents were early risers, Nica set her alarm for seven o'clock on Sunday morning. When the alarm went off, she heard Lucia groan from the twin bed three feet away from her. She tiptoed out of the room and found her parents in the kitchen, drinking coffee.

"Morning, *mija*," her mother said. "You're up early."

"Early to bed, early to wakey, makes a young girl prosper and cranky," her father said, laughing at his own rhyme.

"You're too much, *Papá*," she replied, pouring a cup of coffee from the pot. "And it's too early for silly rhymes."

She poured a little honey in her coffee and sat down. "I was hoping to have a chance to talk to you both without a lot of distraction."

"Oh, no, that doesn't sound good," her mother, the worrier, said.

"Nothing to fret about. I just need to tell you both that I've made some decisions about my future."

"You're marrying that young man that you brought to Evie's *quince*?" her mother questioned, with raised eyebrows.

"No! Come on. Don't you think that would be a little sudden? Besides, you know my thoughts on marriage. I'm not trying to rush to the altar."

"But it's a possibility, yes?"

"Sure. Maybe. Someday. I don't know. That's not why I'm here. I've told you in the past that I want to flip houses, but you have repeatedly said that I should focus on steady work, and you've pushed the teaching degree—"

Her mother gasped. "You're dropping out of college?"

"No. No. I'm not dropping out. I'll still get the degree in education. I'll even teach while I get on my feet financially, to put me in a position to flip houses."

Her father shook his head in disbelief but remained silent. She turned to him. "*Papá*, you saw what I did in that lobby. You said I did good work. I don't know how you can continue to dismiss my dream."

"You did do good, Dominica," Arturo said, "but one job does not make a career. This is hard, hard work. Not right for a girl."

"But I want to do it. I know what's involved. I know the physical aspects. Heck, I'm studying to be a physical education teacher. I'm not afraid of hard work. I love using my muscles. And I love the construction work. I love the creativity, designing, I love making something better. I like salvaging something that is no longer loved and making it loved again."

She paused and thought about the tour in Duncan Manor the day before. She still felt giddy over seeing a hundred-and-fifty-year-old house revived and loved.

Arturo shook his head and groaned, but before he could say anything, Juanita laid a hand on his arm. "That's enough. It's not our job to interfere in our children's lives. We've raised them, we've taught them, we've loved them. Dominica is an adult. And she's an intelligent one. She knows what she's doing. Our role is to support her."

As her mother finished speaking, Nica waited to see what her father would say. She listened to the hum that the coffee pot was making on the counter. Looking over at the machine, she wondered how old it was. She made a mental note to consider replacing it for Christmas.

After several seconds of silence, her father grunted. "You're right. You're right. We will always support you, Nica. Always."

Nica smiled. "Thank you both. It means a lot to me to have your support."

"Now, let's talk about that young man," her mother said, rising to grab the coffee pot. "Who needs a refill?"

NICA FELT LIKE she'd earned an A+ for the success she'd had at her parents. They were behind her; they would support her dream moving forward. She was overjoyed when her father began to describe to her mother the work Nica had done in the lobby. He was obviously proud and impressed with the work. He even said that he was honored to be able to contribute to the overall effort.

Driving back to Bloomington, Nica listened to a nineties pop music channel and used the music to keep her positive vibe going. She refused to think about Grady and the conversation she hoped to have with him.

But if the success of the conversation with her parents was an indication, she wouldn't be deterred. She was going to be honest with him and tell him that she didn't appreciate his assumption that the leak was her fault. As long as he recognized his fault in the mess, she'd move past it. People made mistakes, she made mistakes. She was prepared to put it aside and see where they could take a relationship, if he was willing.

She neared the exit for Grady's house. At the stop sign, she glanced in the rear-view mirror at the painting. She had wrapped it in plain craft paper to protect it from dust or other mishaps. She took a deep breath to calm the tingling in her stomach. Nerves.

Ten minutes later, she pulled into Grady's driveway, parking behind his car. She got out and grabbed the painting from the backseat.

At his front door, she rang the doorbell and waited. Thirty seconds later, she rang again. She looked over her shoulder at his car. He was likely home if his car was here. But of course, there were a lot of reasons why he might not come to the door. He was in the shower, he had headphones on, he was out for a jog, he was visiting a neighbor, he had a camera on the front porch, saw it was her, and decided to not answer.

She sighed. She didn't know why he didn't come to the door, and she wasn't going to assume.

She leaned the painting against the railing, turned, and left.

GRADY TOOK A break from drumming and grabbed a soda from the kitchen refrigerator. He could hardly believe he'd spent another two hours drumming, after the long session on Saturday. Maybe it was time to get a band together. He was feeling quite confident.

Checking the time on the microwave, he decided it was time to shower. Matt and Julie had invited him over for dinner, and he was looking forward to hanging out with them and baby Charlie.

Thirty minutes later, he grabbed car keys and headed out the front door. He stopped short, seeing the large package on his stoop. He hadn't ordered anything and had no clue what it could be.

He dragged the package towards himself and looked at the back. Odd, no label on either side. He took it inside and propped it up on the couch. He looked for where it was taped shut and lifted gently. Once the plain brown paper was pulled back, his eyes widened at the sight of the painting of his grandfather's barn. There was no doubt what it was, and he knew immediately who'd painted it. He smiled when he saw that the loft door was open, and hay was floating out, as if on a breeze. The details were amazing, and he thought longingly back to the day with Nica in the barn. That was the day that he first knew there was something special between them.

Knowing that she'd brought this to him even after the way he'd acted this week was a punch in the gut. He still hadn't called her after finding out that she'd finished on time and hadn't caused the leak. He'd kept making excuses, his favorite one being that he needed to see her in person. He still didn't know why he hadn't gone to her apartment to find her. He'd gotten wrapped up in studying the research that Linda had done, and it was easier to put it off.

But the painting gave him hope. If she had closed the door on their relationship, she wouldn't have brought him the painting after the way he'd acted. He was going to take this assumption and run with it. He could make things right with her, he knew it.

He muttered to himself and shook his head. He was not going to make things right with Nica with a quick apology. He needed something big, something special. It was time to re-prioritize his plans. It was time to put Nica first. He had an idea of how to make things right, but he needed help. Time to call in reinforcements, starting with his brother Matt.

He had a long talk with Matt about their grandfather's farm. They reminisced about their wonderful times on the farm and they envisioned future family gatherings and special occasions at the farm. They hoped to see the next generation of children running and playing in the house and the yard. Grady even imagined his own kids playing with his future nieces and nephews. He smiled to himself thinking about the change. It hadn't been so long since he would have said he was a dedicated bachelor, with no intentions to have kids. Things were different now. With Matt's guidance and example, he could see the allure of having a good woman and a good family around you.

Matt wanted to go in with Grady to buy the property. They spoke to Julie and got her on board, too. He answered all of Matt and Julie's questions and left their house energized and excited.

Matt had questions about Grady's decision to back out of the property near Wesleyan as it had been all Grady had talked about for months. Grady explained that his priorities had changed. He would continue to pursue properties like that one in the future, but right now, the family farm was more important.

On his way home he called Linda. He didn't usually like to bother her on Sundays, but this was an emergency.

"Hey, Linda," he said when she answered. "I'm sorry to bug you on a Sunday night."

"No problem. What's up?"

"Well, I have made some decisions and need your help."

"Don't you always?" she said, laughing.

"Well, yes. I need you to draft a letter to Tom and Marty. I'm not going forward with the apartment building on Chestnut."

"You're not? You've been scheming, I mean, planning for this for a long time."

He chuckled. Linda always called it like she saw it. "You're right. But I'd rather buy my grandfather's farm and I can't do both."

"Cool. What else do you need?"

"Well, now, there's the matter of Nica."

"And?"

"First of all, transfer three thousand to her account for the additional costs. This is in addition to the on-time bonus. Send the two payments separately so it's clear. We can hash out the actual additional costs later."

He could hear the smile in Linda's voice when she answered, "I'm on it."

"I screwed up, Linda. And I need to do something big. I have an idea, but it's going to require pulling in some favors."

"Oh, did you talk to her?"

"No, not yet."

"Grady, that's dumb."

"Maybe, but I think this is the right next step. Hear me out."

He outlined his plan as Linda took copious notes.

CHAPTER THIRTY-THREE

NICA WAS VERY pleasantly surprised when she got an email from Linda on Monday saying that she was transferring money to cover the additional expenses and labor that Nica had to put into the remodel due to the flood, in addition to the on-time bonus! Linda said that Grady authorized the payment and they would look forward to Nica's reply saying if it was sufficient or not.

As nice as that was, she was still disappointed in not hearing from Grady himself by Tuesday. She was worried that maybe he never even got the painting she left for him. What if it had been stolen by a porch pirate?

She tried to not let it get to her. She kept reminding herself that there were legitimate reasons for him not to reach out. It had just been a few days.

After her morning class, she went to her apartment to get ready for a run. She had just put the key in the lock when her text message indicator went off.

She looked down to see a text from Linda.

Nica groaned. *What now?*

> **NICA:** Is something wrong?

> **LINDA:** Oh no, please don't worry. Just want to get your opinion on something.

> **NICA:** Ok. Be there in 20.

Strange. But at least she'd get to meet the mysterious Linda, the voice on the phone. Grady's right-hand person. Shoot. Would Grady *be* there? Surely not. It was a weekday. He had banking to do.

Fifteen minutes later, she pulled into the parking lot behind the building and parked. From the direction of her apartment, she drove down a side street and approached the building from the back.

She was surprised by the number of cars in the parking lot. Most of the visitor spaces were taken.

She entered the back door and heard loud music coming from the lobby. *That's strange,* she thought as she walked down the hallway. *Is Linda throwing a party?*

Walking into the lobby, Nica felt like she was on a hidden camera show. There were streamers, balloons, and people milling around. There was a large banquet table set up in front of the faux fireplace. Grady was standing with another man, and they were both wearing headsets. There was a banner strung along the table with the call letters of a local radio station.

Grady saw her, smiled, waved, and pointed to the headset. He must be on-air.

Seeing him and his smile eased her anxiety. She didn't know what was going on but she was excited to find out.

Looking around, she saw a woman approaching her.

"Hi! You must be Nica," said the woman. "I'm Linda!"

"You look like a mermaid!" Nica blurted. Linda's hair was blue with purple tips. Her eyeshadow was bright purple with glitter. She wore a bright pink sweater, a long flowing purple skirt, and ankle boots. She was several inches taller than Nica and appeared to be a ball of energy. Nica felt an instant connection.

Linda laughed. "Well, I left my tail at home. I'm so glad you could come."

"What's going on?"

"Grady's hosting a fundraiser for The Immigration Resource Center."

"What's that?"

Linda explained the purpose of non-profit, how they provided legal services and citizenship application support. Nica was surprised.

"How's he raising funds, exactly?"

"He's donating twenty dollars for everyone who comes in to get a cup of hot chocolate."

"He's charging twenty dollars for hot chocolate?" Nica asked incredulously.

"No! No!" Linda's eyebrows shot up. "The hot chocolate is free. It's a way to get people in the door. Grady's donating the money out of his pocket. I've got a clicker," she raised her hand to show Nica, "and I'm tallying the number of visitors. Grady's on air with the radio station to get the word out. And," Linda was practically bouncing, "I called a friend who works for Channel 37. They're sending a news crew out to do a feature for the news at noon. It's going to be great!"

"Wow." Nica was impressed. She couldn't believe Grady was doing something like this to raise money for a non-profit. She remembered the rugby game and Grady putting a hundred-dollar bill in the tip jar. She'd seen his generosity but this was taking things to another level. "That's fantastic. But why did you call me?"

"People are super impressed with the lobby," Linda explained. "We've been telling them all about your work. Grady even had me put together these fliers for you. It has your Instagram handle on it. I wanted to show it to you. What do you think?"

Nica looked over the flyer. There were before and after photos. Linda had even taken the simple logo that Nica had created for her Instagram picture and put it on the flyer.

"What do I think?" Nica shook her head. "I think I'm in school, and I can't possibly take on more work. But the exposure is amazing!" She squealed and pulled Linda into a hug. "Thank you! I can't wait to show this to my dad."

Grady approached them, no longer wearing the headset. "Hi," he said tentatively. "We're on a break."

"Gotta get back to the door!" Linda fled.

"Hi," Nica said, smiling at Grady. "This is surprising. Sounds like a great charity to support."

"It is. I'm glad you came. I owe you the biggest apology in the history of apologies—"

"Grady," she interrupted.

"No, please. Let me finish. First of all, this lobby is spectacular. It's even better than I imagined it would be. Residents have been stopping by all morning and saying they love it. I can't believe you pulled it off and finished Friday. You are a miracle worker. You took it all in stride and got it done. I'm so impressed.

"Second of all," he continued, "I was very, very wrong to assume that the leak was your fault. I don't know what I was thinking. I'm usually a better listener. I hope you'll be able to forgive me. I feel like we have some unfinished business."

Nica sighed. He was saying all the right things, all the things she wanted to hear. "From a business perspective, we're fine. The work is done. Thank you for the extra payment. I was pleasantly surprised to get the notification from Linda. I crunched the numbers, and your payment was perfect. We're settled."

"Good. I'm glad we've settled that piece of business."

"Grady, I was hoping we had some unfinished relationship matters to discuss."

Grady gave her the biggest smile she'd seen from him. "You were?"

"Yes. As you know, I've finished the work…." She sing-songed.

"Right, you have. And I have something to ask you."

She waited.

"Miss Dominica," he began, "it would thrill me to no end if you would accept my invitation to our first, of many I hope, official dates."

"Oh, yeah?"

"Yeah. Tomorrow night? Thursday night? When is your soonest availability?"

Nica laughed. "I'm free tomorrow."

"Perfect. We'll be on air until nine tonight, or I would take you out tonight." Grady leaned forward and hugged her, and she felt as though she were glowing from head to toes.

He pulled back and held her gaze, his brows knitting together. "I hope the exposure that you get for the lobby renovation from this event goes a little way to making up for how poorly I reacted. I know I have a lot more to do to make it right and I will do everything I can to make it up to you. I promise."

Nica smiled at him. "I'm glad to hear that you have that self-awareness and want to do better." She took a breath before continuing. "There's one other thing I have to bring up. It really irritated me when you didn't let me answer your brother Matt when he brought the cookies here. He asked me questions, but you answered for me. That's one of my biggest pet peeves."

He groaned. "You're right, I did do that. I'm so sorry. Again, know better, do better. I don't want to do things that tick you off so please call me out when I do."

"Same goes for you. You have to tell me when I mess up. I know I'm not perfect."

"You are in my eyes." He pulled her into another hug.

Linda rushed over. "I'm so sorry to interrupt this adorable moment, but the news crew is here, Grady. And we're up to one hundred and fifty visitors so far!" She beamed as she grabbed Nica's hand. "Let's get some hot chocolate."

AT 9:30 P.M. Grady and Linda walked back into the lobby after hauling the table and miscellaneous equipment to the radio station's van.

Grady sat on one of the swings in the lobby and Linda joined him on the other one.

"Nice job, Mr. Litwiller," she said, setting the swing in motion. "You raised a lot of money today. I'm impressed. And you seemed to have made amends with Nica."

"I hope so. We have a lot to talk about. I'm looking forward to seeing where it may go."

"She's good for you. I can tell. It was great to see how you highlighted her work when you interviewed with the TV station. Though she told me she's worried she may get too much exposure out of this."

"There can be too much of a good thing, but I hope it doesn't overwhelm her. There is more to life than work, you know."

Linda scoffed. "What just happened? Did I just hear Grady Litwiller say that there is more to life than work? Radical! I never thought this day would come! You never fail to amaze me, Grady."

"Miracles happen," he chuckled.

Yes, real estate and investments had been his focus for a long time. But when he'd met Nica, something had shifted. He'd been proud to have her by his side for both his family's gathering and hers. She was joy and light and spice. In hindsight, he realized that life before her had been cold and tasteless.

Linda yawned. "Well, it's been a long day, boss. I'm going to go home."

They both stood. "Thanks, Linda. I could not have pulled this off without you. I'm thankful for all of your connections and your ability to pull off the impossible. I'll talk to you tomorrow."

"No early morning call. You can call me over the lunch hour but no sooner. See ya."

She left and Grady sat back on the swing. He studied the paintings on the wall. He was starting to see Nica's signatures. In every painting, these and the one she'd given him of his grandfather's farm, there was a black cat hidden. They were tiny, and a casual glance might not reveal them. He smiled. Kind of like Nica herself.

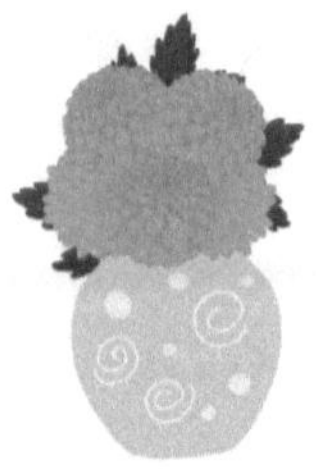

CHAPTER THIRTY-FOUR

NICA WAS READY twenty minutes before Grady arrived to take her on their first official date. For the first time ever, she was excited to go on a date! She had even stopped by In Bloom and picked up a bouquet of orange dahlias. Anna Lee praised her initiative to buy flowers for a man and not waiting to receive them. She had a mischievous smile, but didn't let on what had her in such a good mood.

Nica asked Paige and Izzy to run an errand, to get them out of the apartment before Grady arrived. She was nervous that Grady might scoff at the flowers, and she didn't want to be embarrassed in front of the girls.

There was a knock on the door, and she dashed across the kitchen to open it.

"Hi!" she said. "Come in."

Grady walked in, and she could tell that he'd recently showered. The back of his hair was still slightly damp. He wore a suit, and she chuckled thinking that he'd worn a suit to work, gone home, showered, and put another suit on. This one wasn't rumpled, so she assumed it was a fresh one.

He had one hand behind his back when he entered, and tried to angle his body away so she couldn't see what he was holding.

"Hello, Nica," he said, approaching her, with his hand still behind him.

"What do you have there, Grady?" she asked.

He pulled his hand out and presented her with a bouquet of purple roses.

"Wow! Those are beautiful," she said, laughing.

"Why are you laughing?" he asked, his brow furrowed, as she took the bouquet from him.

"Well, we must think alike because I bought flowers for you today, too." She grabbed a vase from a cabinet and set the roses in them. She'd add water in a moment.

She walked to the dining table and picked up the vase with dahlias, turning to Grady. "These are for you. These are one of my favorite flowers. They're dahlias. I thought they would be perfect for you because they symbolize beauty, prosperity, and wealth."

She waited anxiously for his response.

He took the vase from her and smiled broadly. "Nica, are you calling me beautiful?"

She laughed. "I think I'll call you ridiculous after that comment."

Grady grew somber.

"Oh no," Nica said, putting hand on Grady's arm. "I upset you."

"No, Nica. I love the gesture. I'm just feeling a bit chagrined that wealth and prosperity are the symbols you associate with me. I know I've appeared to be focused only on money, but I want to change that. You made me want to change that."

He took a deep breath. "Nica, I screwed up last week. I know I seemed sour after you asked about the door. I've been under a lot of stress financially, and unfortunately, you saw the ugly side of that. I brought that stress on myself, you didn't do it. It's my responsibility to make sure that doesn't happen again."

He set the vase on the counter and took her hands in his. "I have some news on that front. I decided to not buy the other apartment building. It was going to be too much of a stretch, and I decided there was something more important that I wanted."

Nica furrowed her eyebrows. She had no idea where this was going.

Grady continued. "I told you how much I loved spending time on my grandparents' farm when I was a kid. Well, my grandpa has been talking about selling the property. He's ready to retire, and it was killing me to think about that land not staying in our family. So, with my brother Matt's help, we're going to buy it."

Nica's eyes widened and she smiled just as broadly. "Grady, that's terrific. I saw you let your guard down when we were there. You seemed genuinely happy."

"It's a very special place. Matt and I were just talking about holding family gatherings there. Even long stays with everyone under one roof. It's probably going to take some renovations to make it work for our growing family, but I know someone who is an amazing designer and contractor." He reached and brushed his thumb on her lip.

"Me?" she asked.

"Of course." He smiled and picked her hand back up.

She nodded and raised an eyebrow. "Are you going to take up farming, Mr. Litwiller?"

"Oh, no! That's not for me. I'll stick to banking. We'll lease the land to be farmed. Linda found a couple of local farmers that are interested."

"Nice. Linda is amazing. I loved meeting her. She's a character."

"She is. But you know who else is amazing?" He pulled her to him and wrapped his arms around her back.

She had to tilt her head back to maintain eye contact. She waited.

"You are amazing, Miss Mendoza. I can't believe my luck in meeting you." He looked around the kitchen. They were only a few feet from the door where he'd stood when they first met. "I have to say, it was an unusual meeting."

Nica laughed. "I thought you were going to sue me, and I wanted to throw you out on your head."

"It was memorable. That's for sure." He pushed a strand of hair off her face and tucked it behind her ear. The gesture was so enduring, and his touch sent electricity down to her toes. "We may have had an odd start, but I'm more interested in our future."

"Future?" Nica squeaked. "We haven't even had an official first date."

Grady smiled as he held her. "Doesn't matter. I don't need to date you to know you, Nica. I know you, and I know we are meant to be."

"Together?" she asked.

"Together."

"Grady, wait." She pushed back slightly and noticed the look of hurt in his eye. "I am crazy about you, but…" she took a strangled breath.

"But?" He prompted.

"I am not interested in being with someone who is going to work sixty hours a week and wait until the age of fifty to live a full life. You can live a full life now. Work hard *and* live a life. Travel now. See the world now. Don't wait until later. You don't know what will happen. You could get sick or injured, making it difficult to travel."

As she was still speaking, Grady reached into his jacket pocket. He held his hand up, asking her to pause.

"Nica, I know I've said that was my plan. But plans change. Your coming into my life caused me to look at life differently. I want both now. I want to work, but I want you too. And I know a good woman like you won't put up with sixty-hour weeks. I get it. That will change."

He reached for her hand and gently placed a round object on top of it. "I'm not a patient person, Nica. When I know what I want, I go for it. And I want you. I know, I know, it may seem too soon."

Nica felt a tear escape her right eye.

"But it's not soon enough for me. I'm all in. This is a promise ring." He nodded towards her hand, and she looked down. She saw a simple band with several gemstones. He lifted her hand. "Look."

She picked it up. There was a row of small, multi-colored stones. "It's like a little rainbow," she gasped.

"Yes, like the rainbow you painted above my grandfather's barn. Thank you for that beautiful gift, by the way. I didn't want to freak you out by showing up with a diamond engagement ring." He smiled. "That was my first impulse, though. This is a promise ring. It's a promise that when you're ready..." he paused. "When you've given me the opportunity to show you how much I love you and how much I want to make you the happiest woman in the world, I'll replace this ring with the diamond ring of your dreams."

Nica was shaking her head no, before he finished. "No, Grady. There will be no replacement of this ring. This ring is perfect. I love it. It reminds me of the colors of life. The spices of life." She smiled at him.

"Spicy," he murmured.

She nodded. "Yes, the spices of life. This is perfect, Grady. I'm all in. And I'm not talking about marriage. If it happens, great, if not, great. But I'm all in with you. Our partnership—and I don't mean that in a business sense—our relationship, our understanding, it's enough. We're enough. Together."

"I couldn't have said it better," he agreed. He picked up the ring from her outstretched hand. "May I?" he asked.

"Yes," she said, holding out her right hand.

He slid the ring on, and it fit perfectly.

"How did you…?"

"Your cousin."

Of course, Izzy would have known her ring size. "Well, Grady Litwiller. Will you take me on that first date now? I'm hungry."

"Absolutely, Spicy. Let's go."

WHAT'S NEXT

Thank you for reading *Dahlias for Dominica*. Your honest review will help future readers decide if they want to take a chance on a new-to-them author. Please consider leaving an honest review, or a star rating, on Amazon or Goodreads, or wherever you normally leave reviews.

There is a bonus epilogue available with an exciting occasion for Nica and Grady four years in the future. You can get the bonus by going to https://bookhip.com/SVFMFHJ. This will add you to my newsletter list.

In *Peonies for Paige*, Paige was excited to meet Trevor's friend, Hawk, the software developer that volunteers at a youth crisis center. She thinks he'll be a great match for her smart and driven friend Lauren! Check out *Lilies for Lauren*.

If you missed *Peonies for Paige*, you can find it on <u>Amazon</u>.

Sign up for my newsletter (on my website kasey-kennedy.com) and receive a free novella and to find out about special offers.

ACKNOWLEDGEMENTS

First, I want to thank my husband, Tim, for supporting my writing dream. Thank you for being my sounding board, my inspiration, and my champion. I don't know what I would do without you. I love you!

A huge shout out to the friends and family members that took the time to beta read and provide criticism and feedback–Rebecca E, Marisa F, and Camille D–thank you for your kind words, constructive feedback, and brilliant ideas!

Family is everything and I owe a sincere thank you to my siblings, siblings-in-law, aunts, uncles, cousins, nieces and nephews for all of the encouragement. I love you infinity.

Thank you to the professionals that supported this journey–Rebecca H for editing services; Stacy U for proofreading; and Stephanie and Melissa at Alt 19 Creative for the interior formatting and gorgeous book cover!

Thank you to all the bookstagrammers for your support. What an amazing community of readers.

And a heartfelt thank you to you, dear reader, for taking a chance on this story. I sincerely hope you enjoyed it.

ABOUT THE AUTHOR

Kasey Kennedy is an Illinois gal through and through. She grew up in Central Illinois, completed college at Southern Illinois University Carbondale and soon after, moved to Chicago. She's been in Chicago or the surrounding suburbs ever since.

Kasey is very happily married to her husband Tim and loves nothing more than spending time with him—especially when that involves live music! If not attending a live show, they are usually enjoying evenings on the deck, listening to music; visiting their large families; watching movies; or planning their next trip.

When not dreaming up new characters and new stories, Kasey is reading or planning what to read next. Occasionally, she pulls out the guitar that she has been trying to learn for 30+ years and strums enough to annoy her cat, Pepper.

Keep in touch:

FACEBOOK:

https://www.facebook.com/kaseykennedy8/

INSTAGRAM:

https://www.instagram.com/kaseykennedy8/

WEBSITE:

https://www.kasey-kennedy.com

9 781958 942055